What the critics are saying...

ဆ

"A beautiful adult fairy tale." ~ *Midwest Book Reviews*

"Beautifully captures everything I love in both romances and fantasies. It has earned a place of honor on my keeper shelf." ~ *In the Library Reviews*

"No collection of fantasy will be complete without it. It's that good." ~ *Romance Reviews Today*

A Cerridwen Press Publication

www.cerridwenpress.com

The Gazing Globe

This book printed in the U.S.A. by Jasmine-Jade Enterprises, LLC.

Electronic book Publication May 2007
Trade paperback Publication September 2007

Also by Candace Sams

ဆာ

Tales of the Order 1: Gryphon's Quest

About the Author

ဆာ

Candace Sams is also known as C.S. Chatterly. Before writing award-winning paranormal fiction, she was a police officer for eleven years and a crew chief on an ambulance for eight. She is also the senior woman on the U.S. Kung Fu team and is now receiving Olympic-level training for her fourth black belt. At the age of fifty, she works out a minimum of about nine hours per week.

Currently, Candace lives in the deep south with her husband, Lee. Two dogs and four cats have adopted her. Besides writing and martial arts, she enjoys gardening, weight lifting, and getting email from readers.

Candace welcomes comments from readers. You can find her website and email address on her author bio page at www.cerridwenpress.com.

Tell Us What You Think

We appreciate hearing reader opinions about our books. You can email us at Comments@EllorasCave.com.

TALES OF THE ORDER:
THE GAZING GLOBE
ᔥ

Dedication

❧

I'd like to thank my husband, Lee, and my family and friends for their wonderful and generous support. They've encouraged my active imagination and have been patient with me as it grew and flourished. And my gratitude goes out to all the kind readers who keep the Tales of the Order alive. Enjoy this second Tale in the series.

Prologue

∞

"I've found them, and they're dead, Shayla. Both died recently. I would have called you, but this entire situation has been very hard to take. If only I could have gotten here sooner." Hugh McTavish ran a hand through his hair and sighed.

Shayla Gallagher gripped the phone tightly as the news set in. "I'm sorry, Hugh. Sorry for all of us. I loved them as much as you did and had hoped they would return."

"The search wasn't in vain. They had a son. His name is Blain, and he's a grown man with the build of a pure warrior. I introduced myself and he knew nothing about me. It appears my brother and Syndra hid everything well."

Shayla closed her eyes and shook her head. "Damn Freyja! Her hate is still touching us all. Syndra and Arthur's son should be among us. This matter has gone on far too long. How did the young man react when you met him?" She heard Hugh swallow hard and clear his throat.

"He knew I was related to Arthur the moment he laid eyes on me. After so many years, we must have still looked alike. And Blain was so excited to see me, and so full of questions. It was all I could do to keep from telling him everything, Shayla. But there's something wrong here. Blain told me his parents' deaths were coincidental, but the circumstances are too odd. They died of different illnesses that came on quickly — and now Blain is ill as well."

Shayla quickly stood and pushed her desk chair away. "Tell me everything, Hugh. Don't leave out a single detail."

"According to Blain, Arthur was as healthy as any man could be. Then, he suddenly dropped dead of heart failure while working in the fields. Soon after that, Syndra became ill and died. It seems some of her organs stopped working."

"Forgive me for asking this Hugh, but is there any way Blain could have discovered some powers of his own and used them adversely? Even by mistake?"

"I've thought of that, but there isn't any way he could have harmed them, Shayla. Blain loved his parents and was crushed by their deaths. Even in the few days I've known him, his love for them is evident in everything he says and does. I can't sense any deception, and he says the doctors ruled his parents' deaths as natural." Hugh paused and took a deep breath before continuing. "I'm convinced that someone had a hand in Arthur's and Syndra's deaths, and now they're after Blain. I've found hexes and talismans connected with black magic around the farm. Whoever is using this black magic obviously has enough power to finish him off, but it's like they're torturing him for a reason. Playing with him as though they're testing him and his abilities. He is a blend after all, and I'm afraid this may all lead back to the events surrounding Freyja. I...I believe someone may know about us."

Shayla shivered at his words. "I need to know exactly where you are."

"New England. A place called Harvest, Maine."

"Shayla quickly motioned one of her waiting assistants to come forward. She put her hand over the receiver and gave the girl instructions to book an immediate flight to New England, then she gave Hugh her full attention again. "I'm already booking a flight, and I'll be there as quickly as I can. Now, tell me anything else you can. Nothing is too trivial."

"I've told you everything I know. Whatever is happening, I'm not about to stand idly by and let my own flesh and blood die as his father and mother may have."

"There, there, darling," she soothed as Hugh's anger and pain echoed in the tone of his voice. "If the Goddess allows, I'll not only save his life, but get him back here safely. I owe Arthur and Syndra that much, even if it turns out they never wanted to return or to have anything to do with us."

"Could you blame them if they didn't?" Hugh angrily asked. "What kind of world did we live in where two young people had to run and hide because they loved one another?"

"I agree with you, and I'll be there, soon, darling. I might not be able to get away tomorrow, but…"

"Please, my love, I need to ask a favor of you. Let me have some time with him before you come. Just a few weeks alone. I want to get to know my nephew better, and I can protect him against whatever is happening to him for that short period of time."

"Absolutely not! You could both end up dead."

"I beg you, Shayla. I'll begin reversing the hexes or at least slow their effects. But I think Blain needs to get to know me before we tell him who he really is or he may reject the Order and endanger himself further. If his health worsens or I begin to feel ill, I'll phone you immediately."

Shayla considered the request. "All right, dear. But I'll be there three weeks to the day. And if you don't check in regularly, I'll be bringing warriors with me."

"Thank you, my heart." He paused and lowered his voice. "I miss you."

Shayla gripped the phone with both hands. "Being without you is agonizing."

"My love is yours no matter where we are."

"Take the greatest care, Hugh."

"I will. And sleep well, my darling. I dream of you."

"And I dream of you," she whispered and slowly hung up the phone. As soon as she placed the receiver back down, Shayla turned to her staff member. "Bring me everything we have on old Freyja. Start with the battle thirty years ago and work your way back."

The young assistant bowed his head and hurried from the room to do as he was commanded.

Chapter One

ဢ

"Don't do this, lad. You should get some rest."

"We've had this argument before, Hugh. Don't worry about me. I'll feel better after I've been outside." Blain stared out the back screen door knowing his uncle was right. He couldn't get over the illness plaguing him, keep up with the farm work and still go out in the woods at night. But it wasn't something he could help. He simply had to go or face being even sicker. He dragged his gaze away from the woods and glanced over his shoulder at Hugh once more.

"What about tomorrow? If you go out tonight, how will you feel then?" Hugh asked, frustration in his voice.

"I'll worry about that later. I appreciate your concern, but don't wait up. I can deal with this," Blain lied.

Once he was outside and away from the farmhouse, he stripped off his clothing and ran naked, as though his life depended upon being in contact with nature. In fact, he believed it really did. Because he was weak, he had to push himself, but the effort paid off. When he finally reached the end of a very long forest path, he stopped and rested against a tree. The illness already seemed to be leaving his body. He dragged fresh, clean air into his lungs and sank to his knees. The doctor had been unable to tell him why he was sometimes so weak he could barely move. Was his sickness something rare? Something they couldn't diagnose and for which there was no cure? He didn't know why running naked made a difference in how he felt, but he had to do it. It was an obsession. And because that yearning was so abnormal, he wondered if his mind was failing along with his health. Would he not only end up dying slowly, but going insane as well? The fear that he might, scared the hell out of him. There were only two people in his life that he could go to with his fear—his girlfriend Rhiannon and his Uncle Hugh.

He'd tried telling Rhiannon about the malady plaguing him, but talking wasn't one of her favorite pastimes. She preferred raw, unadulterated sex. As much as she could get. At one time it had pleased him to give it to her. Now, even sex made him feel drained and weak. Only by running in the woods at night did he find any peace. Afterward, he felt whole again. Strong and ready to face a new day. Hugh was the only one who knew about his nightly nude dashes through the woods, and he didn't seem to consider Blain's actions odd. And that in itself was bizarre. Anyone else would have called a shrink and had him committed by now. But how long could the cycle of work, illness, and running nude in the woods at night last? It was an absurd way to live. But since medical science had no answers, he relented to the call of nature and let that be his treatment.

The longer he stayed in the woods, the better he felt, so Blain lingered to gather more strength. A full moon hung overhead like an ornament, and it vaguely reminded him of something he couldn't quite pinpoint. Had the moon's surface been shiny and cast a reflection, its appearance would seem more appropriate to him. He had a faint sense that what he was thinking of or remembering might have been something out of the past. Something he'd heard one of his parents speak of.

Whatever it was, the moon's surface just needed a little imaginary rearranging, and he might be able to grab onto the memory. The more he struggled to recall that elusive memory, however, the more vague the entire concept became.

He sighed and gave up. Then he looked toward the forest again and saw the symbol. In the moon's strong light, it was clearly visible. Someone had deeply carved a picture of a stick man into the side of an oak tree, then slashed through the image with a sharp blade. He walked toward the image, lifted his hand to touch it, but he immediately began to feel ill again.

But that was not only crazy—it was impossible. Touching a vandal's graffiti couldn't make someone sick. Yet here he was, engulfed by dizziness and nausea all over again.

He fought off the symptoms by trying to replace them with an emotional cure. Anger. This was his property. No one was supposed to be out here defacing his trees. As he stared at the carving, he acknowledged that it was an unusual way to mar the bark. Kids would scratch out their names or something they could see later and lay claim to. This was something all together different—something sinister. The event caused him to add anxiety to the list of the other problems afflicting him. Who the hell was in his woods and what were they doing to the trees?

* * * * *

"You've brought everything?"

"I have it all, just as you asked."

"Then leave it and do as you've been told."

"I will, Mistress. But there are easier ways to do this. I could simply put something into his food. We can't keep sneaking around forever. Someone will see us or he'll discover trespassers have been on his land. It's risky."

The old woman pushed back the hood of her cloak and sneered. "Have I taught you nothing? We'll have the police down on us if we do it your way. His parents died within a short time of one another. That might seem odd to some. But killing the boy now will make those deaths seem positively suspicious. That's why I didn't take them all out at once. My way is best. Slowly, one at a time, and using magic to our advantage. No one must ever know what really happened. Besides, it will be more painful for him this way. And his lingering pain is exactly what I want. We haven't planned all this out only to screw up by rushing. I want Shayla here first. I'll have my revenge." The old woman paused and looked up into the moonlit sky. "You'll do this my way, or you can clear out. Do you understand?"

"Fine. But he knows something is wrong. His powers of resistance are definitely stronger than his parents' or he'd be dead already. We don't know how much more we'll have to do to kill him, and we may not be able to keep this up now that his uncle is with him. We'll surely get caught."

"After tonight, we may not have to go out there again. I'll do my job now. You do yours later, just as I've instructed." The cloaked old woman waved a hand in a dismissive gesture. "Now go."

The other cloaked figure bowed and quietly walked away.

* * * * *

Hugh walked into the hallway, picked up the phone and dialed the special number. He was only on the phone long enough to relay what was necessary when he sensed a presence behind him. He quickly ended the call and turned around. Blain stood there, leaning against a wall.

"Calling friends?" Blain asked as he brought a large glass of ice water to his lips.

"I thought you would be outside for a while longer, lad."

"I felt so much better that I cut my run a little short tonight." No sense worrying his uncle over something the doctors couldn't fix.

Hugh took note of the younger man's sweaty face. "Go upstairs and get cleaned up, lad. I'll bring you some fresh lemonade."

"Sounds like a plan," Blain responded. As always, Hugh was a mystery. He knew the older man wouldn't tell him about the phone call, and it wasn't as if it really made a difference. But it was just one more piece of a puzzle that, so far, resisted being solved. Hugh had literally shown up on his doorstep just a few short weeks earlier. The initial shock that he had a living relative was replaced by the emotional attachment he quickly formed with Hugh. Hugh helped fill the gaping hole that had been left in his life by his father's unexpected death, followed shortly after by his mother's.

He walked upstairs, shed the clothing he'd put on after running and made his way to the shower. It helped knowing Hugh was here, that he wasn't completely alone. But why hadn't his parents told him he had an uncle? From the way Hugh spoke about his parents, they had all loved each other very much. So why all the secrecy? And were there other relatives he hadn't been told about? Even if there were, he'd probably never get to meet them. He wouldn't be able to lie about how sick he really was any longer. The pain and illness seemed to be with him almost constantly now.

A knock on the door brought him out of his somber reverie. He stepped out of the shower and pulled on his bathrobe. Then, he half-jogged to the bedroom door to open it. Hugh walked in with a cool pitcher of fresh lemonade and a plate of shortbread cookies. "These will fix you right up." He smiled as he set the tray down near the bed.

"Thanks." Blain paused until Hugh was through laying out the snack. "I, uh, don't suppose I could finally talk you into telling me about Mom, Dad and yourself?" He had an urgent need to know about the secrecy surrounding his family.

"All right, lad. I'll answer what I can for now. You'll know everything when it's time."

Blain laughed and spread out his hands expressively. "Now, that's exactly what I'm wondering about. Why can't I just get a straight answer?"

"Trust me, my lad. You don't want to know everything right now."

"It's that bad?" Blain asked with a glass of lemonade halfway to his lips.

"No, not at all. But there are some things you're just not ready to hear. I can tell you that your parents and me were very close and that they didn't want to leave Scotland. But they loved one another and had to leave."

"Why did they have to leave? What was wrong in Scotland?"

Whatever Hugh's response might have been was stopped by the ringing of the upstairs phone. Blain sighed in exasperation, put his glass down and walked into the hallway. He returned a few moments later and reached into his dresser drawer for a pair of jeans.

"You're not going out?" Hugh asked in disbelief.

"Yep. That was Rhi on the phone. I don't know when I'll be back, so don't wait up." He saw Hugh shake his head in disapproval. Clearly, his relationship with Rhiannon Stone troubled his uncle. Hugh's expression turned dour whenever Rhi's name was mentioned. But Hugh pretty much kept his opinions to himself. Occasionally, however, he would make an offhand remark about how *he* should get more rest and quit gallivanting. But Blain couldn't help the urge to see Rhiannon. What harm could there be in spending time with a sexy, desirable woman? If it turned out that his intuition about his illness was correct, he might have very little time left. He tried to push his fears aside and concentrate on having a good time.

* * * * *

"Damn! I'll never get this right," Afton O'Malley complained as she pushed her hair over her shoulder. Even the powerful presence of the rowan and oak trees, specially planted for those less adept in Druid powers, didn't seem to help. She knew she'd never learn to conjure if she couldn't focus.

Frustrated and out of patience, she carefully looked around the clearing. Then she picked up a carryall containing crystals, herb bundles, scissors and other paraphernalia needed to make charms. She started to walk into the cool, inviting woods.

"One moment, Afton O'Malley. Where do you think you're going?"

Afton inwardly cringed as Shayla, her mentor, stepped from the shadows. The afternoon breeze blew the older woman's white Druid robe and cape against her body. Her silver hair was braided and hung down her back. Afton knew the woman meant to appear imposing. As she caught site of her oldest brother, however, she groaned and momentarily forgot about the Sorceress. Gawain wore one of his eternal and infuriating *I'll protect you* expressions.

"Shayla. Gawain. I didn't know anyone was around." Afton unsuccessfully tried to mask her anger as she faced her teacher and brother. "I was just going to take a few moments in the woods to gather some wild herbs for a new tea I'm blending."

"You'll not leave this clearing until you've conjured wind or at least a small breeze," Shayla declared.

"May as well break wind," a small voice said from under a large fern. "It'd be a whole lot quicker. More accurate, too."

Gawain turned and angrily addressed the little elf. "Keep quiet, Pluck! When Afton wants your opinion, she'll ask."

"Don't be impatient with Pluck simply because Afton has failed to concentrate," Shayla admonished.

"Who asked Pluck to spy on me anyway? He should mind his own bloody business." Afton placed her hands on her hips and glowered at the little brown-clad man in the foliage. She watched as he hopped up on a nearby rock which made his diminutive height nearer to her own five and a half feet.

"For your information, Shayla asked me to keep an eye on you. You're not concentrating on your lessons." Pluck straightened his brown pointed cap over equally pointed ears.

"That'll be enough out of both of you." Shayla raised a graceful hand to stop the argument. "You may go, Pluck. I want to speak to Afton alone."

When the elf smugly glared at Afton as if he'd had the last word, Shayla clapped her hands together sharply. Pluck jumped from the rock and ran into the woods as if some unseen horror was chasing him.

"You may go, too, Gawain." Shayla waved a hand at him in dismissal.

Gawain nodded and turned to leave. "I'll be in the next clearing, Flower. Come get me when you're through here, and I'll walk you home."

"You sent Pluck to watch me?" Afton asked as she watched her brother leave. Then she dropped her gaze and focused on the bare toes peeking from beneath her white robe.

"I wouldn't have done so had you been more conscientious about your conjuring. But I can't be everywhere at once."

"Yes, but he'll tell everyone in the woods that no matter how hard I try, I still can't summon a minor breeze. Every elf, fairy and gnome in the Order will know I can't do what a child apprentice should be able to do. And I'm no child."

"That's true, but you have only yourself to blame. That's why your parents sent you to me. And Gawain's protectiveness isn't helping matters." Shayla walked to a nearby flat rock and patted the surface next to her. "Are you trying as hard as you can, girl?"

Afton nodded as she sat down. "I am, but don't blame Gawain for being overprotective. He thinks he's helping." She sighed and attempted to get the Sorceress to understand. "I try to concentrate. It's just that there's so much to do and to see. And I wonder about using powers at all."

"How so?"

"Please don't be angry, Shayla. But what are such powers used for other than starting fires and bringing down a little rain now and then? It isn't as if they'll be used against any of our own kind. We certainly can't go into the outside world and display such capabilities. I'd rather concentrate on the Druid rituals, ceremonies and customs."

"Afton, if our kind is to be protected from the outside world, everyone in the Order must learn all they can about their particular faction and their respective powers. You know this. Fairies learn what they must with glamour. Trolls and pixies learn their powers of camouflage, and you must hone your own skills. If a crisis arises, you may need your powers to help yourself or one of the Order. It will be too late for you to learn your craft at the last moment. The power to summon elements won't simply come to you without prior preparation. Those elements must be controlled through practice. Many years of it. Take a look at Gawain. He's very powerful, and he's become so through practice."

"I know. He and everyone else in my family have told me a thousand times that practice makes perfect. But how many times have our kind actually had to use our powers against outsiders? When Gawain goes to London, he never speaks of having to protect himself."

"He uses his powers more than you realize. He probably doesn't tell you about the things that happen to him to keep you and your parents from worrying."

Afton stared at Shayla in alarm. She opened her mouth to ask about the matter, but Shayla held up a hand to silence her. "I'll tell you about all that another time. Right now, I believe a change of scene is in order. You're too attached to these woods and those who dwell within them. Things here are distracting you."

Afton waited as Shayla paused and pulled the front of her robe together. As if it were a portent, a cloud blocked out the sun and shadowed them.

"A matter of some urgent business has arisen, and I'll need an assistant to accompany me on a trip. Would you consider coming along?" Shayla asked.

"Travel? Oh Shayla, I'd love it. I've never been anywhere but England and Scotland. Where would we go? Ireland, or maybe even France?" Afton smiled at the prospect of seeing more of the world.

"I'm afraid the trip will take us farther away from ancient ground than that. This journey will be to the States."

Afton felt her jaw drop. "The States? Why would we be needed there? Europe has always contained our most sacred grounds. And you just returned from the States not long ago."

"Yes, but I've received an urgent message from Hugh. He's found what remains of some deserters," Shayla told her as she rose from her seat and took several steps away.

"Deserters from the Order? What will you do to them?" Afton knew anyone leaving the Order without permission could be put to death. The rule was an ancient one meant to protect the Order from human discovery. In Afton's twenty-three years, she couldn't recall the necessity for that particular law to be invoked.

"You know as well as I what our law states. However, this is quite an exceptional situation. The two main offenders have met their fate. Only their child remains, and this boy is unaware of his heritage."

"How could he not know of his relationship to the Order?" Afton tilted her head in confusion as she stood and stared at her mentor.

"I told you, this is an exceptional situation. I'll explain everything later." Shayla's voice took on a wistful quality. Afton watched as the older woman's eyes grew teary. It was as if she was temporarily lost in the past, remembering something painful.

Shaking her head as if she could clear her mind of distant memories, Shayla walked back to her stone bench and sat down again. "Now, back to work on your conjuring skills. You'll need the practice before we leave in a week."

Afton quickly walked to the middle of the clearing and began to practice her powers again. She looked at the sky and watched the wind move the clouds about. But the phenomenon was only a force of nature, and not a sign of her meager attempts to manipulate the elements. She wondered if she would ever be worthy of her heritage and bold enough to live her own life without Gawain's well-intentioned interference.

* * * * *

"Are you sure about this, Flower? You've never been outside sacred ground," Gawain frowned as he watched his sister pack.

Afton sighed and turned to face him. "If Mom, Dad and everyone else aren't worried, why are you? And why do you insist on using that ridiculous nickname. I'm all grown up, Gawain. Or hadn't you noticed?"

He shrugged. "I've noticed. So have a lot of men in the Order. But I can't help remembering when I first saw you all those years ago. You were two hours old when I was allowed to hold you. I was only ten, but I felt ancient when you were placed in my arms. You were so small and had the cutest little button nose. And the color of your eyes reminded me of the bluebells that grow in the Goblin Meadow. That's when I called you Flower. The name just stuck."

Afton's eyes misted. How could she be annoyed with her big-hearted sibling, especially when this was the first time she'd heard why he'd bestowed her with that stupid nickname?

Gawain leaned against the door frame and continued. "You know, you smiled at me and managed to grab onto my fingers with all the strength of a baby ogre. I knew then and there that I would never let anything happen to you. I know what the world outside the sacred forest can be like. You don't. Despite what the Sorceress says, I just don't want to see you get into trouble, Flower. I worry."

For a moment, Afton was taken aback. She'd never before seen all this emotion pouring from her oldest brother, and she had to swallow down a large lump in her throat. But then she remembered Shayla's assertion that Gawain had been forced to use his powers in the outside world to stay safe. It frightened her to know he'd been at risk.

"How many times have you had problems that you haven't mentioned? The Sorceress led me to believe you haven't been so safe."

"That's different. I've got a bit more experience at this kind of thing, and I—"

"Don't, Gawain. Don't go into that big brother mode. You've deliberately let us all believe nothing ever happens to you when you're traveling. Mom and Dad would be worried sick if they knew you'd had to use your powers to protect yourself. And I'd be just as worried about you, too."

"There was no use letting them know since everything has always worked out. I'm here. No scrapes, bruises or broken bones."

Afton knew he was lying and that he wouldn't tell her about his experiences in the outside world. So she took courage from his nonchalant attitude. "The Sorceress needs me. Goddess only knows why she's chosen me, but I'm going and I don't want to hear any more about it." Afton firmly snapped her suitcase shut, turned and glared at her oldest sibling.

Gawain looked at the floor and glowered. "Something about this isn't right. I don't like it."

"None of us especially likes it when you're away, either, but you have to go. Now, so do I."

"Okay, Flower. But just be careful. Life outside the Order can be a bitch."

Afton smiled, walked to where he stood and hugged him hard. As she stepped back, she asked, "Will you ever let me grow up?"

"Don't have much of a choice, do I?" He grinned and crossed his arms over his chest.

"None. So kiss me goodbye, and I'll get downstairs to say my farewells to the others."

Gawain kissed her cheek, quickly hugged her then grabbed her suitcase. "You'll call?"

She rolled her eyes and let out a heavy sigh. While the rest of her family was understandably concerned, Gawain was proving to be a royal pain in the butt. She loved him dearly, but his interference in her life was becoming annoying. He'd even chased off several beaus, claiming they weren't good enough for her. Given the choice of fighting one of the biggest men in the Order or letting Afton go, they'd chosen to walk away. Gawain had used their desertion of her to prove they weren't worthy. She saw this trip as a way of putting some distance between them—a way of letting everyone else know that she was all grown up and didn't need coddling any more. If the Sorceress trusted her, then so should they. And Afton really looked forward to the adventure, but something Gawain had said stayed in her mind. Her brother hadn't been trying to frighten her, but if traveling in the outside world concerned a Druid as powerful as he, she would be insane not to heed his warning. And there was still that nagging thought that Shayla could have picked someone with a great deal more power than herself. Someone who could actually help if authorities discovered the false identification all those of the Order used, or if some other serious problem should arise. Afton sensed the Sorceress hadn't told her everything. That, more than anything, worried her. But she kept those fears buried as she kissed her family goodbye.

Chapter Two

ഔ

"Baby, that was incredible."

"I'm glad you enjoyed it. I've got to get back to the farm or Hugh will be wondering where I am. And morning comes around pretty early," Blain said as he leaned over and kissed Rhiannon's lips, then watched as she stretched her sultry frame.

"Are you saying that feeding livestock is more appealing than making love to me again?" she asked as she watched him leave the bed and reach for his clothes. She smiled at him, using her sweetest tone of voice in an attempt to lure him back.

Blain ran a hand through his hair. "You know I'd like to stay all night, honey, but I've got to get my seeds in the ground. What would harvest be like without pumpkins? Besides, I'm keeping you from your own work."

"I don't have a lot of clients during the week. Most people only want to buy antiques on the weekend. Stay with me, please?" Rhiannon begged as she put on her prettiest pout.

In the process of dressing, Blain paused. "You really like sex, don't you?"

"Who doesn't?" she grinned and traced one finger across the bedspread.

He simply stared for a moment. While he wasn't a shrink, he felt pretty sure that Rhiannon could almost be classified as having some kind of obsession with sex. From the first time he'd met her, she'd come on to him like a nova—hot as hell and ready to burn. After a while, he wondered if there was really anything more between them than the intercourse. It was good and he loved what they did together, but it was strange that she never wanted to talk like other women did. Or cuddle and hold each other afterward. Their entire relationship was rather cold and impersonal. Still, he kept coming back. Maybe hoping for something more substantial. Or maybe because he was as obsessed with making out as she was. He wasn't sure. But he did know that he felt compelled to return to Rhi over and over.

"Will I at least see you this weekend?" she asked as she lifted her hair off her shoulders.

"Maybe. We'll see. I'll probably have more energy then." Blain finished zipping his jeans and rolled up the sleeves on his cambric work shirt. He stopped when a strange tingling sensation began running through him. His skin felt like someone was running a mild electric current over it, and he knew that the feeling might lead to him becoming physically ill again.

"Are you still feeling tired?" Rhiannon asked as she sat up in bed. "Maybe you should see a doctor."

"I have, and the old quack can't find a damned thing wrong with me. According to him, I'm as healthy as a draft horse. I'm just putting in a lot of hard hours." He was lying. The doctor had run every known test. Nothing wrong could be found.

"I'm worried about you," Rhiannon said as she pushed her hair away from her face with one hand.

"Don't be." He sat on the side of the bed and admired the way the light glistened in her long black hair. "I'll see you later in the week."

He had to leave quickly or risk her seeing how ill he was about to become. He fought off the dizziness and shot her his best smile. He wondered if she'd be sorry if anything happened to him and decided that Rhiannon would easily find someone to replace him. Their relationship wasn't all that deep. So why did he keep coming back to her? All he knew was that he couldn't seem to stay away.

"Be good," she told him as he lowered his mouth toward hers.

"I try my best." He kissed her one more time, grinned and quickly got up to leave. Blain looked back over his shoulder before he opened the door to her bedroom. Rhiannon smiled seductively at him and spread her bare legs. It was an open invitation to stay. He pretended to laugh and quickly left before his illness could overcome him. He knew the impromptu meetings between them should stop. He had too much work to do, and he felt an urgency to get it done. It was as if something was driving him to go further, finish more, before he couldn't do anything. It was a kind of impending sense of doom that wasn't rational, except that he had the illness to prove otherwise.

As he drove back to the farmhouse, he began to feel better again. He wondered if there wasn't something psychologically wrong that was causing these physically debilitating episodes. But he was afraid to consider that option. Talking to Hugh about it to any extent would only put some angst on the older man that he didn't deserve. He thought once more about discussing his physical ailments with Rhiannon, but she really only cared about what they did in bed. And that, in and of itself, was another source for concern. Other than Hugh, he didn't have a single person who gave a damn about what was happening to him. It was pathetic, but it was the truth.

Thirty minutes later, Blain pulled onto the dirt road leading to the farmhouse and saw the lights still on. Hugh was, despite his request, waiting up for him. He was bone-tired, and the last thing he needed was having his uncle question him about his sex life. His respect for the older man was the only thing that kept him from rudely telling him to mind his own business.

"You were with Miss Stone quite a while, weren't you?" Hugh asked as Blain entered the house.

"Yeah, though why you've lost sleep just to state the obvious, I have no idea." Blain rubbed the back of his neck. He suddenly felt so damned tired again.

"You should be getting sleep, lad, not cavorting about with that woman at all hours. You look completely done in."

Blain wanted to make some smart retort, but hearing his uncle's gentle reprimand, in the same Scottish accent as his father's, made him smile instead. Hugh was so much like his dad that he sometimes had to remind himself that his father was gone. "You shouldn't worry about me. Did you ever stop to consider that being with a beautiful woman is the most relaxing thing on earth?"

Hugh grinned mischievously. "Aye, I've heard that, though it's been a while since I've had the pleasure myself."

"Maybe you should go out. You know, find a lady in the community with similar interests?" Blain hoped his uncle would get the hint and leave him alone. Or maybe the subject might lead to his uncle talking more about his personal life in Scotland.

Hugh took his time responding. He picked up his pipe, loaded it with tobacco then leaned back in his comfortable chair while he lit it. "Well, since you've brought the subject up, there's an acquaintance of mine living in England. I hope you don't mind, but I've invited her for a visit. That's the real reason I waited up for you."

"You dog! She can stay here and have the room next to yours. Better still, she can stay with you in your room if you'd like some privacy," Blain joked as he straddled a nearby chair. He'd enjoy picking on his uncle the same way the older man had goaded him about Rhiannon.

"Don't be impertinent, young rake," Hugh responded as he raised one eyebrow in an imperious expression. "Shayla Gallagher isn't a woman with whom one toys."

Implying Rhiannon probably was, but Blain let the last comment pass. "Shayla, huh. Sounds interesting. So, tell me about this…friend." If Hugh heard the emphasis he'd placed on that last word, he refused to rise to the bait.

"She's from Cornwall, and you might say she's a sort of cultural expert. She travels from country to country and deals with a variety of people."

"Did this woman know Mom and Dad?"

"She was great friends with your parents. But the same circumstances which prevented me from visiting your father and mother while they were alive also kept Shayla away."

"I don't understand what that means. You've known from the start that Mom and Dad never told me I had an uncle living somewhere in Europe. In fact, they wouldn't discuss anything about family matters at all."

"Aye, I'm sure that's true. It's better that you don't know why for now, but you will soon. I promise."

"That's cryptic. You aren't wanted by the law or anything, are you?"

"Certainly not, young pup," Hugh gasped in mock indignation. "I've never done a single illegal thing in my life!"

"Secret agent? Spy?" Blain questioned as he leaned forward, grinning.

Hugh paused for a long time and stared straight into Blain's face. "I was busy learning to conjure and control the elements of air, fire, water and earth. Does that answer your question?"

"Okay, okay. You win. It's none of my business." Blain laughed, put his hands up in resignation and shrugged.

"Go to bed, lad. If you're going to get up at the crack of dawn, you'll need some sleep."

"All right. Good night, Hugh. I'll see you in the morning."

Hugh watched as Blain left the room. Then he got up and used the fire poker to stir the ashes of the hexes and evil talismans burning there. There was some coal wrapped in black cloth, small dolls with pins stuck in them and poisoned herbs—all things he'd found on the farm earlier that day. "Black magic!" he angrily muttered to himself. "Whoever is using these things won't kill you, lad. I won't let them."

* * * * *

From the back seat, Afton glanced at the scenery as they drove. Then she focused her attention on the distinguished man in the driver's seat. Hugh McTavish was about Shayla's age. He was tall and handsome and had a thick shock of white hair and the kindest blue eyes she'd ever seen. She had liked and trusted him her entire life, and she hoped to have a man like him love her one day.

She tactfully looked out the window again when Hugh lifted Shayla's hand and placed a small kiss on the back of it. Afton knew Shayla sorely missed her consort. Once, she had gotten the courage to ask Shayla why they had never handfasted. Rumors abounded about the reason, but she wanted to get the information straight from the source. But Shayla had waved her hand in one of her typically imperious gestures and made some offhand comment about the fact that she and Hugh were as close as any handfasted couple could possibly be. That since they'd been together for so long, what good would a handfasting do, except take attention away from those couples who came forward on sacred nights and exchanged their vows?

That had sounded perfectly plausible to Afton, but she secretly wondered if the Sorceress might not be averse to commitment of that kind. Everyone had weaknesses and foibles. Maybe that was Shayla Gallagher's.

Knowing she'd probably never know Shayla's real reasons for not handfasting, she dragged her wandering thoughts back to the conversation being held in the front seat. Since he'd picked them up at the airport, Hugh had been filling Shayla in on all the information he knew about his young nephew, Blain.

"What are some of the signs of enchantment you first noticed?" Shayla asked.

Afton sat upright. Perhaps her daydreaming had been poorly timed. What enchantment? This was the first time she'd heard of anything of the like.

"The animals began to sicken and go off their feed all at once and for no apparent reason," Hugh replied. "I didn't call a veterinarian when the wild yew I placed over the barn door worked overnight. That was what made me first suspect a foul presence. Then I found a willow wand lying by the road. The last thing I found was an evil hex sign on a tree in the woods. I came across it about two days ago. Blain just keeps getting more ill and tries to hide it."

"Stars!" Afton gasped. "We're dealing with a Druid who's practicing black magic? You never told me about this, Shayla."

"Aye," Hugh agreed. "A black conjurer was my conclusion, exactly."

"Why would an evil presence like that want to harm your nephew, Hugh?" Afton leaned forward so that her arms rested on the seat backs, between the two older Druids.

"Either he's made some kind of powerful enemy or someone knows something of his heritage. It may be he has powers someone is trying to siphon off or they're testing them. If the latter is true, then this evil presence could bring harm to the Order," Shayla answered, wrapping her shawl more tightly around her shoulders.

"I don't know of a single soul who'd really want to harm the lad. But in the short time I've been with him, I've learned there are a few who resent his presence," Hugh admitted.

"And who would that be?" Shayla asked.

"There's a widow named Hannah Biddles. Some time ago, when her husband was still alive, Mr. Biddles sold the best of his farmland to Arthur and Syndra. Uh, those are Blain's parents," Hugh explained, glancing at Afton. "That land now belongs to Blain. The woman has told everyone in town that she strongly objected to the sale. Her land, of course, adjoins Blain's."

"So she'd be close enough to come onto Blain's property in the night?" Afton asked.

"That's possible. But I think the woman is harmless, more bluster than anything."

"Who else?" Shayla questioned.

"There's the Reverend Myers. He resents Blain's relationship with a woman in town. He says it stirs up too much gossip."

"A woman?" Afton's eyes widened in astonishment. What kind of relationship could a little boy have with a woman?

"Who is this person?" Shayla asked.

"Rhiannon Stone. She moved here from New York about three months ago and owns an antique store in town. The lady is quite lovely, and Blain spends a great deal of his spare time with her. What little spare time he has," Hugh added. "Harvest is a small place, and the good Reverend Myers resents anyone corrupting his flock by committing acts of a *lecherous nature*, as he puts it. Blain's relationship with Ms. Stone seems to anger him no end."

Shayla nodded. "That gives us two possibilities to check out, anyway."

"Excuse me, but I'm more than a bit confused," Afton interjected, her voice rising to emphasize her growing irritation. "No one told me that there was evil magic threatening Blain, and how in the world could a little boy have a relationship of the kind you're describing with a grown woman? That's positively disgusting."

Hugh and Shayla looked at one another and began to laugh.

Afton glared at them both. "What, may I ask, is so amusing?"

"Afton, how old did you think Blain was?" Hugh gasped out between laughs. "He's just over thirty."

"I was guessing he was only about ten or eleven," she responded with a blush. "How long had they been living undetected in this area?"

"They ran for more than thirty years, and lived in this community for the last five of those," Hugh answered. "Together, their magic hid and protected them well. No matter where they went, they'd move on if they thought anyone was closing in. When Syndra passed away, so did the power that hid Blain from the rest of the Order. I came looking for my brother Arthur and his mate, Syndra." He paused as if to compose himself. "I found their son instead. Though he's a good lad, I was devastated to learn both his parents had passed on only a short time before I got here."

Shayla patted Hugh's hand comfortingly.

"No wonder old Freyja wanted them found," Afton said. "The mating of two beings from different factions must have worried her terribly. Together, their powers might even have been greater than hers, and she had to fear that."

"Aye, exactly." Hugh nodded.

Afton looked at Shayla. "You didn't tell me someone practicing black magic wants to harm Blain. You should have done so before I decided to come on this trip." Afton sat back, crossed her arms over her chest and chewed on her lower lip in concern.

Shayla simply shrugged. "I needed you here, lass. Besides, would it have made any difference? This is a perfect chance for you to get away from England and the things distracting you there."

"I guess you're right, but from now on, please tell me everything."

"Whatever led you to believe Blain was a child?" Hugh asked Afton.

"I've only heard him referred to as boy or lad," she responded, glaring at Shayla.

"To us he is. Just as you're a lass or a girl." Shayla grinned.

Afton sat back in her seat and silently fumed over being referred to as anything other than a woman. She had a name, and they could use it instead of referring to her by a younger title. There were, after all, others her age whose powers were as lacking or worse than hers. Yet they weren't referred to in such a juvenile manner. It was a constant irritation to be given less respect than they.

She kept quiet and let the two older people talk to each other for the rest of the journey. Aside from the lack of general respect, she was also angry at having been deliberately deceived. Everything her mentor had said portrayed Blain as a young boy. But why would Shayla mislead her? Perhaps it was her mentor's way of testing her mettle. But black magic such as they were describing was powerful. If she wasn't very careful, she could end up getting herself into a real mess. She shook her head and wondered what she would do with the model airplane she had carefully packed as a gift for Blain.

* * * * *

"Here we are," Hugh said as he drove up the narrow lane to the three-story farmhouse.

"Oh, Hugh, it's lovely." Shayla clasped her hands together and smiled.

"It is nice, isn't it? Blain works very hard to keep things just right. He's quite a dedicated worker," Hugh bragged.

As far as Afton was concerned, he had something to brag about. The farmhouse was wonderfully warm and welcoming. It was built entirely of logs and had a porch running all the way around. In the front yard, colorful flowers bloomed abundantly in beds and containers. Stone fences contained fat cattle in nearby pastures. Thick woods surrounded the pastures and looked as though they stretched for some distance behind the house itself. Afton wondered what kind of man outside the Order loved flowers so much. But then, Blain wasn't really an outsider. He was just raised as one.

"Where is Blain?" Shayla asked as the car came to a stop. "I can already feel something wrong. There's an evil ambience surrounding the land."

Afton felt it, too. And if someone with her lack of powers could sense the evil, it was powerful indeed. She shivered, but her fears fled when a very tall, massively-built man of about thirty opened the front door of the house and strode toward the car. Afton's mouth went dry. She had never seen a man with shoulders quite so broad. With every step he took in their direction, he exuded a masculinity that was almost tangible. This was a person who physically worked hard every day of his life. Her image of him as a small boy dissipated forever. What would happen when he found out his parents had been running from the old Sorceress' wrath for years? Without his parents' combined powers, Freyja would have found and killed all of them. It seemed someone was determined to continue that dark ambition.

Hugh helped Shayla out of the car and began the introductions. "Shayla Gallagher, this is my nephew, Blain McTavish."

Afton watched the older man's face light up with pride. Surely, there was much to be proud of. Blain was one hundred percent pure warrior.

"By the stars," Shayla murmured as her hand came to rest within Blain's, "you're the image of your father. But you have Syndra's lovely gray-green eyes. Hello, Blain."

Blain liked the woman immediately. There was something strong, dignified and trustworthy in the older woman's gray gaze. Though time had weathered her features, her face was uncommonly beautiful. No wonder Hugh had wanted her to come to Harvest for a visit. It seemed his uncle was a sly old fox with an eye for definite femininity, and he wondered if Hugh wouldn't be letting Shayla stay in his bedroom after all.

"Hello, Shayla. I'm so glad you were able to come. Hugh has told me about you." Blain offered his best smile and gently took the hand she held out. The second their palms touched, Blain felt some kind of energy go through his entire body. But the sensation wasn't sickening or debilitating. It actually made him feel stronger and more in command. And he had the strangest feeling that Shayla Gallagher was more than she appeared to be.

"Come, meet Afton O'Malley." Shayla stepped aside and drew him to where a young woman stood transfixed near the rear of the car.

He gazed into her summer-blue eyes and, for a moment, forgot to speak. But only for a brief moment. "Hello, Afton. I hope you enjoy your stay," he said lamely and held out his hand.

As her hand slid into his, his first thought was that he'd never seen eyes so blue or a face so pretty. Strangely, pictures began to enter his consciousness. He looked at her and imagined a summer day, fields of flowers and sunshine. Her light brown hair was pulled back with a white scarf and when she smiled, the sweetest dimples appeared. She was truly an enchanting girl. Freckles faintly dotted her sweet face with its perfect, even features. Her slim body invited closer inspection. She could only be summed up in one word—adorable. Something about her radiated innocence, laughter and fun. And why did a picture of her walking through a thick forest wearing a white robe enter his mind? As bizarre as the image should have been, it somehow seemed right. The thought of it made him want to hold her hand longer, to imagine more. But his gaze came back to her eyes again. They were gorgeous.

"Blain, are you going to stand there all day, or are you going to help me with the luggage?" Hugh's voice broke into Blain's obvious gawking.

"Coming!" Blain reluctantly dropped her hand and grabbed the nearest bag Hugh placed on the ground. He was embarrassed at having stood and stared at Afton for so long. She'd think he'd never seen a woman before, or that he was some ignorant plow boy. Hugh had told him Shayla would be bringing an assistant, but he hadn't mentioned her age, or the fact that she was one finely crafted piece of work.

* * * * *

"Sorry I wasn't able to go to the airport with Hugh, but I had a feeder to fix. My livestock couldn't get food during the day without it," Blain said, sipping at his second cup of coffee and looking around the dinner table at his guests.

"No problem, dear boy. We quite understand." Shayla reached out and patted his arm.

Afton watched her mentor closely. The old woman was absolutely gushing over Blain. It seemed that every syllable the man uttered was of vital importance to her. Afton had never seen the Sorceress behave in such a way. Shayla had always been more reserved and dignified, tending to be aloof with everyone except Hugh.

Then Afton turned her attention toward Blain and saw the unusual gray-green eyes of many of the fairy race. He wore his thick chestnut hair tapered long in the back. It curled near his collar, and the breeze blowing through an open kitchen window pushed strands of it over his forehead. She had to physically stop herself from raising her hand to push them away. Like his forebears, he had a noble countenance. His jaw was square and his expression intelligent. The power of his bright smile invaded her senses.

She'd almost swear she was being enchanted with fairy power, but she had little experience with such things. Gawain had throttled the only fairy who had ever tried to come near her.

"So, Afton, are you from Cornwall, too?" Blain leaned forward, propped both elbows on the table and held his coffee cup between his hands.

"Yes, my parents and brothers all lived there, but we've made our home north of London in recent years." Afton wasn't sure how much she should reveal. If he knew she came from a family of Druids and that they lived in an enchanted forest, what would he say?

"You're the youngest. Right?"

"How did you know?"

Blain shrugged. "Just a guess."

"What crops do you grow on your farm?" Shayla asked, accepting a cup of tea Hugh brought to the table.

"Right now, I'm putting in corn, pumpkins, tomatoes and some other summer crops. I expect to have a good year. But then the land here is very fertile. I haven't had a failing crop yet."

"I remember Syndra had an amazing green thumb," Shayla remarked as she added cream to her tea and stirred it slowly.

"She did. I learned practically everything I know from her. I went to an agricultural college for a while, took night courses. But everything that really matters came from Mom. Of course, Dad knew everything there was to know about herbs. Even wild ones. Both of them were always in the woods or the garden." Blain stopped speaking, the memories suddenly becoming too painful.

Afton watched Blain's expression as he spoke of his parents. They hadn't been dead all that long, and he obviously missed them. There was no hiding the sadness in his beautiful eyes.

"They'd be proud of what you've done here, lad," Hugh said as he lit his briar pipe.

"I'd like to think so. I've kept everything as they would have wanted it and made some improvements we'd discussed. But I'm afraid I haven't had time to complete the new plans Mom had for her herb garden. Maybe I can get to it later in the summer."

"Were these plans on paper or just something you talked about?" Shayla asked as she put down her teacup.

"She drew a rough blueprint, but she never got the chance to start the job. Her heart just gave out." He paused and looked out the back screen door. He desperately needed to be outdoors, though the obsessive feeling was not as bad as usual. For some reason, he really did feel better.

"May I see the plans she drew?" Shayla asked quietly, breaking into his thoughts.

Blain wasn't sure he wanted anyone else looking them over. He hadn't brought them out for a very long time, and doing so would open a book of memories he'd tried to bury. But he had to get on with his life. After a moment of hesitation, he finally pushed himself away from the table. Several minutes later, he returned with a long, rolled up length of paper and spread it out on the table so Shayla could look at the drawing.

"This is wonderful," she said as her fingers slid over the sketch. "All of the old-fashioned plants are here. All of the most powerful curatives. Come and see, Afton."

Afton moved from her seat at the far end of the table and stood to look over Shayla's left shoulder. She nodded in agreement. "This is grand. It's a perfect place for fairies." She could have bitten her tongue off at her careless remark, but Hugh and Shayla didn't seem the least bit annoyed.

Blain smiled, pleased by her reaction. "It's funny you should say that. Mom said exactly the same thing when she finished the design. For some crazy reason, she loved fairies and anything to do with them. She said it was a childhood interest."

Hugh, Shayla and Afton all glanced at each other meaningfully. "She told you she believed in fairies?" Afton asked.

"She believed in everything," he responded with a slow smile. "Mom was a dreamer. I think she and Dad believed the whole world could be a better place if more folks loved nature and kept an open mind about things."

"And what do you believe?" Shayla asked, her gaze meeting his.

For a time he didn't answer. Then he shrugged. "I believe I'd better get to bed. I've got a lot of work to do tomorrow. Good night, everyone." With that, he nodded, rose and left the room. As he walked upstairs, Blain felt he should have made an effort to quiz Shayla Gallagher about his parents and her relationship with them. But some sixth sense told him she probably wouldn't answer his questions. At least, not yet. And there was a kind of...aura about the woman. When he'd shaken hands with her, he'd sensed a great strength—the way a person might feel if they were standing in the presence of a leader.

Not being able to pinpoint his feelings more precisely than that, he dismissed the sensation as his own response to someone who looked like they were in very good health. Something that had been denied him for a long time. While he was better physically right now, something about his mental state was beginning to trouble him. There was a dark hole in his thoughts whenever he pictured the future, and that scared him as much as his physical symptoms. Before the fear could escalate, he emptied his mind, determined to get a good night's rest.

Later that night, Afton stood outside the old farmhouse, closed her eyes and tried to gain a sense of her surroundings. She could still feel the evil that had been present on this beautiful farm. It was readily apparent because the source wasn't natural. It didn't fit with everything else. Its presence was much like a thorn on the land, a shard of broken glass tearing at the earth's crust. It was an abominable thing.

She opened her eyes and turned to face the bedroom in which she knew Blain slept. "Be at peace. Help is here, Blain. We won't let whoever this is destroy you. Whatever it takes, we'll save you. Even if we have to fight the blackest evil on earth." She shuddered, because even as she finished the softly spoken promise, she felt strands of a horrible evil creeping toward them all.

Chapter Three

ℰℴ

"What smells so good? Hugh, are you actually baking something?" Blain walked into the kitchen and poured coffee into a large mug. The appetite he'd felt deserting him had suddenly reappeared with a vengeance.

"No, lad. Afton started muffins baking for breakfast. She's outside looking around."

Blain looked at his watch. It wasn't even five o'clock in the morning. "You mean she flew in all the way from England yesterday and got up this early? What's wrong with her?" Blain shook his head, deciding to go find her. Just as he was heading for the door, Afton walked in. She was wearing a floral print shirt with the sleeves rolled up. It was neatly tucked into blue jeans, and her small feet were shod in hiking boots. Her shining hair was pulled up into a high pony tail, and she looked all of eighteen.

"What in the world are you doing up? And baking, too?" Blain wondered how she could look so well-rested and gorgeous at such an early hour. She was as bright and open as a Morning Glory. All blue-eyed and ready to greet the day. Her appearance reminded him that he had a packet of those particular flower seeds he needed to plant. And why did he feel the need to wrap his arms around her and hold her? Every time she got close to him, he wanted her closer.

Afton immediately looked toward Hugh for some backup, but he just smiled and left her floundering. Blain wasn't supposed to know she'd been in the garden looking for anything that didn't belong—dead wood with figure carvings, noxious herbs that had been bundled, cloth dolls that could be used in black magic. Hexes that would harm or sicken the very man who now stood before her. Flustered by his appearance, coupled with his questions, she swallowed hard and made something up.

"I hope you don't mind, but I found blueberries in the fridge, and I love blueberry muffins. I always get up early back home. There's so much to see and do." She knew she was babbling, but she wasn't good at making things up on the spur of the moment. No one had prepared her for this, and Hugh wasn't helping a bit. He was the one who had instructed her to go look for the talismans in the backyard in the first place. She was supposed to have been replacing anything evil she might find with articles of protection, like yew, oak, and ash branches. So far, she hadn't found any hexes. But she suddenly remembered the one yew branch sticking out of her back pocket, and that made her even more nervous. Blain would certainly notice it.

Blain watched Afton move about the kitchen, setting the table for breakfast. He listened to her bright chatter with suspicion. If ever anyone was hiding something, it was the pretty Englishwoman skittering around his kitchen and trying to force small talk. She also had a yew branch stuck in her back pocket, but there wasn't a yew tree anywhere near his yard. Something weird was up. But he kept silent and amused himself by watching her cook and listening to her chatter. Strangely, Rhiannon came to mind, and he didn't know why. Rhi wouldn't be caught out of bed before noon if she could help it. Why he'd think of that at this precise moment was absurd. Comparing the two women was like comparing the sun to the moon.

"I'm a little confused as to why you were outside. You couldn't see anything out there. It's still dark," Blain pointed out.

"Oh, I was just getting a feel for the place. You know, listening to the last of the night animals and the first sound of birds," Afton replied, keeping her gaze averted. Every lie she told sounded so stupid. Why wouldn't Hugh say something?

Blain looked at Hugh when she topped off his coffee cup and motioned for him to sit down at the table. Whatever was really going on, Hugh was in on it. His face was a smiling mask. What the hell were they up to?

"Oh, these came out well. I wasn't sure they would because I'm baking in an oven I'm not used to. We have different settings on them in England." Afton babbled as she pulled a tray of huge blueberry muffins out of the oven and began to pop them into a bread basket.

Despite all the ridiculous subterfuge, Blain's mouth began to water and his stomach growled at the wonderful smell.

"You don't mind do you?" Afton turned to the men and placed the basket on the table in front of them.

"Um...excuse me?" Blain's look was blank. For the moment, he wanted nothing more than to dive into the muffins, slather them with butter and reach for more.

"That I've used your oven. I love to bake. You don't mind, do you?" She nervously twisted her fingers together, caught him watching the small gesture and quickly put her hands behind her back.

"No. Of course not. It's just that I hope you didn't think you had to get up and make breakfast. You're a guest, and it's really early." When she began to babble again, Blain became even more suspicious. Clearly she wasn't used to hiding things, and it didn't come naturally. He'd love nothing more than to get her alone and question her. Or just get her alone.

"Good morning, everyone. It's going to be a lovely day, isn't it?" Shayla walked into the kitchen.

Blain looked the older woman over and noted she was wearing a long skirt and long sleeved blouse in matching soft blue shades. He likened her attire and quick, graceful movements to those of a butterfly. It was as though the woman was trying to present herself as airy and flighty. Something told him otherwise, and he closely watched as Shayla took a seat next to Hugh. He saw Afton pull the yew branch out of her back jeans pocket, nervously look for a place to put it then stick it behind some crockery. At the same moment, he saw Shayla nod at the younger woman as if some secret message had passed between them.

Things were getting more intriguing by the moment, and Blain began to wonder what Shayla's story was. Afton placed a pitcher of freshly squeezed orange juice on the table, along with a plate of cheese. Then she opened the refrigerator and pulled out an appetizing bowl of freshly cut fruit.

Blain continued to watch the other three people. When they talked, they were congenial, but he had the impression there was some secret scheme going on to which he wasn't supposed to be a party. And it wasn't even being cleverly hidden. There were little furtive looks and gestures that couldn't possibly be normal.

"Okay. What's up?" he finally asked.

Shayla, Hugh and Afton stopped what they were doing and looked at him.

"Whatever are you talking about?" Hugh asked.

Blain let out a frustrated sigh, shook his head and shot them each a suspicious glance. "I'm gonna eat my breakfast and go to work. Since I don't have a decoder ring, I'll assume I'm not a member of the club."

Afton guiltily lowered her gaze and turned away.

Hugh cleared his throat and muttered something unintelligible.

Shayla met Blain's stare, but she said nothing.

"Okay. Whatever you're up to, I guess you'll let me in on it when you're ready. I'm not as clueless as you seem to think. I may be big, but I'm not stupid," Blain advised. He kept his gaze on his coffee cup or plate for the remainder of breakfast. Then he silently got up and left the kitchen.

After she was sure he was gone, Afton turned to the two older Druids. "I'm sorry. He has a fairy's acuity, even though he hasn't a clue about his heritage. I think all my incessant talking is making him even more suspicious."

"That's all right, my dear," Shayla said as she thoughtfully rubbed her chin. "That intuition could save his life one day."

* * * * *

Hours later, Blain was mending a fence when it dawned on him that he felt better than he had in a long time. The chronic weariness he'd suffered seemed to have abated. He hammered a nail into a fence post, smiled and began to whistle. As he bent to retrieve another nail, he glanced toward the items at his feet—the bundle of poisonous herbs, which had been tied with black yarn, a small piece of new rope with knots tied in it and a little pictograph carved into bark. They lay at his feet, ready to be burned. All the strange objects had been gathered from his early morning inspection of the farm and its surroundings.

Deciding to get on with that chore, he cleared a small space for a fire and threw all the objects into the space. As soon as he put a match to them and the flames began to rise, the illness that lingered with him diminished even more. It was an odd coincidence that left him puzzled and again questioning his sanity.

Finding the superstitious items around his farm was odd, but this was New England. There were folk living here who still believed in the power of hexes, omens and the like. It did bother him, however, that the stuff was on his property and near his work area. When he went out at night again, he'd make sure to keep a wary eye out for trespassers. He turned to pull off a broken fence rail and saw Afton approaching. He could hardly miss her—his eyes widened in suprise. A cow, her calf and two sheep were following the woman. He grinned as the thought of the Pied Piper came to mind. And what a pretty piper she made. The sun lit her up even brighter, if that was possible. Just like a sunflower.

"What's going on?" Blain asked, thinking she had some kind of animal food in the basket she carried. Why else would the livestock be following her like a litter of puppies?

"I brought you some lunch. It's past midday, and when you didn't come back to the house, I thought you'd be hungry." She flashed a brilliant smile at him, and he readily responded by smiling back. He watched as she put the basket on the tailgate of his truck and pulled out some sandwiches. His mouth was already watering.

"I'm starved, and you didn't have to do this, you know."

"I don't mind. Besides, walking out here gave me an excuse to see more of the farm. You have the most lovely animals. They're very well cared for." She stopped and stared at the small fire. When Blain saw her gaze linger on the flames and their fuel, he watched her closely.

"What's that for?" She pointed at the contained fire pit.

"Just burning some trash. You know. Vines, rotting wood. Things that will catch fire if I don't keep them picked up."

Afton chewed on her lower lip as she saw the last of the hex mark, carved into oak bark, burn away. She took a deep breath and tried not to show the fear she felt. Blain knew she had some kind of knowledge about the burning items—and that she wasn't pleased.

"What's wrong, Afton? It's just a fire."

She immediately took her eyes off the small blaze and stared at him. "Want to tell me what's going on?" he asked, pulling off his work gloves.

"W-what are you talking about?" she responded, and he heard the fear in her voice.

Blain took a deep breath and let it out slowly. Clearly she didn't want to talk about what she'd seen in the fire. He began to understand what a cop must feel like at the scene of a crime where no one would say anything. He let the matter drop and turned his attention to the animals surrounding her. "What did you feed them to make them follow you around like this?"

She stared at him, her expression confused.

"The animals, Afton."

She shook her head as if the slight motion could clear it. "Um, nothing. They just followed me. I...I made cucumber and tomato sandwiches. Hugh said you told him your mother used to make them."

Blain looked at her, looked at the sandwich she handed him, then looked at the livestock vying for her attention. It was as if the animals hung on to every gesture she made. He took the sandwich, bit into it and knew it was the best he'd ever eaten. There were some unusual herbs in the mayonnaise and he immediately felt as if his appetite had doubled. He watched as she gently shooed the animals back toward the barn. Though they backed away, the livestock stayed near.

"Go on now. I'll come pet you later," she told them softly and laid a gentle hand on each of their heads.

To Blain's surprise, they turned in unison and began to walk back in the direction from which they'd come. Weird. But so far, everything about Afton was a little strange. The same went for her employer, the dauntless Ms. Gallagher. They'd been at the farm less than twenty-four hours, and Blain was certain neither of them was normal.

"Were you raised on a farm?" he asked as he finished off the sandwich.

"I grew up around animals," she said. "I love them. I can tell you do, too."

"You can, huh? How did you figure that out?"

"They're happy and well kept. By the way, when will the foal be born?" she asked as she handed him a cup of lemonade from a thermos.

Blain almost choked. He swallowed the rest of his sandwich with difficulty. His mare wasn't even showing yet.

The veterinarian had only just determined she was carrying a foal.

"How did you know that? No one knows about her except me and the vet. Not even Hugh." He watched her closely. His intuition didn't give him any uncomfortable vibes, but Afton O'Malley needed to start answering some questions.

"I told you, I grew up around animals. My guess is that she's early along, and she'll probably foal late. Well, you're very busy, and I should let you get back to work. I promised to help Shayla with something." She smiled, handed him the last of the sandwiches and walked away.

Blain felt as if he'd had a rug pulled out from under him. She knew too much, tried to act like she didn't and was doing her level best to actually say nothing of consequence. Who was this girl? What was her experience with animals and superstitious objects? He ran a hand through his hair, unable to resume his work until she was out of sight.

Afton had done exactly as Shayla told her, but it felt like they were moving too fast. Blain's expression had been open and friendly at first. Now, it was down right suspicious. She could sense the man staring at her as she walked away. Like most Druids, she'd always had a close relationship with animals. Shayla had sent her to expose Blain to some of the power her kind had in that regard. However, she couldn't help wondering why the Sorceress didn't just come right out and tell Blain he was half fairy and half Druid, and that a black conjurer was trying to harm him for some unknown reason.

Of course, he wouldn't believe them, and he might even ask them to leave. But that would be better than antagonizing him and playing mind games with the man. He'd probably be wondering about her knowledge of the mare's condition all day long. Like many of the Order, she could sense renewal. New life carried great power. All she'd had to do was lay her hand upon the mare's flank to feel the tiny life growing inside.

The worst part of leading the animals around and mentioning the foal was that Blain would think the incident was completely abnormal. And she was pretty certain she hadn't been able to hide her surprise at having caught him burning some evil talismans. His sense of disturbance would be aimed at her, and she didn't want his disapproval. She wanted him to trust her and consider her a friend.

"Who am I kidding?" she quietly mused. "He's gorgeous, and I want him. Period." But she knew he didn't share her feelings. When she'd walked away from him, she'd felt like she had a target on her back. He might never trust her.

* * * * *

After driving back to the farmhouse, Blain stopped to put away some tools in a nearby shed. A movement in the woods caught his attention. He crept around the shed in hopes of catching whoever had been sneaking around on his land and leaving strange objects. What he saw amazed him. He ducked behind some blueberry bushes and watched Shayla Gallagher gathering wild herbs and putting them in a basket. She was dressed in some kind of long white robe. The same kind he'd imagined Afton wearing when they'd been introduced. Wanting to keep his presence a secret, Blain quietly backed away. As he did so, the older woman turned in his direction. He could almost swear she knew he was present. He continued to back away and quickly left. The incident had him questioning not only his own sanity, but the sanity of those living in his house.

Near suppertime, he wanted to believe his imagination was working overtime, especially in regards to his guests and all the strange objects he'd found. But he had a sense of weird foreboding that was different from anything he'd known, and the feeling had nothing to do with his physical afflictions. In fact, the illness that had been ravaging him seemed to be gone, but he still felt as if something wasn't right.

Then he found more bundles of herbs on the window sills of the barn and several more on the sills of the house. He wasn't sure who had put them there or why, but the herbs in these new bundles weren't poisonous, as previous bundles had been. They weren't hemlock or stinging nettle. Instead, harmless yarrow and mint had been bundled with lavender and rosemary. But even though they were harmless, Blain decided that if someone didn't come clean about the shenanigans soon, all hell was going to break loose. He was getting tired of it, and he began to attribute his fear of the future to finding all the odd little bits of superstitious paraphernalia. The problem was, some of what he found was old and dried up, and some of it was fresh. It was impossible to tell how long the stuff had been lying around, so he couldn't come out and accuse his visitors or Hugh about something so odd. So while the others ate supper and made small talk, he answered when spoken to but kept his eyes on them. If he concentrated hard, he could imagine that he knew what they felt. But if that was true, he was worrying over nothing because everything he imagined he felt about them was non-threatening.

When everyone decided to turn in early, he remained outside on the porch. If he had any sense, he'd go to bed and get some sleep. But a restless urge hit him. The moon was full and the night was young. He decided to go into town, knowing where the trip would take him. Rhiannon. He felt a kind of pull, as if something beckoned him to her. When he drove up in front of the antique shop and parked, he saw the lights were on upstairs. He made his way up the steps to the side entrance. The wooden frame creaked as he ascended. Before his fist could even make contact with the door, Rhiannon opened it.

"Baby! What a wonderful surprise. I thought I wouldn't see you until later this week." Rhiannon pulled him into the apartment, slammed the door behind him and threw her arms around his neck. The kiss they shared started slowly, but Blain abruptly ended it. Where the touch of her lips had once been sweet, they now seemed sour. With all the makeup she wore, she looked a little harsh instead of alluring and sophisticated as he'd once thought her to be. And suddenly, there was something dark, almost seedy about her. He stared at her longer than he normally would have, and she seemed to notice some change in him. Her expression altered, going from open lust to a thoughtful, pensive stare.

"You feel tense," she said as she began to massage his shoulders. "What's wrong, baby?"

"Nothing's wrong. It's just that Hugh's friends showed up yesterday, and they're the strangest couple of women you'd ever want to meet."

"Tell me about them." She continued to rub his shoulders.

He moved away from her so that he was slightly out of reach. Something inside him—an unknown warning—made him want to back away from her touch. He attributed his attitude change toward Rhiannon to the new people in his life whose actions had his nerves on edge. Without warning, the old tingling that usually proceeded a bout of nausea rushed over his skin. It was almost as if he'd developed a sudden aversion to being too close to Rhiannon.

Recalling she'd asked him to tell her about his visitors, he said, "There's an older woman, Shayla. Hugh says she's some kind of cultural expert, but she wears weird clothing while looking for wild herbs in the woods. Then there's Afton." Blain stopped. What could he say about Afton that wouldn't sound absolutely ridiculous? And why didn't he want to talk about Afton with Rhiannon? Something inside him didn't want to have the women associated with one another, not even in a conversation.

"Go on. Tell me about her, too," Rhiannon coaxed as she moved closer and let her hands drift over his body.

"Afton bakes good muffins, and she's got a knack with animals." It was the best he could do without sounding absurd.

"What's so strange about wearing odd clothing while looking for herbs, being a good cook and liking animals? I think these new friends of yours sound sweet." She softly blew into his ear and took the lobe into her mouth.

Again Blain moved away. At any other time, having a woman like Rhiannon come on to him would have been so sexually arousing that he wouldn't have been able to stop the urge to throw her down and have his way with her. Now, however, the idea not only left him feeling cold, it actually began to irritate him.

"Sorry, I can't do this." He gently disengaged her outstretched arms from his body and moved away from her.

"What's wrong? You've never acted like this before."

He noted that her tone of voice had become as cool as their relationship was about to. "I don't know what to say. I've led you to believe I came by here to make love, and that wasn't the case. All I wanted to do was talk."

"Talk? Well, that's something you've never really had an interest in, baby. Can't we talk in bed?"

Blain shook his head, and his mind quickly went back to all the empty times they'd shared. There wasn't one substantial moment in their encounters. "Every time I'm here, all we do is have sex. I haven't meant to use you, but that's exactly what it feels like I'm doing." He watched as her hard expression became even harder and colder.

"That's what I suddenly seem like to you? Used? Is this the part where we start being just friends? You know, the beginning of the royal flush for me?" She put her hands on her hips and glared at him.

Blain held out his hands in a supplicating gesture. "I can't explain it, Rhi. Please try to understand. There's got to be more between a man and a woman besides sex. When we're together, we hardly ever leave this apartment. We never go out to eat, to a movie or a drive. It's just sex, and some of what we do is…well, kinky. We never talk. Never. Doesn't that bother you? For crying out loud, Rhi, I don't even know your favorite color or what music you like. I hardly know anything about you."

"No, none of that has ever bothered me," she snapped. "And it didn't bother you until now. What the hell is wrong with you?"

He dragged one hand through his hair. He didn't know how to articulate that he wanted to be with someone who could have thoughts deeper than what sexual position to try next. There had to be more to a relationship than that. He remembered the way his parents had loved each other. It had only taken a glance between them and one knew what the other was thinking. He had grown up watching that kind of passion. It was deep and pure, and he wanted that kind of devotion. That kind of communication. Sex would be all the more fulfilling because of it.

"If your silence is any indication of the way we're headed tonight, I suggest you leave until you get your head straight. I don't know if your uncle has finally convinced you not to like me or these people from England have gotten to your head. Or maybe you're starting to listen to the town gossip. Whatever it is, Blain, I don't like it. I've only done what you wanted, and you enjoyed it. So don't play pious with me."

"You're right. And I'm sorry. But can't we talk about this?"

She adamantly shook her head. "Not right now. You've made me feel like the whore everyone in town thinks I am. Just go." She turned her back on him.

"I'm sorry, Rhi." He was on the verge of telling her she deserved better, but her sullen tone made him feel even worse about his treatment of her. He could easily justify his actions by saying they were both adults, and she could have altered their relationship at any time. But his parents had raised him to love a woman, not use her. And that was exactly what he'd done, whether she'd agreed to it or not. Of course, he wasn't being completely fair to her. He could have also slowed the relationship down, or changed or altered it at any time, and he hadn't. Worse, he was actually seeing her differently...and comparing her to Afton. He *was* judging her. He quietly turned away and left her apartment.

He was walking to his truck when he saw Reverend Myers standing on a nearby corner. The clergyman's house wasn't far away, and Blain had often seen the man walking in the vicinity. He guessed Myers was on one of his nightly constitutionals and had seen his retreat from Rhiannon's apartment.

"Good evening, Reverend." Blain nodded at the tall, wire-thin man, refusing to be intimidated by the preacher's presence and his glowering, holier-than-thou expression.

"Young man, I'd like to have a word with you." He raised his hand as he stalked over to Blain's truck.

"Look Reverend Myers, I know what you're going to say, so you can just keep it to yourself. Okay?" Blain was in no mood for the soul-scorching the man would give him and started to walk away. But his path was suddenly blocked by the Reverend's lithe body. A bony finger was planted firmly in front of his nose as the man began to lecture him for the hundredth time. Blain watched Myers' face turn a dark shade of rhubarb red, and his angry expression made his sharp features even more pronounced. The man reminded Blain of an overactive, mean-tempered terrier that needed medicating.

"Blain McTavish, this is a small town. If you must proceed in your carnal activities, can't you and that woman find some place else to meet? You have this whole place talking, and Harvest is a God-fearing, Christian community. Even our children know of your liaisons with that...woman from New York. Must you flaunt what you're doing in the faces of parents who are trying to raise their children with morals? Can't you even pull the shades in that apartment so the rest of us aren't inflicted with your debauchery?"

Blain watched the thin man's face twist and prune up, and his stringy, dark hair fall into his eyes as he lectured. Blain took a deep, calming breath and tried to be tactful. "Look, Reverend Myers, what the rest of the town does is none of my business, just like what Rhiannon and I do is none of theirs. Your parishioners would better serve their children and the community by watching out for drug dealers instead of spying on other people's private lives. Now, if you don't mind, I've had a long day and would like to go home."

"You should be worrying about a home for your immortal soul, not in satisfying your lustful needs with a daughter of Satan."

Blain raised his hands in frustration and walked around the preacher. He was tired of dealing with the man. Time and time again Myers had confronted him about his affair with Rhiannon, and the old doomsayer didn't seem to care where the confrontations took place. He'd just come out of the feed store the last time the hawk-faced clergyman berated him, and half the town's farmers had been present to hear the lecture.

On that occasion, Blain had also held his temper and walked away. The man was annoying, but he figured that sooner or later another citizen would transgress so the good Reverend would have somebody else to chase after.

"Mark my words, young McTavish. You'll be punished for your sordid behavior. You'll be punished," Myers yelled portentously as Blain got into his truck and drove away.

* * * * *

For days, everything at the farm went on much the same. Blain got up early in the morning and would pretend not to notice Afton's excursions into the garden, where she continually looked for something, and Shayla's walks into the woods, where she collected her herbs. During this time, his physical strength returned to normal, but there was an increasing feeling that something bad was about to happen, and that put him in a constant state of wariness. He also kept finding more strange talismans and bundles of garden herbs. Lemongrass was tied together with wild flowers and ordinary sage with lemon balm. If he kept collecting them, he'd have enough dried herbs to cook with all winter long.

And some of the livestock he'd been treating for various illnesses seemed to suddenly get better without his having to call the vet.

Then, there was Afton. The more she tried to keep out of his way, the more he wanted her to get back in it. During the day, he found himself returning to the farmhouse for some stupid excuse or another just to be near her.

One warm evening after supper, he saw her exit the house and walk toward the woods. He quickly excused himself from Hugh and Shayla, sensing the two older people might want some time alone. He caught up with Afton in the yard at the back of the farmhouse. She was sitting on an old log and looking up at the twilight sky. Her smile warmed him as he approached. "Nice night to sit and watch the stars come out." He took a seat beside her.

"It's beautiful here." Afton paused for a moment. "This is where your mother wanted to put her garden, isn't it?"

He nodded. "Yeah, this is the place. One day, when I catch up on all the work, I'm going to drive into town, get the plants and spend a long weekend getting it all done."

"You should. It would be a wonderful way of remembering her and your father."

He didn't speak for a time, too caught up in memories to converse. Just quietly sitting there with her seemed to make the subject matter a bit more bearable.

"Hugh said your parents passed on quite suddenly," Afton said suddenly, making him feel as if she could read his mind.

He took a deep breath. "Yes. I'd never known them to be sick. I came home from a trip one afternoon, and Mom was sitting on the front steps crying. Before she said a word, I knew what had happened. But she never explained exactly how Dad died. She just sat there crying as though her heart would…" Blain stopped, unable to continue.

"How did you find out what cause your father's death?" Afton gently urged.

Blain shrugged. "The doctor at the hospital said it was a massive heart attack."

"Is that what you believe?"

Strange question. What else should he believe? "I…I want to believe he died doing what he loved. That it was quick and painless. So, I guess that's as good a way as any to go. But I never got to say goodbye, and that…that was hard."

She looped one arm around his. "I'm sure he knew you loved him."

Taken aback by the sudden contact, Blain gazed at her for a moment before pulling her a bit closer. He wanted to talk all night with her. It seemed so right. "It didn't take long before Mom started to get sick. The doc said she was suffering from some kind of general organ failure. It didn't make sense, and I wanted her to go see a specialist. But she wouldn't and said…she wanted to be with Dad." He tried not to let his emotions overcome him.

Afton tightly held his hand, and he was grateful for her touch. "One night, not long after that, I got up to check on her," he continued. "She was taking her last breaths on this earth. I wanted to call for help, but she wouldn't have it. All Mom wanted to do was go to Dad. And she told me…she said…"

Afton held his hand tighter. "It's okay, I'm listening."

"Right before the end, Mom said not to worry. She said that someone would be on my side, would defend me, and that I would understand when it was time. Then she was gone." He pushed back his hair and looked into the distant forest. "I didn't know what she meant, and it didn't seem to matter at the time. Then, out of nowhere, Hugh showed up a few weeks later. All I had to do was take one look at him and I knew he was Dad's brother. There are a lot of things that didn't make sense, but I was so glad to see him. To know that he was alive and that I had some family left."

"Blain, if it isn't too painful for you to talk about, what did you do with your parents' remains?"

He looked at her and wondered where the hell that question had possibly come from. And why she'd asked it. But Afton was as strange as his life seemed to be at the moment. So he said, "I had them cremated. Their urns are on the mantle in my bedroom. For some reason, I just couldn't bury them. We moved around for most of our lives, so I guess I wanted to find someplace suitable to scatter the ashes. A place they could call home. And Harvest just didn't seem to be home for them."

Afton nodded in agreement. "You'll find that place. I know you will."

He turned to look into her blue eyes. "I don't know why I'm telling you all this. I guess it's because you're so easy to talk to."

"I want to be a friend, and friends listen to each other and try to help."

For a long moment, he considered her comment. "What if a guy needs more than just friendship? What if he needs and wants some real commitment? What then, Afton?"

She swallowed hard and took a deep breath. "I think a friend is what you need most...at the moment."

He slowly leaned toward her. "You're right. But sometimes that's awfully hard to do...especially at the moment."

Afton felt his lips brush her hair and wanted to fall into his arms. She could feel a strength about him that she never had with any other man. He was gentle with his animals and loved the land. But he was warrior class at the same time. His build, carriage and the power she sensed within him all said so. And what would happen when he found out about his heritage? Would he want anything at all from her? Or Hugh and Shayla?

She gently pushed him away, though it was one of the hardest things she'd ever had to do. His touch made her insides weak and trembling. "Why don't you bring out those garden plans tomorrow? Maybe we can start on them."

Blain sighed when he sensed Afton's reluctance. She wasn't ready for his advances, which was just as well. He had someone else to think about. Rhiannon. Though he knew it wasn't fair, he couldn't help comparing the two women. One of them was a like a glittering gem—cold and lustrous. The other was like the reflection off a pond—deep and entrancing. And of the two, Afton was so much easier to talk with. "All right. We'll look at the plans tomorrow," he said.

"Good. I guess I'd better get inside. Shayla will be wondering where I've gotten to, and she's sort of my boss."

Blain watched her rise and walk gracefully away. "How can I let her go?" he murmured to himself.

* * * * *

Blain woke up in a cold sweat. It had been so long since he'd felt ill that he'd thought he was permanently over whatever had weakened him. Using his nightstand for support he tried to rise, but a sudden bout of dizziness sent him and the table straight to the floor. He tried to sit up and everything went black.

Afton woke up immediately at the sound of furniture and a body hitting the floor. She turned on her lamp and grabbed her robe. By the time she was in the hallway, Shayla and Hugh were there as well.

"What was that sound?" Afton asked as she stood beside Shayla, her hand gripping the older woman's arm.

"It came from Blain's room. We'd better check on him." Hugh began to move down the hallway. "Blain, lad, are you all right? He rapped sharply on Blain's bedroom door. When there was no answer, he opened the door. Blain was lying unconscious on the carpet. He was bare from the waist up and a fine sheen of sweat covered his torso.

"Hurry," Shayla urged as she rushed into the room. "We need to get him back into bed."

It took all three of them to move Blain's six-foot-three-inch frame onto the bed. Afton left the room, but quickly returned with a bowl of cool water, a clean cloth and some herbs. She watched as Hugh sat on the bed and tried to wake Blain. "Do you think he can hear us?" she asked as she handed him the cloth.

"No, lass, I'm sure he can't." He began to clumsily dab at Blain's forehead. "While I've been living here, nothing like this has ever happened, and I don't mind telling you it scares the bloody hell out of me. Why is he so ill?"

Afton could see the distress in the older man's face and the clumsiness of his movements. She moved forward to take the cloth from Hugh. "Here, let me do that."

Shayla looked around the room. She studied the rows of books on a nearby shelf, walked to the fireplace then slowly turned and said, "We need to check this room thoroughly."

"What are we looking for?" Hugh asked.

"I don't exactly know, but we need to search everything. Look for an amulet, something small." Shayla began to run her hands over the items on Blain's dressing table.

As the two Druid elders searched the expansive room, Afton did her best to lower Blain's temperature. From her robe pocket, she added a small sprinkle of herbs to the cool water and dipped the cloth into it.

Blain sighed in apparent relief when she gently touched the cloth to his face and bare chest. It was the first time in her life that she'd ever been so close to a half-clothed man, other than her own father and brothers. She tried not to stare at his muscular shoulders and chest, but she couldn't help it. He was the most beautiful man she'd ever seen. The muscles of his flat abdomen and sculpted arms were equally well developed. Anyone unfamiliar with the Order would look at him and attribute his wonderful physique to hard manual labor, but Afton recognized him as one of the fairy race's finest warriors. Afton guessed he could easily wield one of the heavy, ancient weapons fairies or Druids sometimes carried. Her gaze traveled down his abdomen to the top of the gray sweatpants he apparently wore as pajama bottoms. She inappropriately wondered if the rest of him was as well-endowed.

"Look!" Shayla cried out as she held up her hand.

"What is it?" Hugh asked as he walked toward her.

Shayla held up her palm and showed Hugh the long lock of hair with a thin black thread tied around it. "This is Blain's hair. Someone has tried to hex him with it. This is a binding amulet. With it, someone practicing black powers can bewitch their victim."

"Will it kill him?" Afton asked as her gaze rested on Blain's handsome face.

"No, this isn't powerful enough for that. It wasn't meant to be. Someone only wanted to weaken him." Shayla paused. "Whoever did this may be after something he has, or this may be an effort to seek revenge. They could only have gained access to his room by using some kind of magic. And they would have to be very powerful or we would have sensed this sooner."

"Can you undo the spell?" Hugh' gaze was fixed on the amulet.

"Of course I can. Just leave this to me." Shayla carefully unwound the thread from the strand of hair. Though still unconscious, Blain sighed as if he found relief the instant the thread was loose. She tossed the thread aside, walked to the bed and handed the long curl to Afton. When Afton placed it next to Blain's head, there was no mistaking it was his. It was the same light brown color.

"Someone had to have been very close to him to get a lock of his hair," Afton observed.

"Aye, that's true," Hugh said. "But the only one with that kind of personal contact is Rhiannon Stone."

Shayla turned to Hugh. "What do you mean?"

"I told you he's having an affair with the woman. He might even be in love with her," Hugh responded.

"Have you been close enough to this woman to sense anything evil?" Shayla walked to an open window and stared into the woods.

"I've met her and haven't perceived anything wrong in a spiritual sense. I just never particularly cared for her, but she truly seems to care for Blain."

"He left the house tonight, didn't he?" Shayla asked, looking at Hugh as she turned from the window.

"Aye, he did. He went out very late to check on a new calf in the upper pasture. If there are more evil amulets that far from the house, anyone could be placing them about."

"Well, this will stop once and for all." Shayla nodded in determination. "His life energy is being drained by some source. Unless we isolate that source, this kind of thing will happen again."

"If I can make a suggestion?" Afton stood and looked at Shayla and Hugh. "Perhaps we're going about this the wrong way. If we try to isolate the source of the problem, it might take too long to find out who's behind this and what they may know of Blain's connection to the Order. My instincts say that Blain doesn't have that kind of time."

"You have a plan?" Shayla crossed her arms and waited.

"Maybe we can find a reason to get the source of Blain's problem to come straight to us. We could find an excuse to bring everyone he knows to one place. Something like...like a party. We could invite people he knows to come here. With everyone present, we could use our combined powers and find out who might be behind this. It might not work, but at least we could try."

Hugh stroked his chin thoughtfully. "Yes, we could do that. But what if everyone won't come?"

Shayla smiled. "We'll make it an affair people won't want to miss. If someone chooses not to accept the invitation and we find nothing suspicious about those present, that will narrow the field of suspects considerably. Even though this person or group of persons is very powerful, I doubt they can keep hiding their identity from all of us for long. And with us keeping watch, Blain will be safe enough, no matter what happens."

"Aye, I think this will work. People in a town this size don't care what the reason is. They're always looking for an excuse to party." Hugh rubbed his hands together in a conspiratorial fashion.

"Well, since it doesn't look like we're going to get much sleep tonight, let's search the rest of the house for more amulets," Shayla suggested briskly. "Afton, you stay with Blain. Hugh and I will be making plans. And good thinking, girl. Perhaps I'll make a warrior class Druid of you yet."

Afton beamed at Shayla's compliment as they exited the room. She sat on the bed next to Blain. His color had returned to normal, and his forehead was much cooler to her touch. Chewing on her lower lip, she looked toward the door to make sure Hugh and Shayla had truly gone. Then she gently placed her hand on his chest. It was rock solid, warm and smooth. His heart beat steady and strong beneath her palm. She placed his loose lock of hair in the pocket of her robe. It was only to keep someone from misusing it again, she assured herself.

He moaned softly and turned his head toward her. She knew he'd sleep the rest of the night. That was fine by her. She could look at him all she wanted without anyone being the wiser. She kept him cool by applying more of the herbal water and occasionally straightened the sheets. Some time later, he moaned softly and finally opened his eyes.

"What the hell hit me?" He tried to sit up despite the pounding in his head and weakness in his body.

"Lie still, Blain." Afton gently pushed him back down. "You've been ill and shouldn't try to sit up yet."

"I've never been sick. At least…not this sick," he croaked as he realized Afton's small hands were able to force him down.

"Well, you were quite ill last night, and I've been given orders to keep you in bed."

"Orders? Whose orders?" Blain looked up at her, his vision clearing.

"Shayla. She says you're to stay in bed, so stay you will."

Blain looked at the young woman sitting on the bedside. Her blue eyes were determined, and he knew she'd do everything possible to follow the older woman's command. From what he'd seen, Afton practically hung on every word Shayla said. But he had work to do. "Look, I'm grateful to you for watching over me, but I have to get up. The animals won't feed themselves, and there's other work to be done."

"Hugh, Shayla and I will see to the chores. But if you leave this bed, I won't be responsible for what Shayla does to put you back here."

"What's that supposed to mean?" Blain wanted to laugh at the silly threat, but his head was pounding so hard that humor escaped him. How could Shayla, Hugh and a slip of a girl keep him from doing as he wished?

"I know what you're thinking, Blain McTavish. But trust me when I tell you that if Shayla Gallagher wants to keep you in bed for the next month, she can do it. So rest."

As he contemplated what she'd said, Afton raised the cloth to his forehead and chest again. Hugh's friends were certainly presumptuous in his home. Relaxing another half hour or so wouldn't matter. The herbal water Afton was using had a soothing effect. The scent reminded him of deep forests and plants which grew there. When he closed his eyes, he could almost see the picture the fragrance conjured. It was cool and inviting.

"There now," Afton crooned, "let the herbs do their work. That's much better, isn't it?"

Blain smiled. There were worse things a man could be subjected to than the tender caresses of a lovely, soft-voiced English girl. He opened his eyes, turned his head sideways and gazed at her face. Her eyes were now the deep blue color of forest violets. He decided to rest just a few more minutes. Somehow the minutes slipped away, and he fell into a placid sleep. Later, he thought the herbs must have been responsible for the strange dreams of mythical creatures cavorting in his woodland fantasy world.

Chapter Four

ဆာ

Afton turned her head as Shayla quietly opened the door and crept into the room.

"How is he?" Shayla whispered, tiptoeing to where Afton sat.

"When he awakens, the pain will be gone, but he'll still be weak. I don't think he should work for a couple of days," Afton responded as she carefully pushed a thick lock of hair off Blain's forehead.

"Hugh and I discovered more amulets hidden within the house and barn," Shayla said. "Separately, they're so weak we couldn't sense them, but then they weren't meant for us. Some have been put in places where only Blain works. Some of his personal belongings, such as a button from his shirt, a work glove and a comb, have been used to make the hexes. They're slowly sapping his life essence. Especially since there were so many and he was exposed to them for so long."

"If the person doing this is so powerful that they can get into and out of this house without being seen or having us sense them, why would they have to hide the hexes so close to Blain? Seems like they could use black magic from a distance." Afton tucked a strand of Blain's hair behind his ear.

"The spells used were intentionally weak so as not to alert him to the seriousness of the situation. Obviously, weaker spells work best in closer contact to their victim. He thinks he's merely been working too hard or the malady exists in his head. This draining is being done slowly, methodically. It's as though someone is testing his endurance. Whatever the reason, you're right about the power of these evil beings. They may be able to materialize where they wish if the conditions are right, and that's the worst use of black magic."

"Do you think whoever is doing this means to eventually cause him serious harm?" Afton asked. "And you suspect someone and have some ideas about the motives for all this, don't you?"

"Yes, girl, to all your questions. But all I'll say for now is that someone means to kill Blain. Of that, I'm certain. This farm and the woods surrounding it are being visited almost nightly by some evil. Why this person hasn't just got on with it is a mystery."

"Shayla, if even I can feel that he has inherited powers, someone more potent will discover them soon. Surely they already suspect he's a blend of two powerful races, or this hexing wouldn't betaking place. He's going to have to be told who he is."

"That's quite true, my girl. I was planning on having a ritual bonfire on the Summer Solstice. He'll be told then, though I don't pretend to know how he's going to react."

"He'll think we're crazy." Afton looked down at the sleeping man.

Shayla sighed. "I'll make him believe. What he does after that is what concerns me most. He must come back to the Order and learn the ways of both his parents."

"I'll help him in whatever way I can, Shayla. You can depend on it."

"I know you will." Shayla placed a hand on Afton's cheek. "You're coming to care for Blain a great deal, aren't you?"

"Well...uh...no more than you and Hugh are. We're all interested in restoring his heritage to him and finding out if he has powers he can use for the benefit of others."

"Aye," Shayla responded with a nod. "Come with me. We have a great deal of work to be done. Keeping evil at bay will be more difficult since we're on ground which isn't sacred to us. Let Blain rest alone. When he awakens, he'll find his world greatly changed."

"As you command," Afton reluctantly agreed as she turned and glanced once more at her patient.

When Blain awoke he felt much better, but he was still tired to the bone. He knew whatever was happening to him physically wasn't going to stop, and it frightened him more now than ever before. As ill as he'd been, nothing in his life had ever caused him to pass out. He looked around the bedroom. It was afternoon. He could tell by the setting sun. But his clock had been moved from the nightstand, so he had no way of knowing the exact time.

He carefully sat up, swung his legs over the side of the bed and stood. So far, so good. The only thing he felt besides the debilitating weariness was extreme hunger. Surely that was a good sign. Sick people didn't want to eat much, did they? He moved to the closet, pulled on some jeans and one of his work shirts. His boots took a bit more time as he had to fuss with the laces and rest a bit. Why was he so damned tired? And where was everyone? He was certain Afton had been in the room with him earlier. He couldn't have imagined her soft voice or her hands on his body.

"Ah, you're awake." Hugh smiled as he poked his head around the door.

"How long was I out?" Blain looked at his uncle and tried to stand. When he wobbled, the older man rushed to help him.

"You've been resting for almost three days now. Afton came in earlier and gave you a bit of broth, but I don't suppose you'd remember. You've been quite exhausted, lad."

"I've been out for three days? That's not possible!"

"Possible or not, that's how long it's been," Hugh declared.

Blain shook his head, let out a long sigh and clenched his hands. "Help me downstairs, will you?"

"Are you sure that's a good idea? You're still unsteady on your feet."

"I think I might feel better once I get some food in me. I'm so hungry I could eat everything in the house."

"Good. That's a healthy sign. I'll help you, but you must take the trip downstairs slow, lad. If you pass out again, none of us is big enough to get you back upstairs, even if we combine our efforts."

"I'm surprised you didn't call an ambulance. Maybe you should have. Nothing like this has ever happened to me before."

"If you don't feel better after the wonderful meal Afton is preparing, then I promise we'll get you to a doctor, lad."

Blain used his uncle's strong shoulder for support, and they made their way downstairs. As soon as he was halfway to the first floor, his nose twitched at a tempting smell emanating from the kitchen. The aroma already had him feeling better. It seemed to energize him.

As they came down the last few steps, Shayla rose from a living room chair, positioned herself on Blain's other side and helped support him as they walked into the kitchen.

"You're a winning lad, Blain McTavish. Make no mistake about it." Shayla patted Blain's shoulder as he lowered himself into a kitchen chair.

"I hope that was a compliment," Blain said as he accepted a glass of ice water from Hugh.

"It was." Shayla smiled at him and pushed back his unruly hair.

"Thanks." Blain paused to drain the entire glass of water. "I'm sorry to have been so much trouble to everyone. Man, I'm hungry!"

"You've been no trouble at all, lad," Hugh said. "We're all glad to see you up and about again. And speaking of being hungry, where's Afton? I'm a wee bit empty myself."

"She's gathering herbs to mix with the soup. You like vegetable soup, don't you Blain?" Shayla turned to Blain, handing him some more water.

"I feel like I'm starving, and soup is one of my favorite things to eat when I'm really hungry," he responded.

The back door opened and everyone turned as Afton walked in. She was carrying a small basket in one hand and a pair of herb scissors in the other. She stopped to place them on the kitchen counter before walking to where Blain sat.

"I'm glad you're up. How do you feel?" She looked down at him, restraining the urge to hug him hard.

"Better. Thank you for sitting with me. I don't know how long you stayed, but I know you were there quite a while." All the attention made him feel both guilty over their concern and wonderful that they cared.

"You're not quite steady yet, but you will be after a bowl or two of my soup. I don't like to brag, but you've never tasted anything like it. It'll have you back on your feet in no time. You must eat every drop."

She smiled at him again, and Blain thought someone should try to bottle her warmth. It would go a long way toward curing more than just illness. She briefly covered his hand with hers then left to set the table for supper.

It was all he could do to keep from grabbing the basket of homemade bread she placed on the table. The aroma was so tantalizing his stomach was doing flips. When Shayla placed a steaming bowl of the soup before him, he wasted no time diving in. Fears about his health fled as he slaked his appetite. The others seemed to enjoy the meal, but Blain swore he'd never tasted anything so good in his entire life. There was something about the soup that filled every part of him with warmth. He reacted to the food as if it were a drug, and he wanted more.

"Another bowl?" Hugh asked, rising to fill his own again.

Blain nodded and smiled his thanks as he reached for his third piece of bread. "You were right. I actually feel like part of the human race again. Afton, you're a wonderful cook."

Afton rewarded him with a brilliant smile and pushed more bread and butter toward him. As Blain continued his meal, she studied him. His remark about being part of the human race couldn't have been more wrong. While Druids were human, fairies were not. They were ethereal creatures whose existence depended upon nature. If something about Blain was attracting an evil presence, there was more to him than a human aura. What was it this foul presence wanted from him? Since she knew that only time would give them the answer, she listened as Hugh told Blain how he'd tended the farm animals with help from Shayla and her.

Blain was ashamed of the weakness which had caused him to stay in bed for so long. Whatever had been wrong was rapidly vanishing. With each moment that passed, he felt stronger. Doubts about his health seemed to fly away. Again, the attention made his chest tighten with warm emotion. It just felt plain good. He didn't want it to end.

"I don't suppose anyone wants the last of that soup?" Blain raised his eyebrows and looked around the table.

Everyone laughed and Afton rose to fill Blain's bowl with the special brew. The soup he had eaten had been filled with some of her best herbal remedies. While it was no more than healthy fare for the rest of them, Blain had badly needed its curative ingredients. His color and humor had already greatly improved.

After supper, Afton waited for a signaling nod from Shayla and Hugh. When it came, she took a deep breath before saying, "Blain, why don't you go out onto the back porch. I think there's something you should see."

Blain looked at her curiously, then rose to do as she'd asked. He walked out onto the porch and gasped in surprise. His mother's herb garden had been landscaped according to her final plans. Every last plant, arbor and stepping stone was in place. Fresh plants had been carefully planted among the old ones to complete the designs she'd drawn. Everything was as she'd imagined it. But for his father's death, his mother would have completed this lovely garden herself. Her heart had simply not been in the project after her husband died.

Shayla spoke very quietly. "Please say you like it. Your uncle, Afton and I did everything we could to make this place exactly right. We stayed up all night digging and made dozens of phone calls during the day to get just the right plants. Every stone has been placed by hand and the paths have all been dug to last. The borders have been aligned down to the last inch as the diagram specified. Because of our efforts, this garden will be here forever. And this was what we wanted. A monument to your parents. We worked very hard. Tell us it was worth it, Blain."

Even after her heartfelt explanation, Blain could only utter, "It's the most amazingly beautiful place I've ever seen. There's magic here. I wish my mother could have seen it."

Blain looked around in wonder and began to slowly walk down one of the paths. His strength increased with each step. Occasionally, he bent to inspect an herb. Smell, color, texture and design were all perfectly balanced. Soft ferns mixed with baby's breath. Purple, frilly-flowered ageratum bordered the beds. Ornamental clover bloomed in pots and hanging baskets of variegated ivy hung from low branches of oak trees. A wind chime tinkled in the evening breeze, and benches invited a weary soul to rest. Blain could almost hear his parents' laughter. How they would have loved this special place.

Then something caught his attention and lured him to the center of the garden. Within a round bed of yarrow stood a wrought-iron pedestal. Ornate, metal vines curved around the base and up to form a well. Within the well rested a striking silver globe. The globe was more than a foot in diameter and reflected the surroundings with an unearthly quality. He tilted his head slightly and gazed deep into its depths. The gleaming, setting sun reflected off the brilliant surface. It was the most enchanting piece of artwork he'd ever seen. The thing had a mesmerizing allure, and it captivated him. Then he remembered the last time he'd run nude in the forest. He recalled viewing the moon in the same way as he was now seeing the gazing globe. That's where the memory had come from. Long ago, his parents must have described this type of garden art to him, and he was only now piecing the memory together. On the night when he'd been running, the moon had looked like a giant gazing globe.

From somewhere deep inside his being, haunting images of another life flooded his thoughts. In this other place, forest beings of legend and myth dwelled. They gracefully drifted among the plants and beckoned him to come. Oh, how wonderful it would be to go to that fantasy place! It was peaceful and safe there.

"Though it wasn't in her plans, the gazing globe is something your mother would have eventually put here. I knew her well, and she would have loved it," Shayla quietly explained as she walked up behind him.

Blain heard her, but her voice didn't break the spell of the moment. Rather, it added to it. It was as if her voice was a part of the world he dreamed.

"Legend has it that its reflective surface could turn away evil spirits. Anyone practicing black magic can't tolerate seeing their reflection in it." Shayla paused before continuing. "We thought it might bring you peace and renew your strength to walk here. Your illness isn't of the body, Blain. It's of the spirit. The only way to combat such an affliction is to renew your strength from Mother Earth herself. If you close your eyes and let yourself feel, you'll know what I say is true."

Blain closed his eyes and felt his every care drift away. The cool night breeze stirred branches of the nearby oaks. An owl hooted from its roost. Something inside him yearned to be free, but he couldn't put a name to that feeling. All he knew was that this strange pull seemed older than time, and his senses became more attuned to everything. He could smell every herb and flower in the garden and knew their names. As the sun dropped lower, the yearning grew. Nothing about the desire was painful. It was just there. He wanted to be alone here and to be one with nature.

"Are you all right?" Shayla asked.

"Yes, I'm fine. Thank you for this," he said, waving a hand to encompass the garden. "All of you must have worked very hard. I don't know that my gratitude will ever be enough, but you have it all the same."

"If you enjoy the garden, that's thanks enough," Shayla said as she placed a hand on his shoulder. "Now, rest here a while. You'll have no more problems with your health. I promise you."

He heard her and the others walk away and believed what she said. Shayla Gallagher was an odd woman, but he thought her heart might be as big as the globe into which he gazed. She was right about feeling at peace. He walked closer to the globe and saw the first of the evening stars glimmer on its lustrous surface. His own reflection, however, seemed dim and far away. As though he needed to be closer. In his mind, Blain interpreted that to mean closer to nature, and not necessarily the globe itself. He recognized that thought as being strange. It was more of an impression, really. And no matter what else he believed or what his mind conjured up, his heart felt calm. He smiled. It was as if his parents were here again. He could almost feel the joy they shared at being together. He wondered if he'd ever share that same emotion with someone.

Suddenly, a memory pushed itself into his mind. He turned and ran into the house, up the stairs and into his room. At the foot of his bed was an old trunk. He hadn't opened it since his mother died. He quickly rummaged through the contents until he found what he wanted. Then he rose and made his way back downstairs and into the garden.

The lights in the house were all off. He assumed everyone needed their sleep after sitting up with him for hours and working so hard to landscape the garden. In the garden, Blain found a stone bench to sit upon. He could see the moon above and its glowing reflection shimmered on the gazing globe. He waited. As time drifted by, there was no sensation of its passing. He'd never felt so extraordinarily alive in his entire life.

He looked at the object in his hands. His father had carved it from a piece of old wood and given it to him when he was about five years old. His mother had taught him to play it. Though he wasn't sure he could do the music justice anymore, he raised the flute to his lips, closed his eyes and played.

Inside the house, Afton heard the sweetest music that had ever been created. She went to the window to see where it was coming from. The musician was Blain. The flute he played was a common instrument among the fey. Some of the fairy race were known to gift their newborns with all kinds of musical instruments the children would later learn to master. Except no fairy of her acquaintance had ever played in such an exquisite way. The vibrato was pure and clear, and she could feel its power pull her to him. Only one of the Sidhe, or spirit race, could play so enchantingly. She could feel every fiber of her body responding to the call he was giving. She wanted to run to him and be one with him. But now was the time to listen, not act.

* * * * *

"Good morning, everyone." Blain smiled warmly as he entered the kitchen. As he sat at the kitchen table, he rolled up the sleeves of a brown flannel work shirt.

"Well, you're looking much better this morning," Hugh remarked and patted Blain on the shoulder.

"I do. In fact, I feel like anything is possible." He grinned broadly at his uncle. Hugh poured them both a cup of coffee as Shayla and Afton walked into the kitchen. Afton went to the refrigerator and began to place items on the kitchen counter for breakfast. Shayla sat beside Blain.

"You know, you don't have to do this every morning," Blain said to Afton as he watched her begin cooking breakfast.

"I love it." Afton shot him a bright smile. "I cook all the time at home. My six brothers and my father need a hardy start to the day, and Shayla isn't much of a hand in the kitchen."

"Enough of that, young lady. I have other urgent business to attend rather than a family's oversized appetites. Hugh, pour me some tea, will you?" Shayla requested.

"How many brothers did you say you had? Six?" Blain grinned. He was glad to finally see Afton stand up to Shayla, even if only jokingly.

"Yes," she replied. "There's Gawain, Taurus, Drew, Sean, Ian and Bolt. Then there's Mother and Father, of course."

"And you're their little girl." Blain stated it as a fact.

"Yes, that's what I am, and it's the bane of my life. How did you know?" Afton stopped her work to look at him.

"Just a hunch." He winked at the others. "You have a sheltered air about you."

"If you mean she's a virgin, then you'd be correct," Shayla mumbled as she sipped her tea.

"Shayla!" Afton turned quickly and glared at her mentor. "That's no one's business. Now, eat your toast!"

Blain watched Shayla smile wickedly as Afton slammed the plate of fresh toast onto the table. "Temper, too," Blain shot the older woman a mischievous grin. "I'll bet she gives those brothers hell."

"I do! Now, all of you be quiet and eat. Your breakfast will get cold," Afton ordered as she stalked back to the stove.

The rest of the breakfast went by without incident. Blain felt a little ashamed that he'd joined Shayla in teasing Afton. She was obviously sensitive about her lack of worldliness. Somehow, he found the fact that she was a virgin refreshing. It was a sad statement of the times to admit he might never have met one. The more he thought about it, the more endearing Afton became. She was just a little slip of a thing, and from the things she'd said, he'd suspected her brothers were probably hulking farmers or construction workers. The kind of men who would gladly mangle anyone who looked at their charming sister for more than a glance.

He once again found himself comparing Afton to Rhiannon. Rhi was dark, alluring and sophisticated, while Afton was sweet, warm and as inviting as sunshine. He mentally shook himself for the comparison. Doing such a thing was like comparing two prize chickens at a county fair. Since he didn't want the same ever done to him, he redirected his thoughts. Like a storm coming in off the ocean, something dour suddenly entered into his consciousness again. A warning of some kind that he just couldn't understand. Everything seemed perfect. The sun was up, he had friends and family around him. Why did he feel like some ominous, dark cloud was on the horizon? Why couldn't he just be happy with what he had and forget the dreaded premonition that was constantly haunting him?

* * * * *

Afton walked to the field where Blain worked. His current project was fixing a pump on a stock tank. She had his lunch in her basket and, as usual, half the livestock at her heels. She turned and laughed at their antics as they tried to keep up with her. Animals knew when there was someone in their midst who loved them. She knew they understood she could never harm a single one of them. And Hugh had told her Blain's farming instincts seemed to stop in the fields. He never butchered any of the animals he personally raised. And that fact was about as sweet a thing as Afton had ever heard. Warrior class he might be, but it sounded as if his heart was pure honey.

Blain watched Afton walk toward him and laughed out loud. She'd added a stray cat, two geese from a nearby pond and several more horses to her menagerie. As she neared, he turned and splashed cool water onto his face and bare chest. It no longer bothered him that animals gravitated to her. He had been raised loving them and the land. Afton simply had that in common with him. Strangely, his thoughts drifted to Rhiannon again. She'd phoned earlier in the day. When he'd made excuses about needing to stay near the farm and work on the weekend, she'd become angry and refused to talk. So their contact had ended badly again.

Somehow, her anger should bother him more than it did. He tried to imagine Rhi's sultry figure gathering herbs, working in the garden, feeding livestock or bringing him lunch the way Afton did. The picture wouldn't come, and he chided himself yet again for the comparison. It was a bad habit he was drifting into. Just like the bad habit he had of looking to the future and feeling some disastrous event looming there. By sheer force of will, he let his mind go blank and thought of only the beauty in front of him. And that made him smile.

"What are you grinning about?" Afton laughed when the cat meowed for attention and bent to scratch its head.

"You and the entire contents of the Ark." He took the basket from her and walked to a nearby tree for shade.

"I know. I haven't the heart to send them away. Besides, they keep me company while I explore your woods."

"And what do you find so fascinating about my woods, young Afton?"

"Herbs. There are different kinds here than in the forests back home. And I'm not that young, young Blain," she countered.

"What are you? Nineteen, maybe twenty?" Blain opened the basket and almost drooled over the fresh bread, honey, fruit and cheese he found.

"I was twenty-three last October." Afton placed her hands on her hips and grinned.

Blain sat beneath a tree and openly stared. "You look much younger, though you wear the ripe old age of twenty-three well."

"You're as bad as my family and Shayla. No one takes me seriously. And, just for that, you can eat lunch by yourself. You're much too old for me," she joked.

She turned and made a show of dramatically flouncing off, but Blain jumped to his feet and caught her arm before she got far. "Afton, I'm sorry. I was just teasing," he said earnestly.

She looked at him and tried to pretend she was upset but ended up laughing instead. "Well, I guess I don't mind eating with an older man. After all, it isn't as though someone your age could pose a threat to a girl. I've heard older men find it difficult to get up to anything, if you know what I mean."

"Why you little...I'm not *that* harmless." He laughed at the cut to his virility and made a mock pass at her.

She countered by running behind an oak tree to hide, laughing as she did so. "What's the matter, Blain? Winded already? Maybe someone your age shouldn't exert himself so much. You might break something vital," she playfully provoked as she dodged him yet again. "Maybe you should find some older woman to chase. You know, someone who's desperate enough to let you catch her?"

"That's it!" Blain laughed again as he faked going one direction around the oak tree. She was caught off guard and he tackled her to the ground.

Laughing hysterically at the mock battle, Afton tried to squirm free and almost succeeded, but Blain was on her in an instant. He momentarily pinned her arms over her head and rested his weight on his elbows. His body pinned hers down.

"All right, you little minx. I promise I won't make any more remarks about your age if you don't make any about my manhood. Besides," he stopped to pant and grin at her, "I'm only seven years older than you. That's not really old now, is it?"

"No Blain. It isn't that old." Afton's chest heaved as she looked up at him, trying to catch her own breath. "I just want people to quit treating me like a child."

"You're no child." Blain gazed down into her blue eyes and felt her soft body beneath his. Suddenly, the situation turned more serious. The laughter was gone, and he was all too aware that the body beneath his was very womanly. There was nothing immature about her. Every desirable female attribute was in the exact right place.

For moments, he searched her face. His hands released her arms and moved to her soft hair. It had come loose from its fastener and lay about her in long disarray. He'd never before seen it down like that, and the sunlight glowed in its depths. He felt her hands come up to his shoulders and tentatively caress them. He realized she was uncertain as to what to do, and she was searching for an answer in his gaze.

Blain knew he should leave her alone. She was an innocent and certainly not the kind of woman who usually appealed to him and his experienced needs. But need her he did. The evidence of that need lay heavy and thick in his jeans. And she was so sweet and inviting.

He lowered his mouth to hers and gently wrapped one arm around her shoulders. To his surprise, she responded with all the urgency of a woman long denied. Her mouth opened to his, and their tongues explored each other, thrusting as their bodies might. The soft moan that came from deep within her throat almost drove Blain crazy with desire. For someone who was untouched, Afton O'Malley responded with astonishing passion. It drove him to the edge of control, and he knew that someday someone would hold this beautiful miracle in his arms.

He recoiled at the idea. The thought was beyond unacceptable. It actually angered him. He kissed her more forcefully because of that anger.

Afton had never believed a man like Blain would be interested in her. But there was a powerful feeling that came with the newfound knowledge that he was interested. From the first time she'd seen him, she'd been attracted to him, but she'd never thought that she would find herself in his arms and that being there could be so glorious. All the handfastings she'd seen in the Order had been nothing more than rituals to her before now. Once, she'd come across two fairies making love in the woods, but she had quickly turned away. Their passionate cries had been little more than an embarrassment, and she'd never believed she'd allow herself to lose control that way. Until now. Now she knew what she'd been missing, and she also knew that Blain was the only one who could fill the need stirring inside her.

Blain could feel the deep passion within Afton. It was in her gaze, her touch and the way she moved beneath him. And he had never known contact with another being could be so elemental.

What they were experiencing wasn't just sexual—it was a kind of spiritual joining. Every moment brought about a profound bonding as he held her closer and traced small kisses along her jaw and her neck. She arched for him beautifully as he began to caress her body. He wanted their clothes gone, and he wanted them together in some peaceful place deep in the woods. He knew of such a place, and some instinct told him how to get her there, but he had to go slow. Afton was new to passion and shouldn't be rushed. She had to come with him knowing they'd make love and wanting it to happen. He'd made monumental mistakes with Rhiannon by moving too fast. It wasn't going to happen this time. This was a completely different kind of relationship—one that had all the promise of the future. It deserved greater care and respect.

He used every ounce of control he had and pushed himself away from Afton. The sudden withdrawal from her was unusually painful. It was almost as if someone had physically torn something away from him. For a moment, he had to close his eyes against the pain. He'd never felt anything like it before.

Afton wanted Blain to hold her again, but common sense pushed itself into her consciousness. What would Shayla do to them? The Sorceress had been unusually lenient with her and highly tolerant of Blain and his circumstances. Would she continue to be so if she knew what had just happened between them?

"Afton, we'd better slow down and get a grip here. Don't think for a minute I don't want you. I sure as hell do. But it'll be better between us if we know more about each other first. I want to know everything you feel and need. What you like and don't like. I want that connection before making love with you. Call me old-fashioned, but that's the way I am."

Afton sat up nodding. "Of course, you're right. I...I don't know what got into me."

He adamantly shook his head. "You haven't done a single damned thing wrong. I came on too fast. I'm sorry," Blain said as he pushed his hair off his forehead.

"There's no need for apologies on your part. It was just one of those things. And you're probably feeling guilty because of Rhiannon. You think you've betrayed her." Afton quickly stood and began to pull the grass from her hair.

"Rhiannon? How do you know about her?"

"Don't worry," Afton said, ignoring his question, "neither she nor anyone else will ever know about this. It was just a silly game that got out of control. I would never cause problems between you and someone you care about, Blain." She sighed inwardly, feeling terrible for him—for them both. Blain could never be with Rhiannon, though he couldn't know that, and she could never be with him. Not while he held her and thought of another. And not so long as she couldn't summon the powers she was meant to control.

She walked away from him, and a strange tightness formed in her throat. For the first time in years, she wanted to cry. Friends of hers had blathered on for days about the loss of someone who wouldn't respond to some ardent gesture. She thought their behavior was silly and time-consuming. Why would anyone actually cry over someone who obviously didn't reciprocate their feelings? In this case, Blain had admitted he was attracted to her, but she knew Rhiannon was his lover. Now she understood what her friends cried about. It hurt to be rejected by someone you cared for and wanted.

Blain wanted to go after Afton, to tell her that Rhiannon hadn't even entered his mind. But that was a lie. He had been comparing them almost from the moment he set eyes on Afton. What kind of man did such a thing? He knew it was wrong, but he kept doing it anyway. Afton probably thought he was the worst kind of bastard for craving two women at the same time. Despite any woman's opinion, some men would see that as a very desirable position. Blain didn't. His confusion about his conduct left a bitter taste in his mouth. It made him feel like he was using people.

He ran a hand through his hair and watched Afton walk away with the animals, realizing he'd never wanted anyone so badly. His relationship with Rhiannon didn't even come close to what he was feeling for Afton. His desire for her wasn't just based on sex. It was something deeper. There was such a connection between them. It was as if the Fates were pushing them together, finding things they both loved and emphasizing those similarities. But Blain remembered there were things about Afton that weren't normal, and the abnormalities weren't anything he could sensibly articulate. He was sure she was keeping secrets, and for some unknown reason, that scared the hell out of him. And with the fear came that strange, bloodcurdling feeling about the future. Every single time he got close to feeling all right emotionally, that dark premonition raised its head. And it came back now with a vengeance. The hair on the back of his neck stood up and he felt rage over his helplessness. In frustration, he walked to a fence and drove his fist into the top rail, snapping it in two. What the hell was wrong with him? Why, when he reached out for a small measure of true happiness, did this awful presentiment of impending darkness reappear? Instead of finding a way to go after Afton and work things out with her, his escalating fear made him suspect her of something nefarious. It was almost as if someone was conjuring a way to keep him unhappy and off balance.

He backed away from the fence and silently cursed. Whatever this feeling was, it was constantly coming between him and all he wanted. But like a terrible omen, he knew that whatever was frightening him was closer than ever. It was taking on an actual life and a presence. It was becoming as real as the rail he had just broken. And he believed this dark entity wanted more than just his life. It craved the last bit of his sanity. What was it, and why wouldn't it leave him alone? And how could he stop it?

Chapter Five

ɞ

Blain threw hay into the mare's stall and kept his mind on that one task. There were plenty of chores that always kept him busy. But they became lifelines now. Each of them kept him from thinking about his desire for Afton, his guilt over Rhiannon and the blackness in the future. If his body wasn't failing any longer, his mind surely was. The chores became a way of keeping his sanity. They were endless physical preoccupations that kept his brain functioning in a productive way. And though more work than ever was getting done, his emotional state was becoming more precarious. Something was wrong, but it wasn't. His visitors were up to something, but they weren't. Nothing was right, but everything seemed fine. It was like living in a dream or a nightmare, depending upon what was happening at any given moment. By focusing on one chore at a time, he thought and felt nothing more than what was necessary to finish the job at hand. But it was tearing up his nerves.

"Ah, lad, here you are," Hugh said.

Blain jumped and quickly turned when he heard his uncle's voice. Forcing himself to calm down, he set his pitchfork aside and picked up a curry comb to groom his mare. "What's up?"

"I wanted to ask a great favor of you." When Blain paused in his work to look up, Hugh continued. "I thought it might be a nice gesture if we were to invite some of the townsfolk over to the farm this Friday evening. This is Afton's first visit to the States, and I thought she and Shayla would like to meet some of your neighbors before they go back to England. You could use the diversion yourself, and there's always Ms. Stone to think of. You haven't seen much of her lately and—"

"All right, all right, Hugh. You're looking for an excuse to have a party. Go ahead. I won't have time to help you plan much, but it sounds like a good idea. And this is your home too, you know. You don't have to ask for permission to entertain." Blain smiled and was gratified to see his uncle's answering grin.

"Thank you, lad. I'll take care of everything. You won't have to lift a finger. It'll be something you'll never forget. I guarantee it."

Blain watched Hugh walk away. Maybe bringing Rhiannon to the farm and letting her see Afton wasn't a good idea. He'd thought that given a little time his feelings for Afton might change, but they'd only grown stronger. He'd stayed away from her knowing she would go back to England soon and be out of his life forever. Still, he found himself wanting her more every time he saw her. The only time he could forget the constant feeling of doom was when she was near. And when he didn't think about whatever secrets she harbored.

When his mare gently nudged him, Blain went back to work. He still wanted to make amends to Rhiannon for his behavior, but he also wanted Afton to stay in his life. She had him absolutely beguiled. But Hugh had just reminded him that she would leave soon. He couldn't go to her and express his feelings. Even if it was possible to work out a way to be together, he was afraid of the future and whatever horrible darkness lurked there.

He could be slowly going insane, imagining horrors where none existed. He could be delusional. He couldn't ask anyone to share a life with a man whose mind was being torn apart. Some demon kept eating away at his rationality and he didn't know how to articulate what was wrong, let alone how to stop it.

Later that evening, Blain took his flute into the garden and began playing again. Since the garden had been redesigned, it was his favorite place to rest. The gazing globe's reflective surface calmed him. But when he looked at his own image in the orb, all he could see was a blur. No matter how he changed positions or how good the light. Something was there but it wasn't distinguishable. And that reflection compounded his fears about what was coming. The former urge to run nude in the night air seemed to be satisfied by sitting near the globe, however, so perhaps it could help him hold on to his sanity. What else could be wrong with a man who had suffered so many physical ailments no doctor could diagnose? The cool evening breeze blew as he played. He poured his heart into every note, just as his mother had taught him. He wished his parents were alive, and that they'd told him about Hugh earlier in his life. He wanted to know more about where they came from and why they never spoke of their home. Most of all, he wanted to end the terrible fear in his heart. If he had to pinpoint the exact time it had begun, he'd swear it was on the day Shayla Gallagher and Afton O'Malley arrived here. Life had been pretty ordinary up until then. Now, there was only the past to hold onto. The future was a threat he didn't want to think about. He stopped playing, listened to the night sounds, and stared at the gazing globe. It glittered in the darkness.

"You play as beautifully as your mother did," Shayla said as she joined him. He moved over to let her sit on the stone bench beside him. Although he'd been deep in thought, her presence hadn't come as a surprise. It was as if he sensed her before actually seeing her. Again, it was another indication that something wasn't right with him.

"Hello, Shayla. I thought everyone would be in bed by now."

"I was up helping Hugh with his party arrangements. It's grand of you to have a get-together so we can meet your friends."

"You can thank Hugh. It was his idea. But I guess I've neglected some of my social activities lately. This will be a good opportunity to make amends for not keeping in touch." The way his brain was working lately, he believed he would dearly need friends one day. Instead of following that train of thought, he latched onto the safe and harmless subject of music. "You said I play the flute like my mother. Tell me about where she came from and how you knew her and my father."

"Perhaps you should know part of the story. The time is near enough."

"What's that supposed to mean?" Blain responded impatiently. "What are you hiding from me? And why, when anyone mentions my parents, do I get the feeling I shouldn't ask? Please tell me what you know, Shayla. I have to understand." Blain straddled the bench to look at her.

She paused, as though gathering her thoughts. "Can you imagine a world where myth and legend are actually a reality? Are you open-minded enough to hear the truth, Blain?"

"Try me," he urged.

"Do you believe in magic?"

"I believe in anything I can hold in my own two hands and see with my own two eyes. Where are you going with this?"

"There was a time, centuries ago, when people not only believed in magic, but they lived by its edicts. Magic pervaded all things. Battles were fought to obtain it and men lost their senses through its use. Kingdoms fell while their kings searched for it. Can you imagine such a world?"

"In fairy tales, sure. But what has that got to do with my parents?"

"Your parents were part of a that which still exists on its belief in magic. Because they loved one another, they were forced to leave that world. Afton, Hugh and I are part of that world as well. On the Summer Solstice, three days from now, you will be exposed to strange and wonderful powers."

Shayla is off her rocker, he thought, gaping at her. Would he soon be just as crazy? And did Hugh and Afton really believe in what Shayla was saying? Hopefully they just humored the old woman to keep from upsetting her. Maybe that's why Afton was Shayla's "assistant". Perhaps she was a caregiver of some kind, hired to look after her. Right now, he decided to go along with Shayla's views to get to the bottom of how this strange, silver-haired woman knew his parents. Besides, how could he really judge her when his own mind was so obsessed about the future and his ominous feelings of what lay there?

"Okay. Suppose you tell me why my parents had to leave this, uh…world of magic." Blain tried to be tactful and sound as receptive to the idea as he could.

"Your father belonged to one faction of an Order of beings that exist on magic. Your mother belonged to another. In those days, the woman in charge of this Order—her name was Freyja—interpreted its laws strictly and wouldn't allow your parents to be together. So they left the Order and ran. Under Freyja's command, the Order searched for Syndra and Arthur. As soon as we had word of their whereabouts, your parents would disappear. We believed they used their combined powers to keep from being found. Finally, they ended up here. Hugh found you only because the powers your parents used to protect and hide you disappeared when your mother died."

Blain passed a hand over his face in a weary gesture. "So my parents were hunted because they fell in love and had magical powers?"

"I wouldn't put it in such simplistic terms, but yes."

"All right, Shayla. What powers were they supposed to have?" This gibberish was making him more than a little angry, but he reminded himself that he was humoring someone with a great big problem. A problem he might be feeding into.

"Your mother was a fairy and your father was a Druid. When you're ready to accept yourself and your heritage, you'll be able to look into the gazing globe and see who you really are instead of the ordinary man you believe yourself to be. You might be a fairy. They're made of light and love. All things good. They have extraordinary powers, as do Druids. But you may be more like your father—able to command the elements. Both your parents were very gifted, even among their own kind. As good as they were, that's how evil Freyja really was." Shayla stopped and pointed to the gazing globe. "Freyja could never approach a garden where one of those exists. She would have seen herself for what she truly was—a psychotic, dangerous monster. I think she feared your parents' love because she was jealous of anything she couldn't have herself. And no one loved her. Oh, she had those who sided with her only because she frightened or bribed them into doing her bidding. But she was far too malevolent to deserve real devotion. It may be that your parents' combined powers threatened hers, and that's why she was so adamantly opposed to their union."

Blain again gaped at her. It took a couple of minutes to process what she'd said and form a coherent question. "And what would have happened to my parents if this woman...Freyja, had ever found them?"

"They would have been brought back to our ancient grounds in Europe and put to death."

Okay, that's it! Humoring her is over. Up until now, the story was whimsical, but harmless. When Shayla talked about killing someone… That was where the fantasy stopped. "And where is this person who wanted to kill my parents?" Blain knew his anger was obvious enough for even the densest creature to sense.

"She's dead. I've taken her place and that's enough for you to hear for now." She stood to leave, but she stopped and turned back to him. "Afton wanted you to have this." She took a small velvet pouch from her pocket and handed it to him. "Its power will protect you from most common evil spells. Place it on your windowsill at night and it will absorb the moon's powers. Then keep it with you during the daytime. And one more thing...the next time you think you're humoring a sick old woman will be the last time, Blain McTavish. Before your mother met Arthur, I loved him, but his path led him one way, mine another. If not for the different roads we took, you could very well have been my own son. Still, I will tolerate no disrespect for myself or the Order. Be very certain about that!"

Blain watched her stoically walk away. There was no doubt in his mind that Shayla Gallagher believed every word she was saying. A cold chill crept over him. As a young boy, his parents had told him to never answer questions about where they had last lived, and the three of them had moved often. To a lonely little boy, the traveling and the subterfuge was a bit frightening. His schooling came from his parents or correspondence courses, and most social events were avoided. He'd grown up accepting their secretive behavior as normal, and it wasn't until he was much older that he knew their lives were very different from other people's lives. That was when he began to ask his parents questions that were never answered. He ran his hands through his hair. "Crazy. Shayla's story is impossible and crazy," he muttered to himself. No matter what his parents' reasons had been for their secrecy, he wasn't about to let himself fall for the trash he'd just heard. His hands automatically clenched, and he felt one of them close around the small pouch Shayla had given him.

Picking up his flute, he went inside the house and up to his room. He switched on the beside lamp, opened the pouch and emptied the contents into his palm. An emerald-cut amethyst fell into his hand. It was about three inches square and beautifully clear. Such a large semiprecious stone had to be worth a great deal of money. The long cord on the pouch indicated it was probably meant to be worn around his neck. Had Afton really given it to Shayla, or had Shayla made that up, too? If Afton was a part of this, then she was as batty as the old woman, and he didn't want to believe that. Though her habits were odd, Afton herself was too real and earnest to fall for anything so ridiculous. Fairies? Druids? Bull shit!

Blain wondered if this was the terrible event he'd been fearing. Or was there more to come? He angrily pulled off his clothes, took a hot shower and went to bed. But he didn't sleep. In the starlight filtering through the room, he could see the small stone on his bedside table.

With each moment that passed, he knew he had to get Shayla out of his home and his life. The worst part was, when she left, Afton would go, too. After Friday night's party, he'd ask them to leave. It would hurt Hugh, but it would hurt him worse. He had come to treasure Afton's and Shayla's presence. For a short time, it had been like having a family again.

The next morning, Blain waited until breakfast was over. When Shayla and Hugh moved into the room which served as Blain's office, Blain confronted Afton. "May I talk to you outside for a few minutes?"

"Of course." Afton hung up the towel she'd been using to dry the dishes. She wondered what Blain wanted to say to her after days of their maintaining a mutual distance. She followed him into the garden. Once there, she watched him pace for a few moments. He seemed to be carefully considering what he was about to say.

Something was definitely bothering him. He paced, clenched his fists and shook his head as though something he wanted to say wasn't acceptable. Blain reached inside his pocket. "Afton, did you give this to Shayla to give to me?"

"Yes. People back home carry them around for good luck and protection."

"And that's all it was meant to be? A gift for luck?"

"Yes." Afton watched his expression turn to relief when she answered. She paused for a moment, not sure how to continue. "But its daylight powers are only focused when it's exposed to moonlight." She quickly watched the relief on his face turn to concern again as he ran his hands through his hair in frustration.

"Do you know what Shayla told me last night?"

She glanced down at her clasped hands. "Yes, she mentioned it."

"Please tell me you don't believe all that crap. That you're only humoring Shayla's delusions."

She took a deep breath. None of this was going to go down easy for Blain. How could it? "What exactly did she say?"

"Nothing much, except that I'm supposed to be half fairy and half Druid," he drawled sarcastically. "She also told me my parents had to run from some crazy woman bent on killing them." As he waited for her response, he watched her tuck a long strand of sun-streaked hair behind one ear and turn her back to him.

"What...what do you want me to say, Blain?"

"I want you to tell me what's wrong with Shayla and that you're not buying into this fantasy world she's created for herself. It's not healthy."

"I'm sorry, but everything Shayla told you is true. Hugh brought us here to bring you back into the Order and explain your heritage to you." She turned to face him.

"For the love of..." Blain tilted his head back and closed his eyes. "Hugh is part of this too?" He sat heavily upon a nearby rock. His entire body sagged.

Afton could only guess how Blain was feeling. To an outsider, which was how he'd been raised, she knew how fantastic it all seemed. But for his sake, the more he knew the less apt he was to lose control when Shayla turned on her powers during the Solstice ceremony.

"Blain, please listen to me," she said as she knelt before him and took his hands into hers. "Try to keep an open mind. Your mother was a fairy. She loved gardens and designed yours because I think she must have missed being with her own kind. It reminded her of home."

Blain looked at her. "Do you know how absolutely crazy this sounds? I'm no psychiatrist, but this is sick. Really sick!"

"What if I could prove that what I'm saying is true? Would you listen to Shayla and do what she tells you?"

"I'd sooner believe in little green men from Mars and UFO abductions."

"That's absurd!" Afton glared at him, hurt by his sarcasm.

"*I'm* being absurd?" His eyebrows rose at the irony.

"Listen to me for a moment. People occasionally see fairies, and they attribute what they see to too much alcohol, being too tired or the very same UFOs you mentioned. The absolute unbelievable nature of what and who we are is what has protected us for the last few centuries. People would rather believe they've had too much ale at the local pub than think they stumbled upon a traveling fairy bathing in a woodland pond. Or they explain away trolls, nymphs, gnomes and others of us as night noises of no consequence."

"And who the hell is *us*, Afton? What do you think you are?" He glared at her and his heart began to beat harder. He'd come to care so much for her. That she was as mentally unstable as her employer left him feeling as though he'd fallen into a dark hole. And their delusions were making his own mental state that much nearer to collapse.

Afton took a deep breath then finally told him what she had wanted him to know all along. "I'm Druid. We have limited abilities to control the elements of earth, fire, water, and air."

Blain sat completely still. He stood and pulled Afton with him. "This has gone far enough. It's not sane. You have to stop this. I won't listen to it."

"Blain, you're fighting what, deep inside, you know is true. You have fairy blood in your veins as well as Druid blood. No other creature on Earth could create music the way you do. No one could be so in tune with nature but someone with Druid blood such as yours. If you stop fighting it, your own powers may come to you, and you'll know what I'm saying is true."

"My own powers? Afton, there are no such things as fairies. My mother was bigger than you are. She wasn't some little, flower-hopping creature. Can't you hear how crazy you sound?"

"The idea that fairies are tiny creatures is idiotic. That's a stereotype created by your world. Perhaps someone, at one time or another, mistook one of the smaller sprites or pixies for a fairy. But real fairies exist, and they have the power to change from human to true fairy form. And they're as large as any normal human. Some are as large as you."

"You're saying I have the power to become one of those...things?"

"We don't know what your powers are yet. You're the first child of a blend we've ever encountered."

"All right. For the sake of argument, I'll humor you for a moment. I can't think why I'm having this conversation, but let's just assume what you're saying is true." He paused and took a deep breath. "Aren't there stories of fairies enchanting mortal men and women? If those stories are true, why wouldn't there be other 'blends', as you call them, besides me?"

"In centuries past, there were stories of such things happening, but the stories always ended with either the fairy or the mortal disappearing or dying somehow. There's only one fairy, other than you, who can claim to have human blood in his veins. But that blood is centuries old, and if you mention it, he's likely to take your head off. Any humanity he may have had in him has long since been bred away. Now that Shayla is Sorceress—the leader of our Order—she allows different factions to keep company with each other and even handfast—marry—if they want to. As yet, all of us have kept to our own kind. No one has availed themselves of the opportunity to interbreed with other factions, though they dally with each other on occasion."

"So this mythical Order has its own brand of racism?"

When Afton bowed her head as if she was ashamed, Blain asked, "And who is this half-cast, mixed-blooded fairy with the human in his woodpile and the chip on his shoulder?"

"His name is Lore, and you will meet him if you agree to come back and establish yourself into the Order. To date, you're the only true, modern-day blend in existence."

"And if I don't want to have anything to do with this so called Order?"

Afton didn't answer. He saw fear come into her eyes, and she tried to turn away. He grabbed her shoulders and forced her to look at him. "Tell me."

"That's up to Shayla. If she knew I was even talking to you about this before Solstice…"

Blain watched as she looked over her shoulder toward the house. He felt her begin to shake. Whatever else she believed, Afton was afraid of Shayla's wrath. The older woman had some kind of power over her. "You're really scared, aren't you? Honey, you're trembling." He pulled her to him and held her close. Although he wanted the truth, he hadn't wanted to frighten her.

"Blain, please try to believe. Please try. I can prove it to you only if you'll let me." She wrapped her arms around him and buried her head against his chest.

"Okay. This is the most asinine thing I've ever let myself get talked into, but if you think you can prove your point, then fine."

"You're only trying to humor me. It's patronizing and I don't like it." She angrily pulled away from him.

"Afton, don't push it. I've had about all I can take. I'm willing to let you do whatever mumbo-jumbo you have in mind on one condition."

"And what's that?" she asked as she watched him place his hands on his hips and stare at her.

"If whatever you do doesn't work, you take Shayla and leave this country the day after the party, and you don't come back. Agreed?"

"You...you don't want us here anymore?" Afton felt tears come into her eyes.

"I can't afford the emotional game-playing going on here, and I don't want Hugh exposed to it. He's all the family I have. It's clear he cares for Shayla, and he'll believe whatever she tells him, just like you do. Now, do you agree to the condition or not?"

"All right. I agree. Meet me in the woods behind the far pasture at midnight. But you have to make some excuse to stay away from the house. Shayla can sometimes sense when something isn't right, and you have no ability to block what she feels. Not yet anyway. It'll be hard enough for me to act as if we've never had this conversation."

"Fine. By Saturday, I want you both packed and on the first plane out of here."

Afton watched him march away. Clearly, he thought she would fail in her attempt to prove the Order existed. What if she did? Until now, her powers had been almost nonexistent. What if they failed tonight? Blain would expect them to leave, she would have to tell Shayla what she and Blain had discussed and the Sorceress would be furious. She didn't even want to think about what Shayla would do to her.

She had to plan. There had to be something she could do to convince Blain to believe. If he behaved disrespectfully or sarcastically toward Shayla, she would be obliged to pass the most severe judgment. Blain would be cut off from the Order for all time and have to live as a regular human, or he would be destroyed if he attempted to ever call upon any powers he might discover he had. Whatever happened, Hugh would be expected to come back to the Order, and Blain would be left all alone.

At least she hadn't told him about someone trying to harm him by using black magic. That little bit of information probably would have gotten her thrown off the farm within the hour. She ran into the house, and upstairs to her room. There had to be some way of making Blain believe. She had to think. There were powers available to her if she was strong enough to conjure them.

Blain told Hugh he was going into town for horse feed and wouldn't be back for supper that evening. While it was true that he needed to run the errand, he also needed time and space away from everyone for a while. Especially since he'd agreed to meet Afton later that evening. He was outside the feed store, loading up the bed of his truck when a short, stout figure approached. Her gray-brown hair stuck out from her round head like a thatch of thorns. Her dark gaze held only hatred, and her face was pinched with contempt. As usual, she was wearing one of her awful, dark dresses that made her look as if she was in perpetual mourning.

"Oh, great. Old lady Biddles. That's all I need," he muttered. "Why the hell doesn't somebody just shoot me?"

Like Reverend Myers, Hannah Biddles loved to make a scene. Though he wasn't the only one the old buzzard argued with, Blain's share of her contemptuous outbursts were always the loudest. There must be something about his personality that attracted unstable people. He vowed to find that particular trait and thoroughly root it out. Or perhaps he was the craziest of all of them, and all this melodrama was his own particular plunge into mental illness.

"McTavish, I received this in the mail." She pulled a white envelope out of her purse. "I'll give you two guesses as to what I'd like to do with it!"

He sighed and tried not to picture her inserting the item into any orifice belonging to him. "And what's in the envelope, Mrs. Biddles?"

"It's an invitation to your party." She paused, and when he didn't respond, she said, "Where do you get off? Do you think you can make everything right by inviting me over for sandwiches, you little prick?"

Blain couldn't imagine why Hannah Biddles was on the guest list. He supposed that not inviting her would be interpreted as petty and grudging, especially since everyone else in town would probably be invited. But he certainly didn't have to stand here and take the woman's venomous assault.

"Look, if you don't want to come, then don't. It was a gesture of friendship. If you want to assign some ulterior motive to it, I'm sorry. It wasn't meant that way."

"Ulterior motive is just what it is, you little mongrel! I had plans for the property your father practically stole from that boozer husband of mine." She smirked and moved to within inches of him. "I'll be at your party. That bastard father of yours thought he could outmaneuver me, but he didn't know who he was dealing with. Neither do you."

Blain shook his head. His hands clenched, and for the first time in his life, he desperately wanted to hit a woman. "I don't have to stand here and take this," he growled. "You do whatever the hell you want with that invitation!" He threw his hands into the air, then jerked open his truck door and left. He was so furious it wasn't safe for him to keep driving. He had to pull over just outside of town. He didn't care what anyone said about him, but his father had actually done the deceased Jed Biddles a huge favor.

According to what his father had told him, Biddles' drinking had led to some bad business deals. Apparently Biddles needed money to pay off debts. Added to the entire situation was the fact that old Jed had been illegally dumping trash near a stream for years. After purchasing the land from him, the McTavishes had cleaned up the mess without reporting it.

Blain hit the steering wheel with his fist. The day was going right down the tubes. If things didn't get better this evening, he was afraid he'd end up in a confrontation with gentle, crazy Afton. And that was the very last thing he wanted. He closed his eyes, took several deep breaths and started the engine again.

What else could go wrong? Remembering his promise to stay away from Shayla and Hugh, he drove to a fast food diner and ordered a hamburger. He really didn't feel like eating, but it was a way to pass the time until tonight. Afton would get her chance to prove this mystical Order existed. He didn't want to think about what would happen when she couldn't. He toyed with the idea of going to see Rhiannon. Though he could never care for her as he did Afton, he could apologize for his past behavior and tell her about all the craziness. When Rhi understood what was going on, maybe she would forgive him for the way he'd treated her. And she might make some silly joke out of the whole thing, and they'd laugh about it. But he decided against that idea. After tonight, there wasn't going to be anything to laugh about. Afton would go home, and he'd never see her again. That would be too painful to bear.

Dammit, he'd even miss Shayla. It wasn't as if crazy people could help themselves. He knew nothing about psychology, but he found it odd that one woman's strange beliefs could effect so many others. In particular, Afton. She seemed so intelligent. Why would she fall victim to Shayla's bizarre stories? And how could Hugh believe everything the old woman said?

Close to midnight, Blain drove his truck to a service road near the far pasture. He grabbed a flashlight, walked into the woods and sat on an old oak log. There was a stream nearby that ended at a small grotto. A tiny waterfall trickled down the grotto's edge and pooled among green plants. Ferns and moss, which covered the rocks, grew there. He'd found the place some time ago when his father and he had cleaned up the damage done by old Biddles. It had become very special to him, and he was averse to having a farce played out here. But Afton had chosen this spot. He waited and hoped she wouldn't be badly hurt when whatever gimmick she planned failed.

Within minutes, he heard the rustling of underbrush. "Afton?" he called out.

"Yes, it's me."

"What in hell are you doing, roaming around out here without any kind of light? Are you crazy?"

"I thought the verdict was already in on that one," she responded sarcastically.

He couldn't help smiling at her ready comeback. "Touché."

"I don't need light to roam about the woods at night. From childhood, we learn not to use such devices. If we're too near the edge of a forest, lights can attract too much attention. Only the best Druids can mask the presence of light or fire. So most of us use our senses as best we can."

Blain shook his head. Her response told him she really was into the whole farce. His heart felt like lead. "You spend a lot of your time in the woods at night, huh?"

"Yes, I do. Some of the herbs I use have to be gathered by the light of the moon and stars for their powers to be potent. We need them for curatives."

He aimed the flashlight at her and was surprised to see her wearing some kind of long, dark green robe with a hood. "I see you came dressed for the part, but Halloween isn't until October."

"I said don't be patronizing. One of these days you're going to apologize to me, and I'm going to take extreme pleasure in making you feel foolish! Now turn off that flashlight before someone sees us."

He switched off the flashlight and put it down. "All right. Do what you came to do so we can go home and get some sleep. Hugh and Shayla will wonder where we are," he said, knowing that no matter what happened, there would be no sleep for him tonight.

"Before I start, I want you to promise me something."

"I'm not promising anything."

"That's not fair. For a bargain to be struck between two people, they both have to compromise. I agreed to take Shayla and leave if I can't convince you that both the Order and magic exists. Now you must agree that if you come away tonight believing what Shayla and I've said is true, you'll listen to Shayla and do exactly as she tells you. Is it a bargain?"

"Fine. Whatever. Just get on with this." He stood and put one hand on his hip in frustration.

Afton had thought long and hard about what she'd do. If this didn't work, she didn't want to think about the consequences. For once in her life, she had to concentrate and focus. Blain's future was at stake. Possibly hers, too.

She closed her eyes and listened to the night sounds. She felt the earth beneath her feet and summoned the power to relax. In her mind, she visualized the element of fire. Her hands lifted, palms turned up to the sky. They began to tingle and grow warm.

Soon they began to glow. She opened her eyes and watched as a small flame appeared and hovered above each palm. One flame was a brilliant blue. The other was dark green. She moved her hands together, and the flames interlocked and wove into one another. They slowly expanded and formed a circle, like a Celtic knot, around her forearms. She spread her arms apart and the circle enlarged. It eventually encompassed her entire body. Green and blue sparks shot from the entwined flames.

Blain watched and his heart stood still. It had to be some kind of magician's trick, but Afton's hands never touched the flames. They hovered above her palms. Unless she'd been to the little clearing earlier, she couldn't have rigged some kind of pyrotechnic device. And there were no chemical agents or machinery on the farm that could create the illusion he was seeing.

Afton stood within the blue-green glow of the circular flame. It moved from her and toward him. He wanted to back away, but his feet were rooted to the ground. No matter how hard he tried to move, he couldn't. It was as though the earth itself held him. Afton appeared to be in some kind of trance. He watched as her eyes began to glow. They turned an electric blue, like something in a horror movie.

For the first time in his life, Blain wanted to run away from something. The fiery circle came closer and closer until it formed around him the same way it had formed around Afton. He couldn't move or speak. All he could do was watch her.

Afton raised her hands again and Blain's vision was blinded by the extreme light. Though it was all around him, he felt no heat. Then he saw a vision materialize in front of him. It was a forest, but not the one in which they stood. It was another place far away, and he sensed it was in the present. He saw creatures — ethereal beings of all shapes and sizes — within a great clearing. They moved as if they weren't aware of his presence. And there was a castle in the distance. Human-looking men, women and children walked with and among the creatures as though they had no fear. Some of the beings looked normal, except they had wings like those of butterflies or dragonflies. They were the most beautiful people Blain had ever seen, and he felt strongly drawn to them. In a dreamlike state, he was suddenly walking with them, but they still didn't seem to be aware of his presence. It was as if he was in the middle of some medieval tapestry.

Men and women laughed and danced, and happy children flitted and played under the loving scrutiny of adults. There were men and women situated on the highest branches of old oaks, their keen eyes watching the surrounding countryside. Guarding, he knew instinctively.

Many of the people practiced with ancient weaponry such as swords, bows and axes, though they appeared to be at peace with one another. Preparations were being made for some kind of great feast. Tables were set with pitchers and mugs. Flowers scented the air. Lovers walked in the forest and disappeared within its depths.

Suddenly, he felt himself being pulled away and he desperately wanted to stay. Some kind of tournament or competition was about to be held, and he wanted to see more. But the vision grew dim and he felt the ground back beneath his feet. The brilliance of the blue-green fire diminished, and Afton stood before him. As the last of the circle faded away, he saw Afton put her hands to her face and drop to the ground. It took a second longer for him to be able to move, but he rushed to her as soon as he was able.

"Afton! Are you all right?" He gently lifted her small form into his embrace and cradled her against his body. She was shaking.

"Blain, I've never…never tried anything so…big. I wanted you to see. I…wanted you to see what you've missed. Please tell me…you believe." Afton gasped for air. She'd made herself incredibly weak—the enchantment had been very draining for someone unused to summoning such power. Only a few times in their entire life could a Druid perform such a ritual, and Afton was so beside herself with pride for having summoned a vision circle on the first try that words failed her.

"I saw it, Afton. I saw it all. I don't know what it means, but we have to get you back to the farm. We'll talk about it there."

"No!" She pushed away from him and lay upon the ground. Her strength would renew itself from the earth. "You have to tell me you believe what you saw. That…that you believe in magic. It was no trick, Blain. I couldn't make you see something you didn't want to see."

Blain pushed the hood of her robe back and pulled her head onto his lap. He stared around the dark woods. Everything was back to normal. Everything but him. He'd seen fairies and other creatures he couldn't put a name to. There was nothing that Afton could have rigged to have produced what he'd seen with his own two eyes. Something in him felt as though it was ripping free. At first, it was as if a piece of his soul was opening up to accept something…something new. Then the sensation in his chest quickly changed to physical pain. His back felt as if it was being literally ripped in half. He tore his shirt off and scooted away from Afton.

"Afton! Help me! I…I…pain," he cried out in agony.

Still recovering from conjuring the vision circle, Afton heard him cry out. She frowned, confused. Nothing she'd done was supposed to have hurt him, though she'd realized any success would drain her considerably.

"Blain, what is it? What's wrong?" she asked as she tried to move to him.

"Afton…I…*no*," Blain shrieked as blinding pain tore into him over and over. He pulled at his clothing to get it off. Every scrap of it seemed to bring torture where it touched his flesh. He was able to crawl and drag himself to the nearby grotto. He had to stop the burning pain, and the cool water seemed the only way to do so.

Afton pushed herself to her feet. She still felt unsteady, but she was strong enough to get to him. His pain had to be because of what she'd done. If anything happened to him, it would be her fault. His welfare was all she could think about as she tried to make her way to him.

As Blain's hands touched the water, something ripped away from his back. With one last wave of horrifying pain, he screamed and fell into unconsciousness.

Tears streamed from Afton's eyes causing her to stumble and fall more than once. "Blain, I'll help you. I'll help you," she repeated over and over. Because the flames she'd conjured were supposed to be muted, Afton knew no one from the farmhouse could have seen them. No one knew they were in the woods, so there was no one to help him but her. She was physically too small to lift or drag Blain's hulking form to the truck, and she wasn't about to leave him alone. Something had gone terribly wrong, but she just didn't know what.

She was a few feet from him when she saw the wings in the moonlight. They glittered like sparkling veils. Surely her vision was still clouded. She must be so upset she was imagining things. But when she reached toward him, her hand felt the silken veins connecting his wings together. They were real. Blain was on his stomach and his clothing was gone. Even with limited light, the butterfly-like wings were the largest she'd ever seen on a fairy. Even larger than the wings of the fairy leader, Lore.

Suddenly, Blain moaned and tried to push himself from the ground. Afton was by his side in an instant.

"Don't try to move. Stay still," she pleaded.

For several moments he did as she asked. The pain was gone, but he'd never felt so strange in his life. It was as though someone had lifted some kind of horrible weight from him and tossed it aside. When he was able to raise his head, he could see every leaf, every blade of grass. He could hear frogs, crickets and insects so small that they blended together and sounded like a forest symphony. Finally, as his strength not only returned but flooded through him, he pushed himself up. He had never felt so physically strong. It was as though the pain never existed. And the earth felt like a life-giving force, an actual entity that fed him with power.

When he turned to her, Afton gasped. A faint green aura began to surround him, and she could see that Blain's ears came to beautiful points. His hair fell about his shoulders in long, soft brown waves. His eyes glowed in the dark, and the whites were now silver and the centers were shaped like green stars.

She'd seen fairies enhance their eyesight in such a way so they could see at night, but she'd never seen the centers shaped like stars. The rest of his physical appearance had changed in much the same way as any other fairy who made the transition from human to their real form. But why had it caused so much pain?

Blain tilted his head and looked at her. "What happened?"

"If I had to take a guess, I'd say you believe me now," she whispered. Blain sat up and looked around him. He touched his chest, face and hair, and knew that an amazing transformation had taken place. His skin had a faint greenish hue. He placed his hands on either side of Afton's face.

"What am I? What's happened to me?"

"You're...you're a fairy, Blain. And how beautiful you are," Afton choked out as her fingertips touched his hair.

Blain glanced back over one shoulder, saw the dark wings threaded with silver veins and turned back to Afton. For a full five minutes neither of them said a word. He simply stared at her. "Now what do I do?" he finally murmured, in shock.

"Since you changed, I...think you can change back."

"You *think*?" Blain gasped, and he began to tremble.

"I'm sure you can," she amended. "The only thing I don't understand is why it caused you so much pain."

"It was like being born," he murmured.

"Of course! That's it!" Afton grabbed his biceps and gazed into his lovely eyes. "When fairy babies are born, they get their wings sometime in the first year after birth. I've been told it's very painful for them the first time. Their parents fret over the suffering the little ones go through. But whenever their wings come after that, there's no pain. Maybe that's what happened to you. You've been waiting all these years to become what you really are. Being half Druid must have had some delaying effect. Or maybe you just needed to believe."

Blain stood, and Afton tried to look away from his nakedness. The man was every bit as well-endowed as she'd thought he would be. He'd obviously forgotten how he'd shed his clothing so his wings could unfold and his body could adapt. Muscles rippled as he moved.

"I feel like I'm breathing for the first time, like I'm connected to everything in nature." He slowly turned and looked around him. He held up his hands, looked at them, then clenched and unclenched them.

Afton again gasped in wonder at his wings. They were the most exquisite things she'd ever seen in her life. She wanted to reach out and fondle them. Deep midnight blue, their edges glistened in the moonlight and the veins were shot with glowing, silver light.

Blain turned and pulled her to him. "You did this, or you helped me do it. When I believed in the magic you showed me, it triggered the change. I believe you now, Afton. I believe in it all!" He released her, stretched his arms toward the moon and looked up into the night sky. "How could I not believe?"

"You should change back. We need to get back to the farmhouse, Blain. Shayla will know what's happened, even if you're in human form."

"No." He stepped back and shook his head. "I've spent my entire life being denied what I really am. Now I want to know everything, and you're going to tell me all you know. Neither of us is leaving here until you do."

Chapter Six

✌

"Blain, I don't think this is a good idea. I had no way of knowing what would happen when I accepted your challenge. We should go back to the farm and tell Shayla and Hugh that you're able to shift into fairy form."

"I don't want to go back yet. I feel so alive. It's almost like this was the way...I should have been all along." He paused and looked around him, almost intoxicated with the raw energy. "Tell me what to do, Afton. How do I use this power? What do I do?"

Afton could see by his expression that he was both beguiled and frightened by his transformation. What would the Druid half of him be like? She started to reiterate to him that they should go back to the farmhouse, but she knew he wouldn't go until he had his answers. "I don't know what to tell you. I wasn't prepared for this. You should be asking a fairy your questions, not me. And Shayla should work with you on whatever gifts your father's blood may have bestowed."

"You're all I've got. Help me. Please," he begged, taking her hands in his.

His touch was warm and electrifying. "All right, I'll try. But first, you...you have to put something on." She turned her back to him, suddenly too aware of his nudity.

Blain sensed that Afton was blushing to her roots. His clothing was scattered about the clearing, but it wasn't appealing to him to wear the heavy garments in his present state. He liked the feeling of the night air on his bare flesh and wondered if that was a fairy trait. It would explain his strange habit of running nude through the woods, and it was a huge relief to know why he'd done so.

"Afton, when I made the change, it almost burned my skin off to have any contact with clothing."

"You may be related to Highland fairies. They don't like much clothing at all in the summer. At other times, they wear soft leather. Here, use this." Afton bent and tore some of the soft green fabric from the bottom of her robe. There would still be more than enough to preserve her own modesty while covering him decently.

Blain grinned as she held the green fabric out behind her without turning to look at him. He tied the soft cloth in a sarong fashion around his waist. It wasn't as comfortable as being nude, but it was better than the heavy pair of jeans lying on the ground.

"Are you decent?" Afton asked.

"I'm covered, if that's what you mean."

Afton slowly turned and sighed in relief as she saw that most of the lower half of his anatomy was concealed. "What do you want to know?"

"Tell me about this Order." Blain watched as she sat upon a nearby rock.

"The Order is older than recorded history. Once, centuries ago, our kind roamed about the land freely. We didn't try to hide ourselves from mankind the way we do now. Most of us tried to live in harmony with the outside world, but the problems came when some of our Order used their powers unwisely. Humans began to fear us all and to the outside world, we became evil. We were hunted for decades. Many of our people were destroyed or chased into seclusion, and that's where we remain today. Since then, only legends lived on. Today, that's all we are—legends, stories people tell their children at bedtime."

"And the members of this Order—tell me about them." Blain knelt at her feet and hung on every word she said.

"Well, there are different factions such as trolls, ogres, gnomes, pixies, sprites and the like. Druids are another faction, as are fairies. Each faction is a member of a clan depending upon their ancestry. Each clan has its leader. Within the clans are classes. The fairies, for example, have warrior classes, gatherers and so on. Clan leaders take their orders from Shayla. She holds the most sacred title of Sorceress of the Ancients. She has power and dominion over us all. Our leader is always a woman, and she may handfast or not, at her discretion. At present, Hugh is her consort."

He took a moment to process all that information. Then, another question drilled into his brain. "Who was the person wanting to destroy my parents?"

"That was old Freyja. She was Sorceress many years ago. The Order had a law which stated that we should all keep to our own. While Shayla interprets that law to mean that anyone in the Order may interact with anyone else within the Order, Freyja interpreted it to mean that factions should not intermingle. She wanted fairies to stick to their kind. Druids to Druids, goblins to goblins and so on."

"So she couldn't stand the fact that my mother and my father fell in love?" Blain turned to face the woods and leaned back as close to Afton as his wings would allow.

"Freyja was very strict—cruel, really. Many were said to have feared her. She was prone to practice the very blackest kind of magic. Because of that predilection for the dark side, Shayla challenged her for the right to lead the Order. Had Shayla lost that challenge, Freyja would have had her put to death. But Freyja was the one who died. Their struggle was that fierce."

"So Shayla took Freyja's place by force?"

"It had to be that way. Freyja was intent on keeping the leadership and power at all costs. You see, whoever the Sorceress is, she may choose her own successor. Sometimes that's someone within her own bloodline. Most Sorceresses have chosen the next leader based upon strength of character, wisdom and the ability to lead with equity, regardless of blood ties. With Freyja, it was exactly the opposite. She only wanted the power for herself. To keep that power, she'd have probably mated with any Druid just to get a daughter who could rule after her. Someone she could control. In that way, she would have kept some kind of power for a very long time, or influenced our laws through her own bloodline. It's said that she bragged about doing just such a thing. You might say her belief in ruling incorporated a kind of nepotism. She would have killed a great many in the Order with her dark ambition. There are horrible stories about her."

"But how did such an evil woman get control in the first place?"

Afton shrugged. "Freyja was chosen by the Sorceress before her. She deceived everyone into believing she was good and just. Some say she was a wonderful person at one time, but the dark side was always in her blood, and she eventually chose it over the powers of good and light. There were those who fought on her side, but they were evil as well. And they were killed during a battle which ensued as Freyja and Shayla fought."

"Is it true Freyja would have killed my parents if she'd found them?" Blain's voice was dangerously soft.

"She would have killed them and you. Even though you were nothing but an innocent child." Afton ran her hand through Blain's long hair. The thought of anyone hurting him was abhorrent to her.

Blain whirled around to face her. "I want to see the Order and meet these people. It must have upset my parents a lot to have left their world and run here. They must have constantly hidden everything from everyone. The same way they hid everything about themselves from me." He paused to think a moment. "I remember traveling a lot. We never stayed anywhere very long. My folks were so reclusive that I didn't want to ask why we left so many towns. The past was something we just didn't talk about. Maybe I was afraid of what I'd find out. But we finally stopped running when we got to Harvest."

"Something about this place must have made your parents want to stay. I can't imagine having grown up outside the Order. Especially since Shayla began her rule. She's wise and fair in all things, Blain. She would never have threatened your parents in such a way that they'd feel compelled to run or be forever parted from one another. She's much more open-minded and equitable. But she can be provoked."

"You were afraid the other day when you told me more about who I was. You were actually trembling," Blain said, remembering how he'd felt the need to protect her.

"Shayla wanted to expose you to your heritage. It was her place to do so, not mine. I don't really believe she would ever do me physical harm, but there are things she could make me do when we get home that are quite odious. Certain chores I don't like. I've quite overstepped my boundaries, and she'll be furious." She sighed and pushed her hair back.

"It was my fault for goading you. If I'd known you weren't feeding me a load of crap, I'd have been a hell of a lot more patient."

"Are you really all right with this, Blain?" She gently placed a hand on his shoulder.

"It's part of me. How can I deny it? I'm only sorry my parents felt they had to run all of their lives or be persecuted for loving one another. It seems no matter what world it is, some things don't change."

"What do you mean?"

"Whether it's in this alternate world called the Order or in the one I learned to call reality, people are still prejudiced. Do you think your people will accept me, Afton? Or will I be hunted the way my parents were?"

"No, Blain!" She firmly shook her head and moved closer to him. "Shayla would never allow any of those past prejudices to harm or restrict you. She came here to bring you back, to give you the chance to know what your heritage is. No one will counter her wishes."

He placed a hand on Afton's cheek. "Do you think it will be that easy, honey? Do you think Shayla can change people's feelings just by telling them to think differently? I'm from the outside world, after all."

Afton covered his hand with one of hers. What could she say to assure him of something she wasn't so certain about herself?

Before she could come up with an answer, he sighed and said, "I'd better try to change back into human form. Heaven help me if I can't."

"I don't know how to help you do it, Blain. I don't have shapeshifting abilities."

He took a deep breath and slowly released it. "Then I'm on my own." Blain stood and backed away from Afton. His heart was beating so hard he was sure she must hear it. If he couldn't change back, his future would be limited to hiding on the farm. There would be no escape for him anywhere. He closed his eyes and tried to calm himself. In his mind, a picture formed of his human half. Heaviness engulfed him, like a weight being placed on his entire body. He fell to his knees.

The next thing he heard was Afton's voice calling to him and telling him everything was over. He opened his eyes and tried to focus. Without his fairy alter ego's night vision, everything was black as onyx around him.

"Blain, it worked. You're back the way you were before. You did it!" She wrapped her arms around his neck and hugged him tightly.

"It feels like something's pulling me into the ground," he moaned.

"That's probably because you aren't yet used to what's happening to you. Fairies are air creatures. They have the ability to fly short distances, and they're stronger than humans."

"Fly? Why didn't you tell me that earlier?"

"I was afraid you'd try it and get hurt. You need to be with your own kind before attempting something like that. Now, we have to get back to the house. If Shayla or Hugh wake up and find us missing, we'll be in for it."

"Hugh won't mind. He's used to me being out at odd hours."

"With Rhiannon?" Afton quickly handed him his clothing, then turned so he could dress.

"Yeah. Hugh told you all about my relationship with her, didn't he?"

Afton shrugged, trying to seem nonchalant. "He mentioned something about her."

Blain continued to dress. Afton probably thought he was chasing after her and having Rhi on the side. At the moment, however, there were more pressing problems to deal with than his love life. And finding out he was a fairy was pretty pressing.

Afton wrung her hands and let out a long breath. "Shayla will have a piece of me for this."

Blain finished buttoning up his shirt and put his hands on her shoulders, turning her to face him. "Don't worry, Afton. We won't tell her anything about it."

"She's going to know, Blain. You can't hide something like this from the Sorceress."

"We'll cross that bridge when we come to it. Right now, let's take my truck and get back to the farm. I'll turn off the lights and coast up to the house so we won't bring attention to ourselves."

When he tried to walk, the heaviness he felt caused him to stumble. With Afton's help, he made it to the truck. They made the short drive in silence. Afton didn't seem any more anxious to discuss what had happened than he. It was too overwhelming at the moment.

By the time they got back to the farmhouse, he almost felt like his old self again. He wondered what his life was going to be like from now on. He'd sprouted wings like a dragonfly. What was next?

Before they got out of the truck, Blain put an index finger to his lips to warn Afton to be quiet. They carefully opened the car doors and made it to the porch, but then the lights came on inside the house.

"Oh no!" Afton whispered. "Shayla's awake."

Blain racked his brain for some excuse. "We'll just have to make something up."

"That won't work. She'll sense something's wrong and grill us both with questions until our feelings give us away." Then Afton gasped as an idea popped into her head. She turned to Blain, stood on tiptoe and pulled him down to her level.

"What the…" Blain began.

Afton kissed him as hard as she could. Whatever he might have said was completely silenced.

To steady himself against the unexpected embrace, Blain wrapped his arms around her. She was so soft and warm that her sudden clinch nearly bowled him over.

Afton could sense his complete confusion, but she kept kissing him all the same.

"What are you two up to?" Shayla demanded as she opened the front door and glared at them.

Afton broke the kiss and pushed herself away from Blain. "Uh…sorry, Shayla. We were just…uh…"

"I can see what you were doing, young lady. Get up to your room this minute," she ordered, her gaze lowering to the hem of Afton's torn Druid robe.

Afton nodded and started to walk away, but Blain grabbed her arm to stop her. "Look, Shayla, I don't know what kind of hold you have over Afton, but you can't just order her around like that. She's a grown woman. She has every right to be out with me or anyone else she chooses. She doesn't have to answer to you."

"Don't test me, Blain McTavish. I'm not in the mood…"

"Blain, stop." Afton placed a hand on his chest. "It's all right. I'll see you in the morning."

Shayla waited until Afton walked into the house. Then, she stepped out onto the porch. "What have you two done?" she asked.

Blain saw the queenly arch of her brow and decided retreat was the best option for now. "I don't want to discuss this with you. It's between Afton and me. Now if you don't mind, I'm going to bed. Good night."

Blain walked to his room, but he'd never felt less like sleeping in his entire life. Everything that had happened suddenly hit him in the face like a wall of cold water. He was a fairy! Things like him weren't supposed to exist. What other creatures existed that he knew nothing about? And what in the world was that act Afton had staged? If it was to throw Shayla off, it was debatable whether it worked. But it had certainly thrown him for a loop. He could still feel her lips against his. A second more and he would have been responding quite ardently. But that kind of relationship would only cause more confusion. Everything in his world was in chaos. How could he go on living a normal life with the kind of knowledge he now possessed? According to what Afton had told him, mingling with other members of this so-called Order was acceptable. Mingling with anyone outside it might get him killed. That meant any normal plans he'd made for himself were out of the question. So what was he supposed to do now?

* * * * *

By Friday morning, Afton was desperate to get to see Blain alone. Both Shayla and Hugh watched her like beady-eyed owls. Obviously they knew something had happened, but hadn't yet figured out what. The Solstice would be upon them by Saturday. Both of them would know then what she'd done with her conjuring. As afraid as she was, she was conscious of the fact that a few of her powers had never been so strong. And that left her with a feeling of elation. Back in England, she had never been able to complete the ritual vision circle. Yet she'd done it for Blain. It had drained her, but she'd still accomplished the task. What was different here that gave her the necessary focus she hadn't had back home? She believed it wasn't the place so much as the person who'd been involved.

She was walking away from the herb garden and into the woods when the sensation of being watched came over her.

"Afton, it's me." Blain stepped from behind a large bush. "I finally gave Hugh the slip by telling him Shayla needed something done in the kitchen. Where's Shayla?"

"When they met in the hallway to talk, I slipped out the front door toward the woods." She paused to look behind her. No one was following either of them. "So you're the reason I was able to get out of the house?"

"Yeah. The two of them are bound and determined to keep you and me from being alone. I can't figure out why." Blain sighed in frustration.

"I wasn't aware they were watching you, too. I'm sorry. I'm afraid it's my fault."

"What do you mean?"

"When I kissed you the way I did, I should have known you'd radiate confusion and surprise. Shayla picked up on that instead of what we'd been doing in the woods. She dislikes it when she thinks people are hiding things."

"So the kiss was just a diversion?" He felt a twinge of disappointment.

"Yes. Shayla has extraordinary powers, and I didn't feel like answering her questions."

"I still don't know why they're following us like hunting dogs. What have we done that's so wrong?"

"If I were Shayla and didn't know whether you'd accept your place in the Order, I wouldn't want you becoming involved with someone who was a member of it," Afton explained.

"Like you?" he asked.

"Exactly."

"Well this crap has got to stop! I've only tolerated Hugh following me as long as he has because I know he respects Shayla and takes orders from her. But this is my land, and they're in my house. You and I are adults, and they'd better get used to leaving us alone."

"Blain, please don't anger Shayla. You don't know what she's capable of. She's been far more lenient than I've ever known her to be. Don't push her." Afton put her hand on Blain's arm and gazed pleadingly into his eyes.

"If she's the fair and just leader you've told me she is, then she should be able to handle the truth. I'm going in that house right now and let her know that I'm fully aware of who and what I am."

"Then you'd better know the rest as well," Afton said softly.

Blain regarded her suspiciously. "What else is there?"

"She and Hugh think someone's after you. And so do I."

"Do you want to explain?" Blain crossed his arms over his chest and scowled.

"When Hugh found you, he contacted Shayla. He convinced her to wait a few weeks before coming to meet you herself. Hugh wanted to get to know you, to see how much your parents had told you about your heritage and whether you'd be receptive to finding out about the Order. In the time between meeting you and Shayla's arrival, he learned t someone was trying to harm you."

"Along with everything else that's happened, I'm supposed to have some kind of enemy? Why? I've never done anything to anyone." Blain held his hands out in frustration.

"Do you remember feeling tired? As if something was draining your energy? Do you remember passing out on the floor of your room?"

Blain turned his back on her and ran one hand over his face. Of course he remembered those things, though he'd attributed it to too much physical labor and a deteriorating mental state. It also occurred to him that many of those physical problems left soon after the two English women invaded his life. But conversely, his mental anxiety had grown. He turned back to face her. "Was someone using magic on me? Is that what you're saying?"

"Yes. We found evidence of black magic being conjured, and you're not safe yet." Afton moved closer to him. "You found that same evidence. I saw you burning some of it one day."

He sighed in frustration. "What else?"

"Hugh and Shayla think someone may be using this evil magic either out of revenge or because they're trying to gain control of your blended powers. It may be that someone knows what you are."

"Except for the ability to turn into a damned fairy, as if that isn't enough, I don't know that I have any powers. And how could anybody know what I was before I did?" He paused to think. "I don't know why I'd have any enemies. This is all too crazy." He began to pace. "Why didn't Hugh tell me any of this sooner? Why didn't you?"

"You said it yourself. You wouldn't have believed us. I had to take you into the woods and conjure a vision circle before you'd understand. I think you would have eventually denied what you'd seen if not for the fact that your body changed."

"Tell me one more thing." He pulled her to him. "Have you, Shayla and Hugh had something to do with the disappearance of the weakness I've been suffering?"

She nodded. "We've been putting herbs into your food and placing objects around the farm to keep you and your livestock safe."

"That's why I've been finding branches of yew, ash and oak on the stall doors in the barn, and why you gave me the amethyst, isn't it?"

Afton saw his hand touch something beneath his shirt and knew he wore the pouch containing the fairy stone. She nodded slowly. "The night you passed out, we found a lock of your hair bound with a black thread. It was in your room. Someone was trying to place a binding spell on you, and they needed something very personal to make the spell work. Obviously, whoever is doing this has access to your property. They can come and go as they please, and they can mask their powers from us. But Shayla believes they can't do so forever."

Blain wasn't sure if he wanted to believe any of what she was saying. But how could he not believe? The evidence that magic existed was undeniable. All he had to do was remember sprouting wings in the woods.

"I still don't see what anyone could gain by harming me. I'm not even sure who I am anymore. After finally getting one whole hour of sleep, I woke up wondering what was and wasn't real. I don't understand anything." He sat on a rock and placed his head in his hands.

Afton could see everything was beginning to overwhelm him, and she wondered just how much he could take before the control he'd exhibited so far deserted him. She moved closer to him and pulled him into her embrace. It was a gesture of concern and friendship. But Blain responded by hugging her back with an urgency born of fear. He might be a strong hulking figure of a man, but his life was drastically changing minute by minute. All she wanted to do was comfort him in some small way and let him know he wasn't alone. It comforted *her* to know he wore the fairy stone she'd given him. It would help protect him as well as calm him a little.

Blain clung to Afton. The world and all its realities were rapidly disappearing and being replaced by magic, ethereal forest creatures and things best left in dreams and nightmares. One of them could be out to destroy him. He couldn't fight what he didn't know, and he wasn't sure he wanted to know any more than he already did. He buried his head against Afton's chest and let her sweet presence fill him with a little peace.

Her hands stroked his hair and back, and she softly said, "I know this is so very hard to accept. Please don't be afraid. Shayla, Hugh and I would never let any harm come to you. The world will come together soon, and everything will be right again once you're with your own kind."

"I don't know what to do anymore," he whispered. And the ever present fear he had carried with him was magnified. There was more to come. He knew it.

Afton pushed far enough away from Blain to see his face. She saw the turmoil in his sage-colored eyes and wanted to replace it with understanding and calm. She gently caressed his cheek as her mouth claimed his.

The kiss started slow and sweet, but it quickly intensified as Blain found release from the tempest he was feeling. He gently stopped the kiss and whispered against her lips, "You're so warm. It's like having the sun come out after a cold rain."

They were a breath apart when Shayla saw the couple. "What, by all the stars, is going on? I want an explanation for this sneaking about, Afton."

Blain broke the contact between them. Knowing how the girl feared Shayla's anger, he stood when Afton did and pushed her slightly behind him. Shayla looked absolutely furious and, surprisingly, so did Hugh. His uncle stood to Shayla's left with his hands on his hips. Hugh resembled his father so much that in that moment Blain almost believed his father was present. For a moment the likeness kept him from speaking.

"Lad, you'd better be about your chores. We need to speak with Afton," Hugh said to Blain with a stern glare.

"I'm not going anywhere. Afton and I have nothing to explain to anyone, but the two of you *do*." Blain stared back at both of them. The time for running from his fears was over.

"You dare defy me…" Shayla suddenly stopped speaking, tilted her head slightly and walked slowly toward Blain. When she was just inches from him, she looked into his face and raised a hand to his cheek. "He knows, Hugh. Afton has shown him," she said without moving her gaze from Blain's face.

"Just about everything," Blain admitted. "Afton isn't at fault. I told her I'd throw you and her off my property if she didn't come clean about what the hell was going on. I know it's true. I know what I am."

"You had no right revealing this information to him, Afton. It was Shayla's place," Hugh reprimanded her.

Afton swallowed hard. "I know, but he's been so confused about everything. Please don't be angry with him. The responsibility for revealing our powers to him is mine. If someone needs to be punished, let it be me."

"Just what did you reveal to him?" Shayla raised an eyebrow and looked at her in a threatening fashion.

"I formed a vision circle. He not only saw the Order, but he changed into his true form. Somehow, when he believed in what he saw, his powers came to him."

"You formed a vision circle? *You*?" Shayla asked incredulously. She stepped away from Blain and moved toward Afton. "You've never shown tendencies toward having that kind of power."

"I know," she readily agreed. "Something just happened to magnify my concentration. I'm sorry, Shayla. My intent wasn't to usurp your authority but to help Blain."

Blain spoke up for her. "No harm was done. Afton just helped me learn who I truly am." He wrapped a protective arm around Afton and pulled her to him. "That's what you wanted, wasn't it? For me to believe?"

"And what are you, Blain? Are you Druid, fairy or both?" Hugh asked curiously.

"I changed into a fairy, but I haven't used any other powers—*if* I have other powers."

"What else do you know?" Shayla asked.

"Everything. I know somebody wants to harm me, though Afton tells me none of you seem to know exactly why."

"Aye, lad," Hugh said as he approached him. "That's one of the reasons we wanted to invite your acquaintances over. After tonight, we may know who's wanting to hurt you and their reasons for doing so."

Shayla regarded them both before speaking again. "I should punish you for your meddling, Afton. I would, except that Blain seems to be taking this rather well. Is that what your little tryst in the woods was all about? Why you wore Druid clothing in front of him?"

Afton simply nodded.

Shayla regarded both of them, crossed her arms over her chest and arched her brows. "And when I found you embracing on the front porch, that was to throw me off the scent, so to speak?"

"Yes, but all that was my idea. Blain didn't have a clue as to why I was kissing him." Afton lowered her head in repentance.

"Don't ever try to hide anything from me again," Shayla warned. "What were you and Blain about to do when Hugh and I walked up just now?"

Blain's anger was growing as the moments passed. "That's none of your damned business!" No one had a right to question his and Afton's actions. Afton might have been raised to be subservient to Shayla, but he hadn't.

Hugh glowered at his nephew. "Blain! No one speaks to Shayla that way. She's the leader of our Order and must be respected at all times."

Shayla held up a hand to indicate Blain should continue. "Let him speak, Hugh. He's unfamiliar with our ways, and I want to hear him out."

Blain let her have it. "Afton and I are adults. I wouldn't treat you and Hugh the way you're treating us. We've been followed, watched and probably manipulated. I'm sick of it and won't be treated with any less respect than you demand for yourself. If you're angry with me for expressing my opinions then you'll just have to do your worst. But leave Afton alone. She's only been trying to help me and without her, I don't know what I'd have done." As Blain finished, he clasped one of Afton's hands tightly.

"Are you quite through?" Shayla placed her hands on her hips.

"No. I want to learn everything I can about this Order and my parents' place within it. I'll need help adjusting to this fairy thing as well. I assume none of you have wings, so I need to be introduced to someone who can relate. Someone like me."

Afton stood in stunned silence. She glanced at Hugh and knew from his own astounded expression that he was thinking her exact same thoughts. Very few people had spoken to Shayla Gallagher in such a fashion without spending a fortnight as a toad or some other hapless creature. After years of conjuring and studying, she commanded greater powers than those a normal Druid possessed.

"Hold your tongue, lad, unless you don't want it anymore," Hugh intoned warningly.

"No, I agree with him." Shayla extended her hands to Blain. "If I do as you request, Blain, you must listen to what I tell you and learn. Will you accept my guidance and cooperate?"

Blain nodded as he took the older woman's hands in his. "I promise, Shayla. So long as there are no more secrets or hidden agendas, I'll do anything you want. Just tell me everything from now on."

Shayla smiled. "You're so like your father. Stubborn and proud. But he was driven away from the things he most loved, as was your mother. I won't see that happen to any of our young people again. Freyja was a dangerous maniac." She gripped his hands firmly. "Come now, Blain. We have much to talk about."

As Shayla walked away with Blain, Hugh and Afton stared at one another.

"I thought she'd turn me into a mushroom or something," Afton whispered in relief.

"If the outcome had been different, lass, she might have. But Blain's taking this unbelievably well, and it's clear even to an old fool like me that you're the reason why."

Afton ignored Hugh's last comment. Instead, she voiced her trepidation. "I hope everything will work out. All Blain needs to do now is accept the Order. If he finds it's too much to handle, none of us will ever see him again. Despite what you, me or anyone else may feel for him."

"Aye, that frightens me as well. If he can't accept what he'll see and he won't keep his powers secret, you know what will have to happen, don't you?"

Afton wrapped her arm around the older man's waist and he looped his arm around her shoulders. Of course she knew what would happen. Death was the only other option for such a circumstance. No one could be allowed to live if they threatened the Order in any way. "Let's hope that doesn't happen, Hugh. All we can do is hope."

Chapter Seven

ഇ

"There's no way Rhiannon has anything to do with this," Blain adamantly declared, pushing himself away from the kitchen table. He stood and began to pace. He'd made love with the woman, and he couldn't believe she'd have shared those passionate moments with him for some ulterior motive. Even if there was no commitment involved, she wouldn't do what Shayla and Hugh were suggesting.

"We aren't accusing anyone, lad. It's just that Ms. Stone has been closer to you than anyone else in town," Hugh explained. "She'd have access to your personal things. Like the lock of hair we found." After a moment's pause, he added, "Perhaps she isn't using personal items of yours to do you harm, but someone might be getting your belongings from her."

"Did you ever give her a lock of your hair for a keepsake?" Shayla asked.

"No." Blain stopped pacing and leaned against the backdoor. "Someone could have picked it up at the barber's, for all I know."

"What about the man who sold your parents this land?" Shayla asked, taking a sip of the tea Afton had just poured her. "Hugh tells me his wife resents the fact that her deceased husband sold his farmland to your father, and that your crops and animals seem to thrive while hers wither and die."

"Hannah Biddles? You can't be serious. She resents me, but the woman is hardly a threat. She's all mouth. Besides, I haven't seen her near my property."

"There's Reverend Myers. He thinks you and Rhiannon are reenacting Sodom and Gomorrah in her apartment," Hugh said.

Blain threw an uncomfortable glance at Afton. She seemed uninterested in their discussion, scrubbing the kitchen counter to perfection. "He's a pretentious ass." Blain sat back down at the table. "None of these people have a reason to do me harm. It has to be someone else."

"Is there a possibility that someone Blain doesn't even know may want to drain his powers?" Hugh suggested. "Maybe someone who has sensed his abilities and has been drawn to the area because of them?"

Shayla shook her head. "I doubt someone unfamiliar with this property could get onto it undetected, or when Blain wasn't in the house. No, this is someone who's used to Blain's habits. Knows when he comes and goes."

"What makes you think someone wanting to hurt me will show up at this party?" Blain glanced at both his uncle and Shayla. "Whoever this is couldn't be that stupid."

"Because the opportunity to get close to you and so many personal things to use against you will be too appealing," Afton responded, finally breaking her silence. "That's how these evil spells work. The one casting the bad magic has to have something belonging to the victim or be physically close. Since we've been here and finally understand what evil we're dealing with, it's much more difficult now to harm you."

Blain shrugged. "Seems to me like someone's already done their worst and failed. What makes you think they'll try again since it hasn't gotten them anything so far?"

"Depends on their motives," Shayla remarked. "We'll see who shows up tonight. Something tells me we'll have our answers soon enough."

* * * * *

"This is ridiculous," Blain complained to Afton as he watched her place the last of the food on the kitchen table. "I just can't believe anybody cares enough about me to want to do me in. What possible reason could there be other than these damned powers I'm supposed to have?"

Afton heard the frustration in his voice and tried to calm him. "Together, we'll get to the bottom of this. I know none of this is remotely normal by your standards. It surprises me you've accepted so much. It can't have been easy to hear that you're a creature from some fantasy world and that similar creatures really exist."

"How can I deny what I am? I turned green and grew wings. I probably look like a butterfly with thyroid problems."

"You most certainly do not," Afton vehemently objected. "You're breathtaking." Then she took a deep breath and tried to see his viewpoint. Having lived on the outside for so long, accepting his place within the Order might be impossible for him. "This isn't going to get any easier for you, is it?"

"No." Blain sighed and sat down in a nearby chair. "I'm beginning to have doubts about what's real, and I have about a million questions I don't know how to begin to ask. Everything's pretty crazy."

Afton moved near enough to place a hand on his shoulder. She smiled at him, wanting to be the one he came to for help. But he needed to be near fairies and Druid men. Only they had the ability to teach him. To do that, Shayla would want him to go back to Europe with her. What Blain would find there could send him over the edge. His nerves seemed very finely strung as it was. He'd taken to pacing and running his hands through his long hair. He even jumped when he heard sounds that might have been familiar to him before. She couldn't imagine being ripped apart emotionally as he was. To her, the Order was everything. Even though he was trying hard to accept his predicament, Blain might never see it as his new way of life.

Hugh entered the kitchen and motioned for Blain to follow him. "Guests are beginning to arrive, lad. You'd best come into the living room and help me greet everyone. Remember what Shayla said. Stay close to one of us at all times."

"Yeah, let's just get this show over with. I feel like I'm in the middle of somebody else's weird dream." Right before leaving the room, he turned and looked at Afton. "I'm breathtaking, huh?"

Afton nodded and smiled to encourage him.

"I guess beauty is relative when you're kin to a bug," he concluded sarcastically.

* * * * *

A great many more people arrived than Blain had anticipated. Most surprising of all was the fact that Hannah Biddles showed up. Manners lacking, she was as bitter as ever and rude to people she didn't like. And Reverend Myers arrived soon after her. His behavior wasn't much better. They tended to stay in groups of people familiar to them, presumably those who would listen to their ranting.

The last person to arrive was Rhiannon. She was fashionably late, dressed in a black, skintight dress. Her voluptuous breasts seemed dangerously close to falling out. Blain grinned when she threw her arms around him and lifted her face for a kiss. He gave her a friendly peck on the cheek and noticed that Afton turned the other way.

"I'm still mad as hell at you," Rhiannon muttered so no one else could hear.

"Sorry. If you remember, I did call to explain about things, but you didn't want to listen. Since then, I've been busy."

Rhiannon stared at Afton. "Yes, I can see you've had your attention elsewhere. Your little house guest is the real reason we haven't been having sex, isn't it?"

Before Blain could answer, she backed away from him to get a drink from a table and engage in conversation with someone else. Some of the townsfolk would gladly talk to her, regardless of Reverend Myer's warnings. Not everyone in Harvest judged her any more than they all believed the Reverend was as sinless as he tried to claim.

Regardless of her proclamation of anger, Rhi didn't seem to care what anyone thought. She spent a great deal of time showing her assets to best advantage, sidling up to Blain as she did so. At another time, her antics might have made him laugh. He was sure she posed, primped and clung to him only for the Reverend's benefit.

Myers was smoldering in a corner with some of his most conservative flock, gossiping and hatefully glaring at Rhiannon. But Blain wasn't in the mood to laugh or play along as he normally might have. Things in his life were just too bizarre. He glanced around the room and Afton captured his gaze. She had traded her jeans for a floral sheath that floated about her ankles and was much more modestly cut at the neckline than Rhiannon's attire. Her bare shoulders had been kissed by the sunlight, and her golden brown hair hung softly about her shoulders. She looked as though she'd just come in from gathering flowers in a meadow. Her sparkling blue eyes seemed to rivet the attention of those around her.

Blain desperately wanted to get her aside and explain about Rhiannon, but the opportunity never presented itself. Besides, what could he say? He and Rhiannon had been lovers for a long time. How could he tell Afton about Rhiannon, with whom he'd shared acts so personal they couldn't be mentioned? Even if he'd had the opportunity, Afton didn't seem to notice him. Her time appeared to be divided between several young men from nearby farms. In fact, she seemed surrounded by every eligible bachelor in the county. They were practically sniffing the air like a pack of dogs after a bitch in heat, and it had the effect of rousing Blain's anger. He set down his drink and clenched his fists. Afton was much too innocent for that kind of crude attention.

Rhiannon's brittle laughter broke into his thoughts. She possessively gripped his arm, and he turned to halfheartedly absorb whatever gossip was on her mind. Rhi was like a rare, exotic vine that needed constant attention and care. She couldn't survive without it. Afton was more like a wildflower. Lovely, bright and vital. Needing only sunlight and a gentle touch to flourish. Of the two, Afton was really the strongest. The most secure and everlasting.

Blain poured himself some more whiskey and gazed guiltily into the amber fluid. He pulled at the collar of his dress shirt and wished, yet again, that he had more integrity than to mentally compare the two women. He swallowed his drink and let Rhiannon's chatter sift into his thoughts.

"Blain, baby, despite what a shit you've been to me, it's still good to be with you," she crooned as she pressed her body close to his. Her hands caressed his backside, careless of who looked on.

"You could have come to the farm any time, Rhi. I'm sorry I've been so busy I couldn't get into town." He gave her what he meant to be a brotherly hug in return.

"I would have come out here, but before now you haven't issued an invitation to visit."

Blain lowered his head in shame. He had never invited her because she was as out of place in the old farmhouse as he would have been in a New York nightclub.

Rhiannon trailed a finger down his arm. "The only reason I'm here now is because I'm curious. I had to see your place. And I also wanted an explanation as to why you've been neglecting our relationship. You owe me that much." She looped her arm through his and gazed into his eyes. Then her gaze drifted around the room until she saw Afton. "But you have a little visitor to keep you company. She's quite…adorable."

There wasn't any animosity in her voice. In fact, Rhi didn't seem at all threatened by Afton's presence, for which he was supremely grateful. Some childish display of jealousy in front of everyone was the last thing he needed right now. For the first time in weeks, he began to feel clearheaded. There was really nothing unusual about Rhiannon. She was fun and brought him out of his self-absorbed thoughts. There were no overtones of anything supernatural, no magic spells or conjuring. There was no talk of anything abnormal. Nothing was expected of him except wild sex. It didn't much fit his way of thinking, but it wasn't as crazy as everything else in his life.

As the night went on, Blain's gaze kept drifting over the crowd and looking for Afton. For some reason, her presence reminded him of what his parents had had together. There was nothing shallow or insignificant about the love his mother and father had shared. It had been deep and very rare. Even with all the crazy circumstances in his life, he wanted that kind of commitment. If he couldn't have that, marriage was out of the question. And he did want to marry one day.

Any kind of relationship with Rhi, therefore, would have been impossible. She didn't seem the marrying kind, and again it became clear to him that there was nothing more between them than sex, and there never would be. And even if he had wanted more, she could never find out what he was. He knew instinctively that she would never accept his being half fairy.

That realization prompted him to put down his drink and gently take her arm. It was time for him to end things with her. "Rhi, let's go someplace quiet. I want to get out of this crowd," Blain murmured into her ear.

"That sounds like a good idea to me, baby. I've wanted to get you alone for days now. I believe there might be a way to repair what's wrong between us." She shot him her most suggestive smile and let him lead her away.

From across the room, Afton watched them leave the room. With a sense of shock, she'd watched the other woman enter the house like some sophisticated diva. No one had to tell her who the gorgeous creature was. Rhiannon Stone had made an entrance Hollywood couldn't have duplicated. There was an arresting quality about her that men had to find enticing. The woman could put to shame some of the nymphs in the sacred forest back home. One look at the way Blain possessively held her arm and whispered into her ear told the entire story. He wanted her. That was probably why he was trying to leave, despite Hugh's and Shayla's warnings to stay close.

Pictures of Blain and Rhiannon having sex entered Afton's mind, and she felt horribly jealous. She suddenly wished her oldest brother hadn't kept her from having more experience with men.

She hurried to the nearest exit to try to divert Blain. Perhaps she could say he had a phone call in his office or that something else needed his immediate attention. As she hurried to stop him from leaving, she also tried to convince herself she was doing what the Sorceress would want her to do. That nothing else motivated her actions. Afton ran after them, quickly passed the couple and blocked their way. "Blain, could you help me with something in the kitchen?"

"Not now. I'll be back in a few minutes. Rhiannon and I just wanted to go out back and get some air. She wants to see the new herb garden in the moonlight," he lied.

"So this is little Afton. You're really quite lovely." Rhiannon held out her hand. "I'm Rhiannon Stone. I'm sure Blain must have mentioned me. Can't think why he hasn't introduced us sooner."

"Yes, Ms. Stone. He mentioned you." Afton forced back the pettiness in her voice and took Rhiannon's hand, finding it cold and rather limp. Just like her patronizing remarks.

"Please, call me Rhiannon, or just Rhi for short." Rhiannon turned to Blain. "Darling, you weren't exaggerating at all. Afton is just too sweet for words. She reminds me of one of those young girls on a medieval tapestry. You know, very lustrous and virginal. She has that *glow*. And your name is just too cute. Isn't Afton a river in Scotland or someplace, sweetie?" She addressed Afton directly.

Afton glared at Blain. Surely he hadn't told the woman she was a virgin! He wouldn't have repeated what he'd heard Shayla say, would he? She'd never felt such a sudden burst of anger in her life. "You're right, Rhiannon. I was named after a river described by the poet Robert Burns. As for being virginal and dulcet, I'm sure Blain could say otherwise. Couldn't you, *darling*?" She affected the same nasal inflection as Rhiannon had. Her sarcastic retort caused Blain's jaw to drop and Rhiannon's mouth became a thin line. Afton was satisfied with their response.

"Uh, I think Rhi and I will take that walk in the garden now. Excuse us, Afton." Blain quickly took Rhiannon's hand in his, stepped around Afton and pulled Rhi along the path.

Blain tried to keep his shock over Afton's quick comeback to himself. It seemed his English beauty could stand up for herself quite well when she wanted to. Though Rhiannon was silent, he could still sense her annoyance.

"Sorry about that, Rhi. Afton isn't usually so…intense."

"Oh, that's okay. She was just staking her claim, darling. Or didn't you pick up on that?"

He shook his head in denial and waved off the comment with one hand. There was no sense discussing Afton. He'd brought Rhi into the garden to say goodbye, so he kept silent about the matter and led her toward the fragrant herb plants.

After a while, she seemed to relax and the angry expression left her face. He tried to find somewhere appropriate to say what needed to be said. He noticed other couples strolling about the garden. Even though torches lit the pathways and strings of white lights floated through the flowerbeds, their effects couldn't compete with the full, lustrous moon. It was perfect for viewing the flowers, which had been planted to show up after dark. Dusty Miller and moonflower vines purchased from a nearby nursery, and white

Astilbe glowed in the ambient light. A cloud of white Lady Banks roses covered the archway into the center of the garden. Knowing what he had to do, Blain steered Rhiannon deeper into the growth and down the pathway leading to the gazing globe. He was fairly certain they wouldn't be disturbed there.

He wasn't sure how Rhi would take what he had to say. The last thing he wanted to do was hurt her, but his life had turned in a totally different direction. She couldn't be a part of it, and he had to tell her that.

Rhiannon suddenly stopped before entering the circular area surrounding the gazing globe. "Stop here, Blain. The light is so beautiful on all these roses."

"Rhi, we need to talk where we won't be disturbed."

"I know, baby. We have some catching up to do." She wrapped her slender arms around his body and tried to keep him from moving, but he took her hand and kept going.

When they finally reached the center of the garden, Blain half pulled a reluctant Rhiannon toward the gazing globe. He looked around to make sure no one was within earshot.

"Baby, what's wrong? You're so tense." She turned his face toward hers.

Blain gently pulled her red-tipped fingers away from his face and stepped back. "You know we've had a good relationship. Everything has always been friendly and on an equal footing, even from the first."

"Why do I sense a *but* coming here?" Rhiannon stepped back and looked up into his face.

"There's no way to make this easy. What I'm going to say is abrupt and cold, and I'm sorry for unloading on you like this." He paused to put his hands on her shoulders. "I can't see you anymore. I've had some circumstances come up in my life that are too difficult to overcome."

"Circumstances? I don't understand." She placed a hand on his chest. "We've always been able to get over town gossip.

And we can get over these little issues we've been having lately. What other problems could there be that we couldn't work through?"

The confusion in her voice tore at his conscience. It felt as if he were throwing her out like Monday morning garbage. "Rhi, sweetheart, I'm sorry. It isn't within my power to explain. I wish things could be different. But this is the way it has to be. Some very unexpected and overwhelming personal problems have come up in my life."

"You brought me all the way out to the farm to break up with me? You didn't even have the decency to come into town where we could be alone?" Her tone was icy. "Now I have to walk back through all those people in your house and act as if nothing is wrong. That fucking preacher has half of them believing I charge by the hour, and now he'll be proven right."

"Honey, no! That isn't true. You know I care about you as a friend, and I always will, but things in my life are very different than they were a few months...even different than just a few days ago." Blain tried to calm her by taking her hands in his, but she backed away.

"You used me! I was just someone to get off with until that little English bitch got here."

Blain watched as she unexpectedly smiled, but there was no warmth in it. Her eyes were as cold as a Maine night in January. "Rhi," he said carefully, "you and I never cared deeply for each other, and I think you know it wouldn't have worked. I'm a small town farmer who couldn't have given you the kind of life you want. To go on like we were wasn't right."

"Don't worry too much over it, *darling*," she drawled sarcastically. "You just wanted me for sex. But if we're playing confession, that's all I was after as well. It's just a little humiliating that you could drop me like a bad habit to run around with a girl who won't ever be able to compete with what I have." She ran her hands over her full breasts. "Have your little English rose, Blain. She's young and hot, but she'll never be able to satisfy you the way I can. So when the novelty wears off, don't come running back to me, because I won't be here. You're not the only fish in the sea, and I've had a few bites." She stroked his chin with one finger. "Maybe you could even send Miss English to me to break her in properly. I could show her what you like—make sure she's ready."

"This has nothing to do with Afton. Despite what she said earlier, she's nothing but a friend." He knew that wasn't the truth as far as he was concerned, and he hated himself for not admitting it. But something in his heart didn't want Afton mentioned in what had become a sordid scene. Rhiannon's pride was hurt, and she was taking it out on Afton. This was what he deserved for engaging in a meaningless, empty affair. Someone was bound to get hurt, even if pride was the only real issue.

"I guess everything has been said. Nothing to do now but say goodbye. Have a good life, lover." Rhi quickly turned and left him standing there. As she walked by the gazing globe, Rhiannon's form came between the lights from the garden and the globe itself. Blain saw a blackened shape emerge on the globe's smooth surface. It was very much like looking into a carnival mirror where a person's true form is twisted and malformed into something wicked and inhuman. The clean, glittering lights reflected back on the globe's surface as soon as Rhi was gone, but Blain was nauseated and shaken. He tried to shrug off the eerie sensation. He had to keep his perspective. With everything that had happened, he could easily let his imagination get the better of him.

Through the trees, he watched Rhiannon saunter back toward the house and wanted to stop her. If he could better express what was happening to him, maybe she wouldn't be so angry. But what good would it do? Even if he could tell Rhi everything, there wasn't any way she'd understand. There would never be a way to explain who he was without sounding insane.

Hearing her voice as she laughingly told someone the party was too dull and she had to get out of this country bumpkin scene, he wondered if she wasn't taking the breakup as more of an embarrassment than anything more serious. She was a survivor and would land on her feet. She'd likely find someone new and tell everyone in Harvest that *she* had dumped *him*.

To Blain, the breakup marked the beginning of a great many drastic changes to come. Some of them would be just as harsh, but he knew he'd make it. There were people on his side, exactly as his mother had said on the night she died.

He ran a weary hand over his face and tried to think how hard it must have been for his parents. He was just experiencing a tiny bit of what they had lived through for decades. How much harder had it been for his mother and father to exist all those years without being discovered? How many acquaintances had been left behind in similar scenes like the one he'd just played out? How many lies had they been forced to tell just to survive?

People who might have become friends had been kept at a distance just so the pain of leaving them behind wouldn't be too great. No real friends, no one to confide in, no real home. But he remembered how they'd loved each other fiercely and had been totally devoted to him until the day they died.

Now, their past was his legacy for the future. Except he would be granted a luxury his parents had never had—a way back into this mystical Order and the support that existed in Hugh, Shayla and Afton. For them, he was thankful, but did he even have a future? He ran his hands through his hair and walked toward the gazing globe. When he stared into it, his fairy self stared back. But that had to be his imagination working overtime. The thing couldn't be *that* good.

"Mom, Dad," he whispered. "I'm so sorry for what happened to you, and I now realize that most of what you went through was for me." He wished there was a way they could hear him. He desperately needed some space, and the garden's stillness was the only place that seemed right.

Afton turned from her position behind a tree and ambled back to the house. She'd only come out to the garden to guard Blain in case his enemy showed up. It hadn't been her intention to eavesdrop on the lovers' breakup. It seemed Blain was beginning to understand the serious consequences of his parents' desertion from the Order. That it had been forced didn't mitigate the results. They'd had to leave friends, family and all they cherished behind. Now Blain had to give up a relationship from the outside world. Freyja's horrible work would last a long, bitter time. Her maliciousness seemed to circle back and encompass them all.

Tears stung Afton's eyes. They were for Blain and herself. She had secretly hoped there could be something between them, but as far as Blain was concerned, she was nothing but the sweet virginal assistant tagging along with Shayla. His words in the garden had made that quite clear. She was just a friend. Moreover, she was one of the unexpected complications in his life. She wiped the tears from her face with the back of her hand and made a resolution to give up on whatever feelings might have been between them. Even if Blain had felt differently toward her, there were other complications he didn't know about.

Though traditions of the Order had never been explained, he would come to learn certain differences which would keep them apart. Though Blain was a blend, it was obvious he was very powerful. His size, musculature and physical appearance marked him as warrior class, which put him out of her league. Because she hadn't mastered the very basics of Druid powers, she was relegated to eventually handfast with someone of her own gatherer class.

Most members of the Order still clung to the belief that the strongest men and women should pair. This was an ancient holdover from a need to survive. All the Sorceress had done was make it possible for any warrior to mingle their blood with anyone else who was a warrior. No one had said anything about gatherer classes mixing with warrior classes. Though she was certain Shayla would permit it, the rest of the Order still insisted on mating with the strongest. Therefore, warrior men only chose warrior women and visa versa. This was the way things had been for thousands of years. Only a man whose meager powers matched her own would ever approach Afton. It simply wasn't socially acceptable to do otherwise.

Summoning a vision circle was a great accomplishment, and she was proud of herself for having done such a thing. But it was the basics that mattered to the Order. Conjuring fire and the other elements of wind, water and earth had to be demonstrated on a daily basis. Over and over. These were the skills that would protect a family, not one outstanding display of magic that couldn't be used for defense. And she'd only been able to do what she had because of Blain. He had been her motivation. And now that motivation was gone.

Oh, someone would handfast with her. Afton wasn't worried about that. She'd had offers from wonderful men, but she just hadn't been ready. Or, if she was honest with herself, she'd uncharitably reverted back to instinct when these men indicated an amorous interest. Afton's suitors weren't warriors, and it was the warrior class who secretly appealed to her. Those men offered the best future since they were accomplished in numerous tasks.

The most important of these tasks was defense. They could wield weapons as easily as they could farm, build or create artwork to sell. They were characteristically the largest, physically strongest and the most virile and sensually appealing. They fathered strong children. She couldn't help it that her emotions — and thousands of years of breeding — made her want such a mate. Other women of the Order said they felt the same way.

Even lacking the necessary warrior traits, many of her friends had tried to attract a warrior's attention and couldn't.

143

Some of them eventually became satisfied and happy with men of their own class. Some carried on in hysterics about their failure. Afton had never done either of those things. She tended to linger in the forest, mix herbs and play with the animals, silently hoping that the right man would come along.

There was simply no reason to get all worked up over something she couldn't seem to change. It was easy, therefore, to let Gawain chase off anyone she didn't fancy. She used his interference as an excuse to keep unwanted male attention at bay. And if she didn't practice her conjuring as she should, it was because she feared her powers might never meet her family's expectations. If that was the case, she'd have to settle with what was offered. And she didn't want to settle. She wanted a warrior. Added to her family's anxiety was the fact that every year the outside world came closer and closer to discovering the Order and its secrets. On the day when they were finally exposed to the world, her loved ones wanted to see her mated to a man who could help her defend a home and children. For it was an undeniable fact that a confrontation would evolve when some outsiders learned of their existence.

That was why Shayla was so protective of them all and had commanded that some of the old laws be reexamined or changed. While there were a great many beings in the Order, there weren't so many that defenses should be compromised by chasing people away as Freyja had done. Freyja's interpretation of the laws had almost destroyed their world, and it had wrought irreparable damage on Blain.

Afton smiled sadly and walked up the farmhouse steps. Whatever romantic interludes they'd shared, Blain obviously hadn't placed the importance on them that she had. His announcement of their friendship prompted her to think over other options. If her powers never evolved, there might be some men she would consider as a mate. So what if they couldn't swing a claymore like they were born to it, or shoot a longbow and put the arrow exactly on target? She wasn't special, after all. Who was she to judge them worthy or not?

She stopped walking and contemplated the outcome. No. There was no way she'd handfast with someone her heart couldn't accept. Afton shook her head in anger. "Oh, damn it all! I want a man who can sweep me off my feet, fight dragons and make love like there's no tomorrow!"

"You do?"

Afton jumped in surprise, and her hands went to her throat as she spied Hugh sitting on the porch, grinning at her. Embarrassed, she lowered her head and mumbled, "I didn't know anyone was here." She turned away and fidgeted with the leaves of a moonflower vine as Hugh rose and walked toward her. Where were her Druid senses that she hadn't known he was present?

"It's all right, Afton." Hugh gently turned her around and hugged her. "I may be older, but I understand."

Afton hugged him back as tears welled in her eyes. "Please don't tell anyone you heard me say that. Especially the part about…you know."

"It'll be our secret." He patted her cheek. "Now, go on inside and dry your tears. There are still guests about, and we need to watch over your dragon slayer."

Afton smiled and walked up the stairs to her room. Hugh knew she'd been talking about Blain. But Hugh also had to know Blain would never be hers. She blew her nose and decided to go back downstairs. Shayla and Hugh were depending on her. There would be plenty of time later to feel sorry for herself. She was about to open the door to her room when a strange feeling came over her. It was like ice water dripping down her spine.

Someone was moving toward Blain's door. Her room was closest to his and had been assigned at Shayla's insistence. At the time, it had seemed like a strange request, but Afton had gone along with it, just as she went along with everything the Sorceress wanted. Perhaps her proximity to Blain had been chosen because she was an extremely light sleeper. But it didn't matter why she'd been assigned the room, because she needed to worry about what was happening now. Whoever was moving around radiated menacing, frightening vibrations. Even a Druid baby could have felt the dark intensity of them.

Afton had never before experienced sensations so eerie. Whoever this was was creeping about like someone bent on doing harm. Protective instincts flooded through her. If she could never be anything more to Blain than a friend, then she'd be the best friend he'd ever have. And someone was about to hurt him. She felt it.

Afton carefully cracked opened her door and saw Blain's door closing very slowly. There wasn't time to get Shayla or Hugh. She took a deep breath, stepped out of her room and hurried to Blain's room. Placing her hand on his doorknob, she quickly shoved the door open.

The woman who'd been introduced to her as Hannah Biddles was standing in the middle of the room and holding one of Blain's work shirts. Her gray-streaked brown hair had been pulled away from her face in a severe bun, and she wore a navy gingham dress over her more than ample figure. Dark eyes glared at Afton from a lined countenance more familiar with frowning than showing any kinder emotion.

"What are you doing in here?" Afton asked. She wanted to give the woman a chance to explain her presence before making any accusations. If Hannah was the one hurting Blain, Shayla would show her very little mercy. If the woman knew about the Order, the Sorceress would show none.

"I might ask the same of you," the older woman replied, dropping the shirt to the floor.

"I'm not about to get into a game of twenty questions with you. You're in Blain's room with his property in your hands. What do you think you're doing?"

Hannah's eyes began to glow as if some horrible fire lit them from within. Afton stood her ground. This was the person they'd been seeking. The third and final suspect on their list, Reverend Myers, had long since left the farm. "You're the one who has been casting these malicious spells, aren't you? Why are you trying to hurt Blain? "

"Keep out of my way," the old woman sneered. I can sense you have power, but you haven't got what it takes to stop me."

"You're trying to hurt someone I care about, so I'm not going to let you leave this room." Afton swallowed hard. "You'll have to go through me if you want to escape."

"Whatever you want, little fool. Through you it is." She raised her right arm and began an incantation.

Afton knew she probably wouldn't be alone for long. Hugh and Shayla would sense the magic being conjured and would show up at any moment. But it was important to keep the woman in the room so none of the remaining townsfolk would know what was going on. To ward off anything that might come her way, Afton raised her hands and began to whisper a spell of protection. Not just for her, but for Blain as well. She could feel the evil hit her like a cold hand reaching out and slapping her hard. She stood fast. Others were counting on her. If Hannah was allowed to leave, there was no telling what might happen.

"Leave Blain alone. He hasn't done anything to you. You have no right to harm him." Afton lifted her palms toward Hannah in an effort to fend off the evil. Strands of black plasma like tentacles reached for her. She wasn't sure if it was a manifestation of what she sensed in her mind, or if the tentacles were real.

"Hasn't done anything? You have no idea what you're talking about, little girl. Blain McTavish is as good as dead. And so are you!"

The wavering arms of blackness that reached for Afton were beginning take their toll. She felt dizzy, cold and nauseated all at once. If it had been only her safety at stake, Hannah would have already destroyed her. But others were counting on her—especially Blain. So she closed her eyes and dug deep within herself. She could only hold back the evil a bit longer before all her strength melted away.

"Do you think you can stop a power that spans the bridge of time? You're barely out of your cradle. You and that impotent Order of hapless beings can't stand against someone as powerful as me. My kind have existed since the beginning of creation. I'm just getting warmed up on you. Then I'll take care of that old hag downstairs and her Druid lover. Finally, I'll drag that fairy half-breed into the woods and make him beg to die before this night is through. No one will ever know what happened to any of you." She laughed wickedly. "Your kind has never been, and never will be, as powerful as those who wield the black arts."

Afton opened her eyes and saw that the older farm woman had disappeared. The woman now standing before her was younger and taller, with long, flowing dark hair. Her eyes had turned blood-red, and they glowed with contempt. The gingham dress had been replaced by a black, hooded robe. Jewels glistened from its surface.

Afton felt herself slipping into unconsciousness and wondered if she'd been fighting off the blackness for minutes or hours. She had never felt so weak, but she kept her hands raised even as she felt her body falling to the floor. Perhaps she couldn't stop the menacing witch, but she could delay her until more powerful help came.

As if watching a movie in slow motion, Afton saw Shayla glide into the room with Hugh following. The black tendrils retreated to their source as Shayla raised her hands and chanted.

"*Dion*." Shayla uttered the Celtic word for protection. "I know who you really are now."

"Leave off, you foul daughter of horrors," Hugh cried as he knelt beside Afton, protectively wrapping his arms around her. "You evil whore!"

"What the hell..." Blain gasped as he entered his room and saw the scene unfolding there. Afton was on her knees as Hugh tightly held her. Shayla was gesturing toward some unknown woman dressed like a Halloween figure. The woman was backing into the farthest corner of his room. Black fingers of some bizarre substance were retreating into the corner with the strange woman.

"Die, Shayla Gallagher! All of your kind shall perish with you. And I'll start with that worthless little Druid. I'm disappointed you didn't come with an assistant who was more challenging. But I need no such help. I've gleaned enough of that fairy bastard's power to take you all on at once."

"We'll see, you offspring of darkness! Your kind and mine have always battled. The evil of yours has always lost. So it has been. So it shall always be!" Shayla's voice rose, and wind whipped through an open window. The room's contents were scattered everywhere.

"Take her, lad!" Hugh cried as he pushed Afton into Blain's arms. "The lass is too weak to withstand any more!" He moved to stand at Shayla's side, mimicking her gestures and uttering the same incantation. The figure in the corner cried out in anger as she was buffeted against the wall by what had to be gale force winds. The black strands slowly disappeared. Together, Shayla's and Hugh's voices rose above the sound of the wind. The gale increased, and so did the dark woman's shrieks of pain and frustration.

Blain held Afton very close. He was more petrified than he'd ever been in his entire life. Nothing in any horror movie could have prepared him for what he was seeing. The woman in the corner raised her hands toward Shayla and Hugh. A ball of purple-black light shot from her fingertips, but Shayla and Hugh simultaneously fired a similar ball of pure white light. It blocked the woman's volley, then passed through it and struck the robed woman's chest. She shrieked with pain but seemed to shake it off. Her hands made small circles in the air. The circles gradually enlarged, and red, devilish apparitions appeared.

Each of them changed shape as they moved, but all had horns and mouths filled with sharp teeth. They were more like shadows than real beings, with a smell like sulphur accompanying them. The odor became so strong it almost displaced the very air they breathed.

Blain watched Shayla and Hugh join hands. The wind increased and blew the apparitions back to the cornered figure. They turned on the woman and ripped her robe apart with their teeth. She yelled out profanity and managed to stop them by releasing more of the black tentacles. They wrapped around the red demons and pulled them toward the floor where they seemed to dissipate.

The figure in black raised her fist and shook it at Hugh and Shayla. "No matter what you do, Sorceress, you…still…lose!"

The woman shot a barrage of what looked like black lightning toward Shayla and Hugh. It crackled from her fingertips like electricity. They easily countered her offense with strong, white lightning. Whatever the evil woman did, Shayla and Hugh mimicked those powers with greater intensity. But they never struck out at her first. They only defended themselves against her actions.

Blain could see that the woman's powers appeared to be weakening. Still, she fought on. Her final bursts of magic were aimed toward him and Afton, but Hugh and Shayla stepped in front of them and easily blocked it all. He clutched Afton's body close, vowing that nothing would harm her. Then he pulled her head against his shoulder.

"Hang on, baby, it's almost over!" he yelled, hoping she could hear his voice. As if someone was erasing a chalkboard, the strange figure began to disappear. She howled and convulsed in pain. Even as she began to waft away, she tried to conjure, but the fight didn't go on for more than a few moments. Strangely, she looked him straight in the eyes and smiled as if there was some secret joke he couldn't share. It was as if she knew something he didn't, and fear paralyzed him.

The same fear of impending doom he had been feeling all along.

"*You...still...lose!*" she screamed at him. Then the horrible figure cried out in agony and clutched at the air, struggling to hang on to life only to vanish into nothing. The wind suddenly died, and the contents of the room were all back where they belonged. Just as if nothing had ever happened.

Shayla and Hugh turned toward Blain.

Afton moaned softly.

Without pausing to think, Blain picked her up and walked toward the bed.

Shayla fluffed pillows as she pulled back the covers. "Let her rest. She'll be right as rain in no time. Come, Hugh. Let's gather her some mint from the garden and brew a nice tea. She'll have need of it shortly."

Blain gently laid Afton on the bed then looked at them in amazement. "How in the hell can you talk about brewing tea? What just happened in here? Who was that, and what happened to her?" His voice rose as he pointed toward the corner of the room.

"That was Hannah Biddles in her true form," Hugh replied. "She wanted your powers to use against you and the rest of us."

"What...Hannah...why..." Blain tried to form a coherent sentence, but couldn't. He'd seen too much he couldn't explain, too much that seemed too fantastical.

"Take a deep breath and relax, Blain." Shayla patted his shoulder. "All will be well. At least, for now. Hannah won't trouble you or anyone else." She regarded him carefully. "I know what you've seen is a bit perplexing, but—"

"No, Shayla. Finding out you're a damned fairy is perplexing. What happened in here was frickin' unbelievable!"

"All right, Blain. All right. Just sit with Afton and try to calm yourself. Everything will be explained," Hugh interjected softly. "Keep Afton warm. We'll be back soon."

Blain took deep breaths, trying to slow his heart down. What, in the name of creation had he gotten himself into? He looked down at Afton, then sat beside her. He lifted her hand and pressed his fingers to her wrist. Her pulse was strong, but she looked pale. What had happened to her?

"Afton, honey, can you hear me?"

"Blain? Is it over?" she whispered back. Afton opened her eyes to see Blain leaning over her, concern etched into his features.

"*Some*thing's over. Don't ask me what." He paused, took another deep breath and focused on her. "Are you okay, baby?"

"I think you have an American expression about getting the license of the truck that hit me. The expression seems to apply here," she tried to joke.

"This isn't funny, Afton. Whatever happened, you seem to have been badly hurt."

"I'll be fine. Where are Shayla and Hugh?" she asked, glancing around the room.

"Downstairs brewing you a cup of tea."

"Good. I could use one."

"Afton, some…*thing*…just tried to kill you, and you want a damned cup of tea?" Blain stared at her as if she was insane.

"The thing you're referring to was Hannah Biddles. She was a Druid practicing black powers. I caught her in your room trying to steal one of your shirts."

Blain's brow furrowed. "Why would she want a shirt? This is getting screwier by the minute."

"Remember, we told you whoever was trying to hurt you needed something personal. She was probably trying to steal anything she could get her hands on." Afton paused. "We took most of the protective amulets out of the house, hoping to make it easier for whoever was harming you to show themselves."

"Thanks a lot!" Blain bit out.

"As long as Hugh and Shayla were close by, I knew nothing would happen to you. They wouldn't let it."

"But it wasn't Hugh or Shayla who passed out in my arms. It was you. Weren't you the one who first confronted her?"

"I wouldn't call what I did a confrontation. I sort of acted like a speed bump and slowed her down a little until the real cavalry arrived." She sighed. "I'm a bit tired."

This was the strangest situation Blain could ever imagine, but dealing with his problems could wait. Afton's were imminently more important now. "You'd better rest, honey. When you're feeling up to it, we'll talk. I need your help and…I trust you" Blain stroked her hair.

"I'll do everything I can to help. I'll always be here for you, Blain." She gazed up into his sage-colored eyes.

"Just sleep now. Okay?"

"Will you do something for me?"

"Anything. All you have to do is ask."

"Would you hold me? Just for a while?"

"Sure, sweetness. For as long as you want." Blain pulled her into his arms and let her rest against his chest. Her color seemed better, her breathing was sound and she was coherent. Whatever had happened to Afton was probably temporary. Shayla and Hugh didn't act too upset by the girl's physical state, but he wasn't leaving her tonight. He'd hold her all night long if that was what she wanted. And he vowed that, no matter what it took, no one would fight his battles again. He had powers of his own, and he'd damned sure learn how to use them.

* * * * *

Hugh watched as Shayla put the kettle on to boil. "You know that woman wasn't Hannah Biddles. At least that's not what we called her over thirty years ago."

Shayla nodded. "I know, though I wasn't really sure until she changed into her true form upstairs. She was very good at masking her presence and true identity. I can't believe someone from the Order could practice such black magic, or why anyone would believe it would give them omnipotent powers. But they must have wanted those powers very badly."

"That's the nature of black magic. It lures you in and destroys your sanity. It creates monsters out of those who were once normal people. But did you suspect this all along?" Hugh asked.

"Yes. And so did you, if I'm reading you correctly. I suppose neither of us spoke of it because we didn't want to admit one of them got away or that more could be out there."

"Aye. I wanted to let the dead stay buried. There was so much bloodshed all those years ago." Hugh sighed and ran a hand over his face. "Should we tell Blain and Afton?"

"Blain's feelings are still very precarious. Although this will only muddy the waters for him, I'll tell him tomorrow. I promised I'd keep nothing from him. I must keep my word. You may tell Afton in your own way."

Hugh thought about the past and wished it had been different. "I understand, my love. And I think I can see Arthur and Syndra's position much better now."

Shayla nodded. "We'll never know exactly what they found out. And there are still some things I don't understand. I have a feeling this isn't over, that our confrontation upstairs was just the beginning."

"Aye. But what if Blain won't come with us now?"

"He must, Hugh. He must come with us or he'll surely die."

Chapter Eight

∾

"Blain. Afton. It's morning." Shayla placed a hand on Afton's shoulder and gently shook her awake. She knew Afton didn't want to move. Her head was pillowed against Blain's chest, and Shayla sensed she felt safe and warm there. But today was the Summer Solstice. Preparations had to be made for this evening's celebration. A bonfire needed to be built—but the breakfast feast came first.

Afton came awake feeling a little homesick. She'd never been away from her family during such an event. And the entire Order would be missing the Sorceress.

"You're awake. How are you feeling?" Shayla sat on the opposite side of the bed from Blain. She gently stroked Afton's hair away from her face.

"I'm fine, Shayla. What happened? Hannah—"

"She's gone," Shayla interrupted. "Now if you're feeling up to it, I need some help to prepare for tonight's celebration."

"Wait just a damn minute!" Blain sat up, awake and blinking as the morning light blurred his vision. "Last night you fought some kind of lightning-throwing woman you say was Hannah Biddles. Now you're ready to have some celebration over it?"

"No, Blain. That's not what's happening," Afton told him. "It's the Summer Solstice. It's the time of year when the sun is at it's greatest force. It's a very special day for us."

"Yes, we celebrate the chasing away of evil and a time of plenty. It just so happens that this year, the celebration coincides with what happened last night." Shayla patted his hand reassuringly.

"And what *did* happen, Shayla? What happened to Mrs. Biddles? If that was her." Blain sat up, tensely waiting for an answer. When he saw Afton look toward Shayla and the older woman's responding glance, he knew exactly what had happened to her.

Blain stood, walked to the open window and hung his head. "She's dead, isn't she? You actually took someone's life."

"She'd have destroyed you, Blain. If she had her way, she'd have murdered any member of the Order who stood against her," Shayla explained. "The woman knew about us and came here to fight. If she had to take a number of lives in the process, she wouldn't have hesitated."

"This can't be happening. It can't be," Blain whispered. He gazed out the window and saw a sunny day, just like any other. But a death had taken place in his home.

"Afton, if you're well enough to get up, leave us alone for a time. Hugh is downstairs and has some tea brewed. It'll help you feel much better."

Afton did as she was asked, but she hesitated at the door and glanced back at Blain, wanting to return to him. If Shayla wasn't careful, he could be on the brink of renouncing his heritage. If that happened, he'd be forever separated from the Order—or worse. She quietly walked away, praying to all creation that Shayla could make him understand.

"Come and sit," Shayla said, patting the bed beside her.

Blain turned to face her and was about to refuse, but her expression exuded kindness and patience. The woman didn't look like a killer. But neither did his uncle. He seated himself beside her, and she looped her arm through his.

"No one in the Order is allowed—or predisposed, for that matter—to hurt other living souls without good cause, Blain. But we must protect ourselves. Compared to outsiders, there are so very few of us left, and so few parcels of suitable land on which we can survive. We hide and lurk. We creep about and play at being shadows. Such is our life." She paused for a moment then continued. "Once we numbered in the thousands and walked the earth among men. We held our heads up proudly and dwelled among kings. But now we would be hunted into extinction. Can you imagine what humankind would do to us—and themselves—to gain our powers? Our existence depends upon what each member of the Order does on a daily basis. We scheme and devise ways around the outsiders' laws in order to exist and protect the land. We use magic to forge documents and to travel. There are only a few places on earth where our children can play in the sunshine. Even in those rare spots, they're always guarded and can never move about freely. If they survive to adulthood, they might be allowed to travel, but only as necessity dictates. Our young learn the games of survival, not the games of simple childhood. Everything they're taught is in an effort to help them stay alive and remain undetected. Someday soon, changes will have to be made or we won't exist at all."

"The woman last night—she would have killed Afton, wouldn't she?" Blain asked, his voice breaking.

"Yes. Afton got in her way. I didn't want to tell you this, but there may be more out there like Hannah Biddles. And I must also tell you that she was once one of Freyja's minions. Her sister, if I recall. I only recognized her when she changed form. Her real name isn't important. She's dead now. But if she escaped the Order when I took over, others might have done the same. And those others might do what this woman did to you. They're very good at hiding their real identities. Do you understand?"

Blain slowly clenched his hands. He understood. Perfectly. They might come after him again. "What could I possibly have that they want?"

"I'm not sure, Blain. It could be they wanted to kill you simply to get even with me, or to follow Freyja's bent interpretations of the laws. I'm not certain."

"All of this is getting harder and harder to accept. At first it was new and fantastic. Now it's become a fight for survival. I don't know what to do."

"I can't promise you things will be easy if you pledge yourself to the Order, but I can tell you that you'll never find more peaceful or loving creatures. Like all societies, there are a few among us who are bad apples, as they say. But for the most part, we live happily because we love and help one another. It's the only way we've survived. We protect each other."

"And that woman last night was in the minority?"

"Yes. We don't allow evil to enter our presence. We shun it and turn away if we're allowed to do so. Last night, it had to be confronted. While our magic is normally only used to serve, it may also be used to protect. But it is never abused. Those who do so threaten us all by drawing attention to our existence. If any of the Order misuses their powers to hurt anyone without just cause, they suffer what we refer to as the judgment."

"Death?" Blain asked.

"Sometimes, but that penalty has rarely been used. We live simply and love in abundance. There's little need for judgment or punishment of any kind."

Blain hung his head. He couldn't deny what he was, but the conditions of accepting his heritage scared the hell out of him. His own parents might have been killed if they hadn't run away from the Order. But things had to have changed or he'd be dead already. And he couldn't deny the fact that someone had been trying to harm him. Since Shayla's arrival, the harm had stopped.

Until last night. He stood and glanced around. The walls closed in on him, and he felt more alone than at any other time in his life. How could he forget what he'd turned into in the woods? When the transformation had taken place, he hadn't felt evil or malicious. All he'd felt was wonder, curiosity and awe. But for the laws which drove his parents away, wouldn't he have been born a part of this Order? Wouldn't he have been one of those who now lived each day to survive? And wasn't that what he'd do from now until the day he died? Especially now that he knew what and who he truly was?

"Am I allowed a choice in what I do from here on out?"

"Because you were born never knowing about the Order, you won't be forced to accept it now. But if you don't, you'll never see any of us again. And if anyone should find out about us because of you—"

"You'd kill me?" He turned to her.

Shayla saw the tears in his eyes. "That's one law even I can't reinterpret, Blain. I must protect all those who depend upon me." She closed her eyes for a moment, then stared earnestly at him. "Please don't force me to make that choice. I love you as I would have loved my own son."

He dropped his head back as tears streamed down his face. "I want to believe in all of this. I can't deny what I turned into in the woods, but it's so damned hard."

Shayla pulled him to her.

Like a lost child, he lowered his head against her shoulder and wept. Someone had died in his room, and he was being asked to accept the circumstances which caused the death. Somewhere in the world, a magical order of creatures existed from day to day on no more than the trust they placed in one another. He could deny their existence and lose his uncle, the only living relative he had, or accept the situation and allow magic into his life. It was the same terrible magic that had caused a death, and the same wonderful enchantment that had allowed him to physically alter himself into a creature of legend.

"Think and rest, Blain. Tonight we honor the Summer Solstice. In our tradition, it's a time to celebrate. We shall light a bonfire this evening and observe the goodness and wonder of life. We'll put aside the horror and evil. The bad things have passed away for a time and have left only the good. Until tonight, stay here and rest. We'll see to the chores." She hugged him once more and walked out of the room.

Blain remained motionless for a very long time. He had a choice to make and no matter what he did, nothing would remotely be the same again.

* * * * *

"It's time," Hugh announced. "May I begin?"

Shayla nodded.

Afton watched as Hugh walked forward and stretched out his hands. Using powers she could never hope to imitate, he caused fire to leap from the bottom of the stacked wood. When the blaze was burning well, Hugh joined her and pulled the hood of his long white robe up over his head. She did the same. And as the flames grew even higher, Blain didn't appear.

Afton thought her heart would break as surely as if it were made of brittle glass. If Blain hadn't shown himself by now, he'd probably decided to have no part of the Order or its ceremonies. That meant they would leave for England and none of them would ever see him again.

Afton clasped one of Hugh's hands tightly in both of hers. How horrible it must have been for the older man to have searched so long for his brother and sister-in-law only to find them dead. Then to find a wonderful nephew he never knew existed and lose him as well. But Hugh kept his face toward the flames so she couldn't see his expression. His feelings were being masked from her. Perhaps it was his way of hiding how awful the moment was for him.

"Join hands," Shayla ordered in a voice that shook.

"Wait, Shayla. Please, wait a few more minutes," Afton begged.

"There's no use prolonging this. It seems Blain has made his choice," Shayla responded sadly.

Afton stepped in front of Hugh so she could see his face. There was terrible sorrow in his downcast expression and tears glittered in his eyes. She had already delayed the ceremony as long as possible by walking slowly to the pasture where the bonfire was situated. She moved forward to hug Hugh and tried to convey some hope to him when she felt none herself. He responded in kind, then quickly released her from his embrace.

Afton saw him take Shayla's hand in his. With the joining of their hands, she knew Shayla would utter the ancient words as the sun set. And Blain's final decision would become forever recorded.

"Is it too late to join you?" Blain called out. He saw Shayla whirl around to look into the inky depths of the woods. He hadn't mean his entrance to be so dramatic, but after everything the woman had put him through, it was rather gratifying to see the startled look on her face. He slowly walked forward and watched Shayla's eyes widen in surprise. It had seemed appropriate to make his appearance in fairy form. Their response to him would tell him a lot about what would happen with this mythical Order and how they would react to him.

"By all that's magic," Shayla gasped, "Blain, you're magnificent." With what almost sounded like embarrassment, she added, "And I didn't sense your presence."

Blain stepped nearer to the fire. It was the first time Afton had seen him in well-lit surroundings, and her expression reflected pure astonishment. He'd made the transformation in the woods. It had come much easier than expected and with none of the pain he'd suffered before. In this form, he felt almost invincible. It was as if even the laws of gravity changed for him. His movements were light and quick, like those of a predator. He could see with ease in the coming darkness. His senses were sharp enough to tell him that no human, other than the three people before him, was within miles of the pasture. It wouldn't do to start this new life by revealing his alter ego to some hapless farmer who'd then be destroyed because of his carelessness. Changing at will was something he'd have to be very careful about in the future.

Some instinct told him that Shayla had masked the bonfire's presence, and no one would ever know they'd been in this pasture burning anything at all. Unlike the Druids, he couldn't stand the feeling of clothing upon flesh that seemed much too sensitive. A piece of leather from the barn was tied loosely about his waist.

Shayla moved closer to him and placed a hand on his cheek. "You have the look of your mother. She was a Highland fairy. Depending upon the weather, they move a great deal between England and Scotland. She spent most of her time teaching the children at our ancestral grounds in England. She'd be so very proud of you."

Afton could see that, possibly for the first time in her life, Shayla was hard-pressed to find words. So the Sorceress did what most people do when they were flummoxed—she began babbling.

"Come, Blain," Afton said as she reached for his hand and took him closer to the fire. "It isn't too late to join us." The gaze he turned on her was elemental. Since his irises were star-shaped instead of round, it gave him an even more ethereal look than most fairies already possessed. His skin was green, but a lighter shade than usual. As before, his ears were pointed and his hair had grown much longer than its normal collar length. The light from the fire cast eerie shadows upon his features, which would have frightened anyone who didn't know him.

"What do you think, Hugh?" Afton asked.

"By the stars! He's remarkable. Simply remarkable," Hugh choked out.

"Well, that makes it unanimous. I'm odd even by your standards, whatever those are," Blain quipped. Then he changed his tone of voice to reflect his feelings. His inflection was more serious and primitive. "After I changed forms, I saw my reflection in the gazing globe tonight. I fully accept what I have to do. Whatever happens from now on, I place my future in your hands, Shayla. I can't live with one foot in this world and one in yours. This is what I am. This is who I'll stay. Teach me. Show me what I need to know. If your Order can accept a half-breed, then take me to them."

Shayla took his hands in hers as tears of joy coursed down her cheeks. "The pledge has been made. It will be honored. *So Mote It Be.*" After she spoke, the wind rose and the fire burned a deep orange.

Afton watched Blain's face as he stood beside her. His starry-eyed gaze never faltered, and his solemn expression endured throughout the evening. She'd never known anyone with more courage. She did know she was falling deeply in love with him. This was the warrior of her dreams. Though she believed he might never reciprocate her feelings, she still wanted him so much it actually hurt. If Blain could draw forth the courage to face the challenges ahead of him, then so would she. One way or another, she'd find a way to make him see her as something more than just a friend. And she'd find a way to be worthy of him and obtain the strength it would take to be warrior class. In unison, they all turned together and stepped forward, joining hands as Shayla spoke the ancient Celtic words to celebrate.

* * * * *

"Everything here will be fine, lad," Hugh promised. "Shayla is sending some of our most trusted people to look out for the animals and the crops. After they've arrived and settled, I'll join you in England. It should only take a week, maybe less."

Blain nodded. "I'm not really worried. When Shayla assured me everything here would be well taken care of, I believed her. It's what's waiting for me on the other side of the ocean that I'm more concerned about. But I've made my decision. I'll see it through."

"You make it sound like you're going on a death march. I think you'll have quite a few surprises waiting for you. You may even enjoy it if you'll let yourself." Hugh clapped Blain on the back. "We don't bite, lad."

"We'll see," Blain remarked as he picked up his bag. He walked toward the door to join Afton and Shayla. They had their belongings in the car and were ready for the drive to the airport. Using fake passports and IDs didn't seem to faze them a bit. It scared the hell out of him. But everything had been carefully arranged to make his leaving look like a planned vacation, though no one would know where he'd actually gone.

He paused and turned back toward Hugh one last time. "Anything I should know? Any words of wisdom you care to pass along?" He noticed the trepidation in his own voice.

"Aye." Hugh turned to the bar, poured a large measure of whiskey into a glass and handed it to him. "Drink this and try to relax, lad. At this rate, you'll be giving yourself an ulcer."

Blain took the whiskey and a deep breath. "Here's to fairy tales, magic, and the fools who believe in them." He tossed back the entire contents of the glass, hugged his uncle and walked out of his house.

The drive to the airport went by all too quickly for Blain. He took his cues from Afton and Shayla as they got to the airport ticket counter. When Blain was asked for his identification, he was sure the sweat on his face would give him away. The man behind the counter looked him over carefully before finally processing the ticket and taking his luggage. Blain believed his heart might tear out of his chest. It was beating that hard. He saw how easily the women were getting through the entire ordeal. How the hell did they act so calm?

Finally he was on the plane. But they weren't off the ground yet. Shayla was, as always, full of poise. Afton surprised him. She'd put her hair up in a much more sophisticated style and wore a light blue sheath dress with matching sandals. Except for the night of the party, he'd been used to seeing her in jeans and farm gear. Her new look was quite alluring. Some of the male passengers openly stared at her. He felt a surge of jealousy. They were looking her over like she was a thick, juicy steak.

When they were airborne, Blain forgot about the men's eyes on Afton and breathed a sigh of relief. But Afton's collected calm got to him. While he was sweating bullets, she sat next to him and exuded confidence and coolness.

Occasionally, she looked up from the magazine she was reading and smiled at him as if they were doing nothing unusual. It irritated the hell out of him. The least she could do was show the same concern she had while they were on the farm together. This new Afton seemed too self-assured. He hated being placed in a defensive position. Afton was confident because she knew what she was going home to and welcomed it. He was left to sit and suffer in almost complete silence through the hours it took to get to London. He couldn't talk about his doubts or concerns in the plane's confined spaces. Someone might overhear.

The closer they got to their destination, the happier Afton and Shayla looked, and the more anxious he felt himself growing. He'd never considered himself a coward, but when the flight attendant came by to check with each passenger before landing, he broke into a cold sweat. Then that awful feeling of impending doom hit him. He stared out the window, took a deep breath and tried to shake it off. Whatever he was sensing hadn't, as he'd hoped, gone away with Hannah's death. It was back with force.

He ordered a whiskey, drank it down and ordered another. That dark outcome he felt had to be his own fear of the future eating at him. That was the only plausible explanation. If he told anyone about it, they'd think he was a fool or the coward he already thought himself. He had to find a way to fit into this Order or spend the rest of his life alone. Living as they probably did, Blain believed they wouldn't tolerate someone without courage. So he kept his mouth shut and tamped the black feeling down.

Seeing his hand tightly clenched into a fist, Afton placed hers over it. "It's all right. Everything will be easy from here on out, Blain. Lore is meeting us at the airport."

Blain recognized the name as belonging to the leader of the fairy clan. He remembered Afton saying Lore was the one with the dubious ancestry who never used his real last name. There was some fairy tradition having to do with the magical quality of his surname. As Blain tried to remember everything else he'd been told, he clenched his hands around the arms of his seat and physically willed himself to take deep breaths. When they landed, he only hoped he could get through customs as easily as any other passenger on vacation. Afton took his hand as they disembarked. He squeezed it tightly.

"Ouch! Not so hard, Blain."

"Sorry." He raised her hand to his mouth for a soothing kiss. Showing his current state of nerves wasn't going to win him any points with this Lore person. And apparently, as leader of the fairies, Lore was the one to impress. Shayla hadn't yet decided who was going to train him in the Druid ways.

Shayla led the way to the customs area. Blain held his breath, trying to look nonchalant as the authorities checked his passport and asked a few mundane questions. He surprised himself by being able to joke with the man looking at his documents. It must have worked because the man smiled, handed him back his passport and wished him well.

When he turned and walked toward Shayla and Afton, he noticed a man matching his own height standing beside them. His hair was long, blond and pulled back into a ponytail. He wore a black leather jacket, boots and jeans. He could have been anyone from any part of Europe or the States. As Blain approached, the blond giant pulled off the sunglasses he was wearing. The green eyes gazing into his own were full of curiosity and welcome.

"Blain, I'm Lore. Shayla has told me all about you. It'll be my job to make sure you're properly introduced to everyone. Sure 'n it's good to meet you."

Blain noted the Irish accent and took Lore's outstretched hand in his own. He immediately felt some kind of electric quality in the touch. Since Lore didn't mention it, he chalked it up as something ordinary between people of their race.

"I'm glad to meet you, Lore," Blain said, meaning it. Lore's handshake was made in earnest. This was his first contact with the fairy race — or Sidhe, as they were called. If this had been a dream, he'd have awakened laughing. But it was all too real. It was ridiculous to have ever imagined that fairies were tiny people flitting around in a garden. While Lore seemed genuinely glad to meet him, Blain had a hunch it wouldn't do to anger him. Ever.

"Come. Let's hurry," Shayla commanded. "I want to be home by dark."

Lore led them outside to a large sedan. He quickly drove them away from the airport and headed north. Afton sat in the front passenger seat and smiled at the fairy leader. Blain wondered what their history was together. Did Afton have a thing for the man? In that blue dress, she was down right titillating.

"You look glad to be back," Lore remarked as he returned her smile. "Afton, you're as lovely a sight as ever a man dreamed."

"Flattery will get you everywhere." She laughed. "Now tell me all the gossip since we left."

Lore grinned. "Pluck has been driving your poor mother daft. That wee rascal needs someone to put him back in line."

Afton looked over the back seat at Blain. "Pluck and I have been friends since we were babies. He's one of the elf faction and doesn't know how to stay out of trouble."

"That's the way of elves, I'm afraid." Shayla clucked, shaking her head. "You'll meet everyone soon, Blain. Don't let anything overwhelm you. If you have any questions, simply ask."

"Questions? I don't know where to begin," Blain stammered. He trained his gaze to the passing scenery, just as Shayla was doing. The two of them shared the sedan's expansive back seat, which was wide and very luxurious. This Order must be doing well for itself, Blain thought. As he kept his mind on these mundane thoughts, the horrible, dark feeling he'd felt on the plane disappeared. But that only left him believing it represented something very important. Something he should be recognizing and wasn't. He shook his head as if doing so could rid him of his doubts.

"I can't imagine what this must be like for you," Lore said, glancing into the rearview mirror at Blain, "but you're in for a very warm welcome. Since Shayla told us you'd be coming, members of different factions have been showing up at the estate for days. Everyone wants to meet you."

"The estate?" Blain looked at Shayla.

Shayla smiled. "That's another name for our place in England. The wooded area where we live is part of a very large estate belonging to a member of our Druid faction. The place has been in his family for centuries. It's large enough to offer privacy and very well guarded. You'll also hear it referred to as the Shire. Afton or Lore can show you some of the more historic sites there."

Afton turned around to look at him and smiled. "Oh, there are some lovely ruins, Blain. There are all kinds of sacred stone circles and ancient abbeys to explore."

Blain returned her smile with one of his own. He didn't know what would be expected of him, but it all began to take on the air of an adventure. Talk turned lighthearted as Afton began to ask about her family and explained about each of them for his benefit. The countryside became more wooded and looked as if it were the exact kind of place a creature of legend would haunt. A creature like him.

They drove on and stopped only to get a quick bite to eat and refuel the car. Though the lanes were very narrow and they had to occasionally slow down, they made good time. It was late afternoon when they finally drove through a massive wrought-iron gate and up to an old but beautifully restored castle.

Blain was dumbstruck. The place had towers with flags flying from them as if knights would arrive home any time. A set of arched oak doors graced the front. As they drove up to them, people began to exit the dwelling by the scores. Some walked toward them from the woods.

Blain's heart was in his throat and beating even faster. Shayla took his hand in hers and smiled at him before they got out of the car.

"Welcome home, Blain," she whispered and leaned over to kiss his cheek. He squeezed her hand back, careful not to squeeze as hard as he'd done Afton's. Swallowing hard, he stood as tall as he could. These people had to perceive him as strong. Anyone who might not accept him would use any excuse to start something. He now understood what some of those people claiming to have been abducted by UFOs must feel like. Or a fish in a bowl.

"Welcome, Shayla, welcome." A man and woman the Sorceress' age greeted her with hugs and kisses.

Afton came to stand on one side of Blain while Lore stood on the other. "Steady on, Blain," Lore advised. "There's no one who resents your being here. The two people with Shayla are the Earl of Glen Rowan and his mate, or wife. That's how the outside world knows them. To us, they're James and Gwyneth."

Blain wondered if the man had sensed his fears. If he did, then others would too. He had to control himself better. He had to.

A beautiful woman with flame-red hair came forward. She greeted Lore and Afton with a smile and a hug then stared at Blain.

"You have the look o' a Heelander," she said.

Blain smiled at her and glanced out of the corner of his eye at Lore.

"A Highland fairy," Lore interpreted with a grin. "Bonny has a thick brogue, but you'll get used to it."

"And you've no' a brogue at all?" She winked at Lore. "Come, Blain. My sisters are cryin' ta meet ya."

The girl led Blain toward a group of amazing beauties standing just outside the castle doors. Lore began to laugh as he watched Blain's progress. "Well, it didn't take her long. Bonny has a way of getting what she wants, doesn't she?"

"Bonny needs to slow down or people will think she's forward," Afton groused.

"Well, well, Afton. Anyone would think you were jealous." Lore smiled when he noticed her frowning at the women now surrounding Blain.

Afton's response was a vigorous snort in derision. "That's ridiculous. The man might at least notice other people. There are many members of the Order here to meet him. Not just Bonny and her top-heavy sisters."

"Afton!" a familiar voice shouted from behind her.

She turned to see Gawain waving at her. Thoughts of Blain's present predicament fled as she saw the other members of her family in the crowd. "Gawain! Oh, Gawain, I'm so glad to be home," she cried as she ran toward him. Her parents and other siblings were close behind.

Blain heard Afton's name being shouted, and he saw her run toward someone. The man she embraced could only be described as a mountain with long brown hair. She was soon surrounded by many other men of equally menacing size. One of them had graying black hair and a barely lined face. Her father and brothers, he guessed.

After hugging all the men, an iridescent woman took Afton into her embrace. That was the only word Blain could come up with to describe her. Her hair was lighter than Afton's, but she had the same sweet face, and she moved as gracefully as a dancer. Probably Afton's mother. So this was what Afton would look like in thirty years. Blain smiled just thinking of how Afton's dainty physical attributes would blossom in the years to come.

"Leave off, Bonny. The man needs to meet other people," Lore gently chided as he rescued Blain from the growing crowd of young women.

"May I ask a strange question?" Blain said as he looked around him.

Lore merrily ducked his head in acknowledgement of a quick kiss from a maiden. "There are no strange questions here, Blain. Only strange answers. Fire away."

"Many of the men have very long hair and the clothing is…well, the way some of the people are dressed looks almost medieval. Why? Doesn't that draw attention to yourselves?" Blain looked around at many of the men wearing leather jerkins and leather pants, boots and armbands. Some of the women also wore similar attire or had on Druid gowns.

"While we're in the middle of sacred and protected land, we maintain our heritage as much as possible. No one is allowed on the grounds who hasn't proper business here, and that means customary dress and habits can be followed. There's no real rule about it. But once you've worn that soft leather or loose Druid cloth, anything else becomes bloody uncomfortable. Speaking of which, as soon as I've introduced you around to a few more folk, we'll make our excuses and head inside. We can change and get out of these heavy outsider garments."

Blain took in Lore's explanation and nodded. He wondered when he'd be expected to not only change clothing, but his form as well. What if his appearance was so different from the others they couldn't accept him? As he scanned the crowd, he couldn't see any signs of ethereal creatures lurking about. No little green men and women roaming around. No one with wings. But as he focused on the woods, a strange feeling came over him. He was being watched. There were eyes everywhere. Hundreds. These must be the guards Shayla had told him about. For some reason, Blain felt a pull toward those woods. It was as though he needed to be there, and the more he focused on the trees and the lush undergrowth, the more he wanted to go and explore.

"I know. I feel it too," Lore said from behind him. "We're drawn to the earth and its denizens. Our kind has always been more at peace in the woods than any other place. The first time you sleep in this enchanted forest, you'll be lost to its charm forever. That's what this land does for us. Especially at night."

"You seem to sense everything I feel. Is that common?"

"Most of the time. But we can mask our feelings and thoughts from one another if we choose, though I'm sure you've realized that by now. But doing so depends upon your mood."

"But I can't sense things the way you seem to," Blain told him.

"That comes with time," Lore explained. "When we're in the woods, we'll do some experimenting with your powers. I've a feeling you'll be finding out things about yourself for the rest of your life."

Their conversation was interrupted when hoards of men and women pressed forward to meet Blain. Some of them professed to have known his parents and told him how glad they were that Shayla had changed the way the laws were interpreted. All of them seemed genuinely happy to meet him, and several of them invited him to visit them at their homes. He was surprised to learn that many of them lived in cottages on the grounds. Others had journeyed a great distance just to meet him. He felt flattered and awed. More than that, he felt warm. His apprehension melted away, and he was able to be himself.

"Blain," Afton called from a nearby group, "I want you to meet my family."

Blain and Lore moved toward her and the bevy of hulking giants who were her brothers. They looked like a bunch of lumberjacks. Blain had the feeling that if anyone ever hurt her, the offending party might as well dig his own grave.

Judging by the expressions on their faces, her brothers and her parents so clearly loved her that he had no problem understanding why she was still a virgin. It would take the bravest of hearts—or the craziest of fools—to plot an amorous tryst with Afton O'Malley. But the family was all smiles now. From the way her parents and brothers gathered around her, it was apparent Afton had been greatly missed. After Blain's introductions were made, Lore joined the O'Malley family in friendly banter. Afton's parents, Deirdre and Markham, offered Blain an invitation to visit whenever he liked. They even gave him directions to their cottage and were overwhelmingly warm. He could see where Afton acquired her openness. Smiling and laughing came easily to these people.

Afton pushed her way through her family to stand next to him. "I'm going home for the night, Blain, but I'll be back tomorrow. I'll find Pluck and bring him along. He's annoying, but rather dear to me," she added as she picked up her bags. Several of her brothers came forward and took them from her, and she laughed at their antics when they pretended the luggage was too heavy.

"I'll see you tomorrow then. Have a good night, Afton." Blain smiled back at her and nodded to the others. He was about to turn away when she stepped forward and kissed him on the lips. The kiss lingered for a moment, and he placed his hand on the small of her back. When she finally backed away, Blain forgot anyone was there and wanted more.

"You'll be glad you came. You'll see," she whispered.

"I'm already glad," he responded, grinning.

The O'Malley family waved goodbye and left with Afton in the middle of them, but Gawain took his time before leaving. He stared at Blain for longer than was polite.

Blain returned the intense stare. Then Gawain glanced at Afton's retreating form.

"You and Afton have become close?" Gawain asked, returning his attention to Blain.

"Yes," Blain admitted, not feeling obliged to explain more.

"I guess people can never have too many…friends." He paused and deliberately stared Blain down again. Then, he slowly followed his family into the woods.

As Blain watched him lumber away, it didn't take any fairy sense to figure out that Gawain didn't want him around Afton. Blain's original thoughts about her family were correct. The little Druid had bruiser brothers who weren't about to let their baby sister get hurt by anyone.

"Well, you had to have felt that." Lore grinned. "Gawain was warning you off. The man should have openly ordered you to keep your bloody hands off his sister. It would have been tactless, uncalled for and rude, but the impact would have been the same."

"He can warn away. I'm not giving up my relationship with Afton for anyone. She's been like a rock through this whole thing, and I'm not about to let her go."

Lore burst out laughing. "She'd be very flattered knowing she'd been compared to a rock."

Blain grinned. "I'll have to ask you to keep that description between us. Besides, I now know I can pick up on what others are feeling."

"A graveyard headstone could have picked up on that message, my friend. Be careful about Afton. Gawain is a good man, but where his sister is concerned, he's always looking for a fight." Lore clapped Blain on the shoulder. "Come on. Let's get out of these clothes."

Before walking into the castle, Blain paused outside the door and turned to face the woods. For a moment, he was frozen in place. That terrible feeling was back. It hovered around him like thick black smoke that just wouldn't go away. When he glanced at Lore's retreating figure, he knew the fairy leader wasn't sensing it. That made the feeling even more menacing. Something was coming for him. It wasn't there yet, but it was coming. He could feel it approaching, and he didn't even know how to explain what it was he felt. But whatever it was, thousands of miles and an ocean hadn't stopped it. More than ever, he knew he had to learn about his powers. Instinct told him there wasn't much time, and he couldn't run any more. This was the last place he could go, and he'd make a stand on the ground his parents had been forced to leave.

"No matter what happens, I'll see this to the end," he quietly muttered. Then he turned and walked into the castle.

Chapter Nine

ഗ

Blain stood in the middle of his assigned room and finished drying from his shower. It was late afternoon, and he probably shouldn't have slept so long, but jet lag wasn't something he could control. After last night's initial introductions and a late supper, he'd excused himself and gone straight to bed. Deep, restful sleep had come to him. Given the recent events in his life and his persistent premonition of doom, this was a surprise. But maybe it was his decision to finish this once and for all that had allowed him to rest so peacefully. He was tired of being plagued, hexed, followed and tortured. It would stop. One way or another, this had to end.

He heard sounds of movement about the building and hoped Shayla was among those present. He didn't want to run into one of the denizens of this environment without knowing the correct protocol for establishing his presence. Startled, one of them might turn him into something inhuman. He didn't fancy spending the rest of his life as a toilet seat or something equivalent.

He quickly dressed in the soft leather pants, boots and jerkin that had been laid out in the room. He had to admit they were a definite improvement upon the jeans and shirts he'd brought. The dark green leather pants and matching leather jerkin molded comfortably to his body and moved with him. The feel of the soft garments against his flesh was sensuously appealing.

Ostensibly, the colors would allow him to blend in with the greenery in the woods. And the high black leather boots fit to perfection. They made no sound as he moved. Just as he finished dressing, there was a knock on the door. He ran a brush through his hair before answering.

"Afton," he acknowledged when he pulled open the door and saw her. He smiled as he studied her. She was dressed in an outfit similar to his except the leather was died in shades of brown and she wore a cream-colored blouse beneath her jerkin. He liked the way the tight leather hugged her small bottom, and how the boots accentuated the length of her legs.

"I'm glad you're awake," she said. "I thought we might find you something to eat then take a walk through the woods. Lore is waiting out there. He doesn't like to sleep inside."

"And how would you know about Lore's sleeping habits?" Blain asked as a fierce sense of possessiveness hit him. "Do you sleep in the woods, too?"

Afton stopped talking for the moment. She chewed on her bottom lip, twisted her fingers together and tried to shift her gaze. It wouldn't do to let Blain know how captivating she found him in the traditional clothing of the Order. No man needed to know he was affecting a woman in such a way. But there was no doubt about it. Blain was an imposing, first class warrior. And handsome as bloody sin. Except for where the jerkin fastened together at his waist, the man's arms and chest were bare. Muscles flexed as he moved and caused her to swallow hard. For some reason, she almost wished he'd decided on wearing his regular clothing. Bonny and her friends, as well as hundreds of other unattached women, would be in the woods tonight. Looking like he did, Blain could have his pick of any of them.

"Afton, do you sleep in the woods?" he softly repeated the question.

"Sometimes, when my brothers and I have been out late," she admitted. "Once you've done it, you'll see there are advantages. And as for me knowing about Lore, everyone knows most fairies dislike being inside for very long."

Her response immediately relieved Blain. Her romantic status was still open and he felt guilt at having suspicions to the contrary. "Well, I'm ready whenever you are. Have you seen Shayla?"

"No. It's likely she's still sleeping. The trip from the States was long, and she'll want to be in the woods tonight. I believe there's to be a welcoming party for you in the great clearing. It'll probably last until dawn. Are you sure you wouldn't like to bring a jacket? The evening might be a bit cool for someone unused to our weather."

"No, thanks. I'll be fine. If this is what everyone else wears, then this is what I wear."

Afton sighed and wished she had a sack to throw over him that would cover the majority of his body. "Come on, then. I'll get you something to eat. You've a long evening ahead of you."

Blain followed her downstairs and ate a light meal of scrambled eggs and the ever-present tea. Then, Afton took him outside and led him toward the woods. They were only a few yards from the dense growth when he stopped.

"What's wrong?" she asked when he stared into the under growth.

"I'm not sure. I feel as though I need to change into fairy form," he said, keeping his gaze on the woods ahead of him.

Something about the forest called to him. If he had to describe the feeling, it was almost as if he was being pulled. It felt safe there.

"Then you shouldn't fight it. You should do what you feel is right. No one expects you to be in any particular guise. If fairy form is more comfortable for you, then change."

He nodded, walked forward and took off his jerkin. He handed the garment to Afton, but he couldn't seem to break his gaze from the woods. He wanted the foliage to brush his skin, to have the evening air blow freely across his body. Within seconds he felt the bonds of the earth lighten and his wings expand. It felt so right. He sighed with pure joy. The forest and its creatures called. He could feel the magic all around him — and he was part of it.

Without hesitating, he grabbed Afton's hand and loped for the nearest path into the woods. She laughed and ran with him. When they came to the first small clearing, he stopped. He looked around, then placed his hand on the rough bark of a nearby oak.

"This feels good. I don't know how to describe it any other way," Blain murmured as he closed his eyes and breathed in scents both new and familiar. This place was deeply embedded in his blood. It was his heritage.

"You're so perfect," Afton whispered as she lightly touched one midnight blue wing and gazed at his green skin.

Blain turned to her and moved within a breath's distance. He stroked her cheek with one finger. "Is this what it's like for the others? Do they feel so strong and free here? As if they could fight anything and win?"

"I'm not a fairy, so I don't know. But I do know that their environmental senses are generally stronger than the Druids'. Perhaps yours are even more so. You have fairy and Druid blood. No one knows what you're capable of feeling."

His thoughts seemed to reel with all the input from his surroundings. And Afton's presence was one of the most alluring of all the phenomena besieging him. His fingers tingled where he touched her face. He plunged his hands into her long hair, reveling in its softness.

"What...wh-what are you doing?" she stammered.

"Touching you. You're so damned soft and sweet. Of all the things I'm sensing, you're the most wonderful." He pulled her to him. "Your scent is driving me crazy. Is this some magic, Afton? Because if it is, you're playing a dangerous game."

"No. I'm not doing anything to cause this. Maybe it's some kind of sensory overload. You're on sacred ground now and unused to —"

Blain lowered his head and gently moved his lips against hers. When she didn't try to pull away from him, he grew bolder.

The smell of evergreens, ferns, and wild flowers assaulted him. But Afton's scent was the most pervasive. She'd recently washed her hair with sage water and bathed in herbs. He recognized the smell of the sage most readily. The combination of botanical elements and the forest scents were driving him wild. There was no way to stop himself.

When she looped her arms around his neck, he knew she was giving him permission to continue. His conscience was telling him to back off, but his body wouldn't allow it. He began to kiss her neck and caress her back.

"Blain," she whispered, "what's happening?"

"I need you, Afton, and the need is killing me," he breathed against her throat. His blood turned hot.

"Maybe...I'd better find Lore. This might be something unusual."

"Don't leave me. I won't let you leave." He was in command, the master of their fates. Blain unfastened the jerkin she wore and let it fall to the ground. He stroked the soft flesh beneath each button of her blouse as one by one, he slowly unfastened them. But Afton only gazed into his eyes with trust and growing passion. She made no move to prevent what was happening. Her hands came up to caress his chest, and Blain thought he'd die. Her touch set his sensitized skin on fire. His chest rose and fell as he breathed in her essence more deeply. His heart raced.

When he pushed her blouse away and cupped her small, white breasts in his palms, all feeling of the earth beneath his feet left. The soft mounds of flesh filled his hands perfectly. He teased the nipples until she cried out and moved against him. He kept his right hand over her breast and stroked her bare back with his left palm. Then he slid the hand down her back to her hip. He pulled her against him harder and let her feel how aroused he'd become.

Afton had never wanted anything in her life more than she wanted Blain. Whatever was happening, she wanted it to continue and never stop. No man had ever touched her, and she suddenly knew that no man but him ever would. Her heart was as certain of that fact as it had ever been about anything. She'd die for him. Die loving him.

"You're mine," he growled against her shoulder. "Only mine."

His mouth claimed hers again, this time with more force. When her tongue met his, he moaned, wrapped his arms about her small waist and lifted her against him. Somewhere in the distance, someone called his name. Part of his fevered brain wanted to ignore the summons, but the other part wanting to protect Afton wouldn't allow it. He had to take her, own her, but he had to protect her first.

Blain finally found his voice and whispered, "Afton, someone's coming."

"I know. It's Shayla. She's been headed this way for a few minutes." She gasped as he kissed her neck again. "Maybe we'd better answer."

"Dammit! I don't want to. I have to be alone with you. I need you."

"Blain, she'll find us no matter where we go, and she'll know what we've been up to."

"Does that matter to you? Do you care if we make love and she knows?" Blain pushed her hair back and gazed into her eyes.

"We'll be together later," she promised as she kissed the tip of one of his pointed ears. "Right now, we'd better see what she wants."

When she kissed his ear and pushed away from him, Blain almost lost all control. Among other places, the tip of his ear was extremely sensitive. When she backed away, his breathing slowed slightly. As she moved still further away to dress, his control grew. But his groin still ached, and he wanted her beneath him.

He sat upon a nearby log and closed his eyes. No amount of distance was going to wipe away what had just happened. He still wanted her, and that wasn't going to change just because Shayla had decided to interrupt at the most inopportune moment.

When his eyes met hers again, Afton knew it was only a matter of time before he took her. His gaze and intense expression promised this wasn't the end of the loving, but a precursor to something wild. Her heart beat hard at the thought. The next time, she'd learn what it meant to be claimed. There would be no turning back, no interruptions. The next time he'd take her no matter what happened. It was all there in his searing gaze.

Blain tried to calm himself and could see Afton was trying just as hard to do the same. But something so strong as the emotions churning within them wasn't going to go away just because they wished it. He waited for Shayla to come and was angered by her interruption.

"There you two are! I've been calling." Shayla stopped and stared at them both. "I won't even ask what you have been doing, but the next time, go deeper into the woods. Anyone might have interrupted you."

Afton rolled her eyes. "Nothing happened, Shayla. It's just that Blain's senses are adjusting."

Shayla arched an eyebrow. "Adjusting? That's not what we called it in my day."

"Get Afton out of here, Shayla. Now. Before I forget she's a virgin and you're standing here," Blain growled as he kept his gaze on Afton. His hands clenched into fists as he stood, desire suddenly rekindling in his veins. His control was rapidly fleeing. "Go, Afton. Now!"

"Afton, come to me quickly," Shayla said in alarm. "Something's wrong."

"What do you mean?" she asked.

"He's losing control of himself. If you don't leave now, he'll take you by force. Go, girl!"

"He won't have to take me by force. I'm his anytime he wants me," Afton declared. She looked back over her shoulder toward Blain and saw how desperate he was to gain control. He'd broken into a sweat, his hands were clenched, and his eyes seemed to glow with an inner, savage light. Shayla was motioning for her to go.

Considering their privacy was gone, Afton decided the best thing to do was leave. "Later," she told Blain, giving him a promising look before walking away.

After she'd gone, Blain fell to his knees and panted as if he'd run a marathon. He raised his hands to his face and pushed his hair back. What had happened? He still craved Afton, but his senses had calmed considerably after she left the area. It scared the hell out of him that even though she wanted him, he'd have taken her no matter what. If she had changed her mind during the interlude, it wouldn't have mattered. He'd still have taken her.

"Shayla, what happened to me? I've never wanted another soul in my life the way I wanted Afton. I think I'd have even hurt her if she had denied me. What's happening?"

"In ancient times, it's said that fairies suffered a kind of bloodlust. It was an urge that came over them when a particularly arousing man or woman became available, and it was an instinct that ensured the survival of the race. When this happened, it didn't matter where the man or woman was. The fairy involved simply took what she or he wanted."

"Do you mean this will happen again, and that I won't be able to control the urge? That I'll be like some kind of rutting animal?" Blain gasped in horror.

She shook her head and thought for a moment. "I'm not sure. There's probably something about this ground and Afton's presence that triggered your most primitive emotions. This kind of behavior has long since vanished in the fairy race. They don't need it, you see. Though times are unsafe, there isn't such an immediate and urgent need to preserve the species as in past centuries. Fairies aren't forced to make love and breed on the run. Though I'm told their blood still runs hot, the bloodlust doesn't come upon them anymore. At least, not until now."

"I still want her. What do I do?"

"We'll talk to Lore about this. Take heart, Blain. This never happened until you entered these woods?"

"No. It didn't happen until we got to this clearing, though I won't deny that I've been attracted to Afton since I first saw her."

"Then there's something about this particular area that's causing this physical demand. It could be a particular blend of smells or herbs."

"Wait! Afton was wearing something. I don't know what all of the herbs were, but I could smell sage in her hair. I got close to her, smelled the herbs and everything went out of control."

"That's probably it, then. I'll talk to her about what she was wearing. Whatever it was, she didn't blend it on purpose, Blain. We don't have any known potions or a particular herb that could cause someone to lose control that way. Certainly none Afton would know about, anyway."

"Why do I still want her so badly if that's all it was?"

"If it was a blend of herbs that caused this, they only amplified what you were already feeling, my lad. I suspect that you'll be back to normal in a few hours. Afton just hit upon the exact combination of scents to trigger a very basic need, and this also may have something to do with your mixed blood."

"What do I do in the meantime?"

"First, I suggest you stay away from Afton for a while. Second, find a very cold stream. I'll get Lore." Shayla grinned then walked away.

* * * * *

"The only way to get this out of your system is to work up a good sweat. I've wanted to talk to you about choosing a weapon. Perhaps this would be the best time. You can control this, uh, problem of yours on the training green." Lore mischievously grinned as he led Blain through the woods, toward a large clearing.

Blain was sorry he'd explained his intense need for Afton to Lore. The man would probably think he was some kind of pervert—worse, he might tell everyone else. He'd just have to trust the fairy leader to know what was best. It wasn't as if this new life came with an owner's manual. But the subject of weapons had him intrigued. It reminded him of the vision Afton had shown him. People had been practicing with all kinds of medieval paraphernalia. "What do you mean when you say I need to choose a weapon? What do weapons have to do with me almost attacking Afton?"

"I told you, the only way to rid yourself of the bloodlust is hard physical action. You have to really sweat it out. Only then will your blood cool. As for the weapons, we choose the means by which we defend our families and homes. Most fairies do this when they come of age. Since you were denied that privilege, you'll have your choice now. You're warrior class. That means choice of the best blades, bows, knives and everything else in our armory is yours."

Blain didn't know exactly what all that meant, but it sounded important. When they entered the clearing his eyes widened in shock. If he'd been under the influence of some drug, he couldn't have been more surprised. Fairies of all shapes and sizes walked about. Their wings were unfurled and shimmered in the afternoon light. The sun made the skins of some look as if they'd been dusted in silver or gold glitter.

Though his heart beat wildly in anticipation, he felt no fear. Some of them looked up as he passed by, and he noted their whispered comments. Some openly stared.

He couldn't see any two creatures who were exactly alike, yet they all appeared to sense a difference in him. Maybe that was because he was new. Whatever was happening, he was definitely not in Kansas anymore. Here were real fairies, just like himself and Lore.

When he turned back to his companion, Lore had changed into his true form. The man's hair was pure white and hung down his back to his waist. His eyes glittered a forest green and matched the lighter shade of his skin. As with the others, his ears were now pointed and matched the defined slant of his eyes. The man's wings were large and a kind of blue-green. But they seemed to change shades just a bit as the light hit them differently.

"Welcome home, brother." Lore grinned and clasped Blain's upper arm in greeting. "You're welcome here among us."

"Thank you, Lore. I was afraid I wouldn't be," Blain responded earnestly. "What do I do now?"

"You meet some of the others. There are fairies here from all over the world. Over there are members of the Italian fairy faction," he said as he motioned toward some decidedly Renaissance-looking creatures. "Then there are the Nordic fairies, the Baltic factions and some of your own Highland race. The smaller members of the fairy clan are pixies, sprites and others you'll learn about. Our one common link is that we all have—or had—wings at one time. Many of us can shapeshift, others can't. You may have been told that we can fly. This is true, but only for a very short distance, and it's more like gliding really. Ask any questions you want of anyone. Don't be afraid. No one here harbors ill will toward you for any reason. Your separation from us was old Freyja's fault, not yours, and may she be damned for it wherever she burns."

Blain watched Lore walk away to speak to the others and knew he had a true friend in the fairy leader. What a world of wonders this was. If anyone had told him he'd be in the middle of it, he'd have laughed his ass off at the very idea. Yet here he was. And it was all as real as the sunlight on his green skin, the air in his lungs and the dark blue wings on his back.

He stopped his cursory inspection of the beings when he saw a table at the far end of the clearing. On it, objects of metal and wood lay in carefully arranged groups. He was about to walk toward them when a soft hand grasped his bicep. He turned and was confronted by one of the most enchanting sites he could ever hope to see.

The woman before him was young and light blue-green in color, and had long hair that matched her skin. Her eyes shone like two sapphires from a heart-shaped face. She smiled at him as he openly stared.

"I see thou hast not seen the like of me, Blain McTavish. My sisters, cousins, and I will help thee become accustomed to thy new life in any way we can. We are of an old English faction of the fey race. My name is Morynn."

"Thank you, Morynn. I'll probably need a great deal of help." Blain admitted.

"Come, Blain. You've a weapon to choose and training to begin," Lore said as he approached and led Blain toward the far end of the green. When they were halfway across the clearing, Lore glanced back toward Morynn. "Be careful of her kind. They're lovely to look at, but they thrive on stealing a man's senses away and leaving him a babbling idiot when they're through. It took me three days to get over lying with one once."

"Don't worry. I have no intention of letting anything or anyone with that much seducing magic near me. I could almost feel it closing around me like cement. Besides, there's someone else I want to be with."

"Aye, that would be fair Afton, would it not?"

"It would," Blain heartily responded.

"She's a fine lass. And it's good you can sense different kinds of enchantment about you. The seducing enchantment you're speaking of has led many a good man to his ruin. Morynn and her kin should find themselves some randy Satyrs. Those are the only beings who can satisfy her breed."

Blain started to ask more about Morynn and the Satyrs, but the sun's glare off metal distracted him. They stood in front of a long table. He eyed what looked like museum quality medieval weapons. There were broadswords, axes, staffs, bows of different lengths, maces and assorted other deadly items he couldn't name.

"These things are archaic. Why not just use guns like the rest of the world?" Blain blurted and immediately felt guilty for his tactlessness. "I'm sorry, Lore, I didn't mean to say it like that. It's just that it must be hard to defend yourself against some thug with a gun."

"It's all right, my friend. What you say is quite true. But unlike the weapons of the outside world, ours are made to be totally untraceable. Some can even be carried without authorities questioning their presence." Lore pointed toward the staffs. "These, for instance, don't look like anything but sticks to help people walk over rugged moors. Many other weapons, like wooden crossbows, can be packed in luggage. They don't set off metal detectors at airports, and can always be carried if the right paperwork is filled out. Best of all, virtually every weapon you see here is silent." Lore lifted a bow and arrow. His deft fingers put the arrow to the string and sent it flying soundlessly down the green. It landed in the direct center of a knothole some seventy yards away.

"Holy…" Blain muttered.

"When I have to travel with some of the metal weaponry, the authorities are fooled by false documentation telling them I'm a collector of rare antiquities. In this age of fully automatic weapons, none of the outsiders appreciates just how deadly these things are."

"And you really find a need to defend yourself with these weapons?" Blain asked, vividly recalling the incident with Hannah Biddles.

"The rare occasion arises now and again. Of course, all evidence of our having been involved is completely destroyed, and we only defend when we're cornered. Fairies can't call the elements and use them the way the Druids can. We have limited use of our dust or glamour. That is only used in the rarest of occasions to give us time to flee. It can temporarily blind a foe. So we rely on these," he explained as he waved his hand toward the collected weapons. "Of course, when the Sorceress chooses someone to check out your Druid powers, you may find you have some or all of the elements at your command."

Blain sighed, glanced at the tree Lore had targeted and turned back to the table. He considered the weapons. "I'm supposed to learn to use all of these?"

"Aye, but you must choose your main weapon. Mine is the bow."

"Go figure," Blain quipped, then tried to make his decision. "How do I go about choosing?"

"Look them over. See what appeals to you." Lore backed away from the table and let Blain look over the weapons at his own pace. Others gathered to watch. Blain was aware of their presence. He sensed this was some kind of momentous affair. This business of choosing weapons was probably some kind of traditional ceremony he had to endure. He took a deep breath and began to inspect each object.

He handled all kinds of dirks, swords and other cutlery. None of them did anything for him, so he kept looking. He was almost at the end of the table when a massive, double-bladed battle axe caught his attention. His fingers swept over the long wooden handle, or haft, and he felt a surge of energy. Used to handling axes on the farm, he appreciated the fine workmanship. In fact, he valued the use of an axe over a chain saw any day. Though the axe took more time, it also yielded strength and endurance. Vainly, he enjoyed what it did for his body when he could see the muscle formed in his arms and back.

Without hesitating, he grabbed the axe haft with both hands and slowly lifted the opposite end. As he did so, the double blades rang out. The sound wasn't unlike two pieces of metal striking one another. Blain was aware of the crowds' awed response, but the axe claimed the better part of his attention. The two blades were engraved with Celtic design. The scrollwork etched across the metal like twining serpents. Despite the fact that it was a particularly gruesome item that could dismember a very large man or animal, it was still a riveting work of craftsmanship.

Magnificently carved Celtic animals and knot work circled the haft. All five feet of it were superb. Carefully running his index finger along one of the blades, he knew just how deadly the axe really was. Swung in a circular motion, it could maim or kill many men in close combat.

"You've chosen," Lore stated. "I should say the weapon chose you. It sang out. I've never seen such a thing happen. If anyone else had come forward and picked up that particular weapon, I would have said he was a bit too ambitious. It's an awesome thing to carry and must be wielded with precision. But the choice has been made. The axe is yours. Take care with it, Blain. It may guard your life or the lives of those you love one day."

Applause started from the back of the crowd and worked its way forward. Blain lifted the axe up and felt primitive power flow through his arms and chest. It was as though the weapon really had chosen him. Lore's remark about guarding the lives of others hung in Blain's mind like a threat. There was something he should be remembering. Something of great importance. But he couldn't force the thought to come from the back of his brain where he could make sense of it. He had a feeling whatever he was forgetting would haunt him. He kept the axe very close.

Chapter Ten

&

Until late in the evening, Blain practiced wielding the heavy weapon. He guessed the thing weighed nearly twenty pounds. Swinging it several times was no chore. As the afternoon wore on, however, the weight became grueling. Perhaps he'd chosen the axe because it was the only weapon available that was familiar. No matter how tortuous the swinging became, he did as Lore and the others instructed and practiced the motions over and over. He thought his chest would explode from the exertion, but he wasn't about to let anyone see how tired he was. And all the while, that nagging dark forecast of doom kept persisting.

The hard work hadn't driven it off as he'd hoped. Something was very wrong, and he should be able to put his finger on it but couldn't. But apparently no one but him felt the coming blackness. What could he say to them that wouldn't make him sound insane? For the thousandth time, he stuffed the fear down and refused to give in to it.

"Enough, Blain," Lore called out from the other side of the clearing. "You won't be able to lift a fork tonight if you don't stop."

Blain lowered the axe and wiped the sweat from his face with the back of one forearm. "I was hoping you'd think I could go on forever, even if I couldn't."

Lore laughed and slapped him on the back. "You've no one to prove anything to. It's doubtful anyone will challenge you for Afton the way you were swinging that blade."

"What do you mean? Who would challenge me for Afton?" Blain lowered the blades of the axe to the ground and leaned against the thick handle.

"Our customs are ancient. We claim our chosen mates during special times of the year in a ceremony referred to as handfasting. It's the same as marriage among humans, only we tend to stay with our chosen ones for life. Before the ceremony, if someone vigorously objects to the handfasting of a particular couple, that person may make a challenge to stop it."

"What happens then?" Blain asked, suddenly feeling a bit threatened. He didn't want to fight someone for Afton. She wasn't a piece of meat to be argued over, and anyway he'd seen the size of the other men. He'd surely have to hurt someone if they fought.

"If it's a man challenging, he fights the handfasting male. If it's a woman, she fights the handfasting woman. It seldom happens, but when it does, sparks fly and tempers flare. In the distant past, men and women fought to the death over the right to handfast a particular woman or man. That's how the strongest survived."

"Are you trying to tell me that if a handfasting man is defeated by the challenging man, that challenger can claim the woman as his?"

"That's the way of it. That's why some couples won't announce they're handfasting. They simply come forward during some celebration like Beltane or Samhain. They have Shayla handfast them as soon as possible, then they go into the woods and stay a few nights to consummate their vows."

"Well, no one is taking Afton from me, no matter what kind of weapon they use or what challenge they make!" Blain growled. If it was a fight someone wanted and the outcome was who would get Afton, then some man was going to limp off crying, even if the custom was sordid and ridiculous.

"So you *do* love her." Lore smiled.

"Of course I do." Blain stopped as the realization hit him hard. He was in love with Afton. It was obvious to Lore. How could he not have known it? Somewhere in the middle of all the magic, sorcery, and mysticism, he'd fallen in love. She'd been his friend, confidante and instructor. No one in his life had ever made him feel so complete, so at ease. She was the one he wanted to hold in the night and wake up with in the morning. Her sweetness and warmth had been a balm when he thought he was losing his sanity. She'd always been there for him, never asking anything except his understanding. Her heart was loving and tender.

He smirked. When he'd lost control and almost attacked her, she had wanted more than just friendship then. She'd wanted him as badly as he'd wanted her. If there was anything to this challenging business, he'd have to keep her very close until Lughnasadh — August Eve. If memory served him correctly, that was the next Celtic celebration, and it was still a few weeks away. Until then, he'd find a way to meet with her and win her love. It would be the sweetest task he would ever undertake. He would handfast with her, and to hell with anyone who tried to stop him.

"You're grinning like a dragon eating a fresh knight sandwich. What ails you?" Lore asked, breaking the silence.

"Nothing. But the reference to a dragon sandwich is making me hungry. Let's find some food."

* * * * *

"Remember, Pluck," Afton warned her elfin friend as they walked toward the main clearing, "please don't do anything to humiliate me tonight." His short legs moved efficiently enough to keep up with her longer stride, and he was typically dressed like an elf with his brown suit and pointed cap. The bearded Pluck was about her own age, but he often acted a great deal younger, as those of his kind did. The little man was up to juvenile antics constantly, and she worried about what he might do tonight in front of Blain.

"What could I possibly do to humiliate you? Are you saying that being seen with me is somehow beneath your dignity?" the little man asked, his anger rising.

"Of course not. It's just that you always say something about me that's…well…embarrassing," Afton explained.

"Like what?"

"Like the time you told the story about how I lost my knickers in the river while bathing, and I had to run home holding ferns to cover myself."

"You were only a little girl when that happened. Everyone thought that story was sweet."

"Well tonight is special. Promise me you won't tell any of the stories about the times I've screwed up. Promise!" Afton stopped then turned to face Pluck.

"What's so special about tonight?" He paused and tilted his head while gazing at her. "Afton O'Malley, you have your cap set for this Blain fellow, haven't you?"

Afton ducked her head. Pluck had known her all her life. They'd been infants playing in the woods together. Why she should feel so uncomfortable about the elf knowing she wanted Blain was a mystery. Perhaps she was afraid Pluck would say something that would make Blain think less of her. All she knew was that she didn't want Blain to hear about anything demeaning in her past. Today, she'd been in the woods practicing her elemental powers and had accomplished some unusually potent feats. Perhaps knowing she loved and wanted Blain was all the motivation she needed to concentrate properly. The past wasn't something she could change, and she was certain her powers were growing. The future was what mattered. Blain gave her the will to practice her powers and concentrate harder than she'd ever done in her life.

"Afton, I'm sorry if the stories I told about you hurt your feelings." Pluck paused then continued, "You know that no one would play with me when we were young because I was always the smallest elf and was sometimes picked on because of it. You couldn't control the elements the way you were supposed to, but you were always there for me. We were misfits." He shrugged. "You're the last person in the world I'd ever want to hurt. I always saw you laugh when I told those silly stories, so I thought you didn't mind. You do know I was only joking, don't you?"

Afton heard the contrition in her friend's voice and smiled. "I do know, Pluck. I guess I smiled at those stories you told so no one would learn their laughing hurt me. And I know you didn't mean to cause me pain. It's just that Blain is…he's…"

"I know. He's special to you. Don't worry, Afton. I won't say anything to embarrass you. I promise."

"Thank you."

Afton began to walk toward the large clearing again. Pluck half-jogged along with her as his shorter legs sought to keep pace with her stride. Afton slowed down by degrees so Pluck wouldn't notice and accuse her of patronizing her. The top of his head only came to her waist, so it was difficult changing pace without his noticing.

Earlier, she'd washed away her special botanicsl essence and bathed in sparkling spring water. Afton didn't want Blain lured to her through the use of some "herbal concoction", as Shayla had put it.

As they neared the clearing, reveling voices could be heard. Blain would be among them. Afton had heard he'd chosen the battle axe as his primary weapon. Only the strongest warriors chose such a blade, but she knew Blain could handle it. He had muscle to spare, and it was a source of joy that he had wanted that particular weapon.

"Look," Pluck cried as he ran forward, "Hugh has returned from the States. He's come back sooner than planned."

Afton followed Pluck to the older Druid and hugged him. Hugh smiled, looking in high spirits. She could tell he was glad to be home, and she knew his happiness had as much to do with being close to Shayla as having Blain present.

"Have you heard how incredibly well Blain has been accepted?" Afton asked as she looped her arm through Hugh's.

"Aye, I've heard and am as proud as if he were my own son. I've been told he wields a battle axe. He's a good lad, and he'll make a strong warrior."

"Then you haven't seen him yet?"

"No. In this crowd, I'll have to wait my turn. It seems everyone is standing in line to meet my nephew. Arthur and Syndra would have been so proud of him."

"Hugh!"

The older Druid turned to see the subject of his conversation standing behind him. In an instant, Hugh moved forward and unashamedly hugged his nephew.

Afton could see tears of pure pride in the older man's eyes. And it was no wonder. Blain was in fairy form and looking magnificent. His inspiring wings glowed like jewels and fanned out behind him for the whole Order to see and admire.

"I'm glad you're here. Did your trip from the States go well? Is everything okay at the farm?" Blain quizzed.

"Aye, lad. Shayla sent more than enough manpower to take care of everything. All's well. And things here are going splendidly from what I've heard. I told you everything would be all right, didn't I?"

"You tried to. I just wasn't ready to listen."

"Uh-um!" Pluck cleared his throat, obviously wanting an introduction.

Afton stepped forward. "Blain, this is Pluck. He's my best friend."

Blain took a moment to shake hands and exchange a few words of greeting with the elf. Pluck's smile, Irish accent and leprechaun-like appearance were winning, and he liked the small man immediately. But Blain's attention was soon riveted on Afton. She was lovely in a light green Druid gown. All the leprechauns, elves, fairies and their combined magic couldn't pull his gaze away from her.

"How was your day, Afton?" he murmured, moving closer to her.

"Fine, thank you. And yours seemed quite eventful, from all the rumors. Quite a wonderful impression you've made."

Blain gazed into Afton's blue eyes and wanted to run to the woods with her. Later, he would. Though the hot desire should have abated, he still wanted her with every fiber in his body.

"Come, lad. The feasting is about to begin, but the guest of honor hasn't arrived. I think Lore wants you at the head table," Hugh told him as he saw Lore wave from across the clearing.

Afton watched Blain take his place beside Shayla. She wanted to get closer, but the seats nearest him were all taken. The crowd was growing fast. She chose a place near her brothers and parents, and Shayla formally introduced Blain to everyone as a matter of protocol. By now, everyone in the Order either knew him or knew of him. The feasting and revelry began and went on for a time, but Blain never looked in her direction.

Some of the fairy folk began to sing and dance in the center of the clearing, and Afton noticed Bonny and Morynn vying for Blain's attention. When Shayla vacated her seat to dance with Hugh, the two women practically fought to see who would have it.

Afton's heart began to sink. She wasn't as beautiful or as worldly as those two women. Rumor had it Bonny had spurned several advances from young warrior men who might have offered to handfast with her. But it was said she had enough men after her as to afford her a considerable choice. Afton watched in distaste as Morynn leaned forward, displaying the cleavage of her breasts while pouring Blain some wine. Rather than watch the spectacle, she decided to leave, but someone tapped her on the shoulder.

"Afton, the main fire is getting low. Be a love and give it a little jump start, will you?" Shayla asked.

Afton looked at the fire at the far end of the clearing and saw it had indeed burned to embers. A few months ago, she would have bolted and hidden in the woods at such a request. It would have been a public humiliation for herself and her family to attempt such a feat and fail. But tonight was different. She welcomed the chance to vindicate herself in front of the Order, and she knew she could claim her place as warrior class.

She smiled at Shayla and, to her family's surprise, got up to do as she was asked instead of balking. She walked to the end of the clearing and stood before the circular fire. It was almost twenty feet across and would need to burn the rest of the night. To let it go out during any celebration was considered disrespectful to the Order and a slight against those who were being honored. It was customary that the fire only be allowed to die at dawn. At one time in history, it guarded the clearing against invaders. Now it burned for Blain's celebration. She decided to rekindle it for him. She closed her eyes and held out her hands.

"She isn't going to actually try to light the main fire is she? Not Afton O'Malley?" someone called out then laughed. Afton's anger grew. She was tired of being the butt of jokes. Everyone thought she didn't possess that kind of power, but she'd practiced very hard all day and wasn't going to fail. Not this time or ever again. She concentrated on the words of enchantment.

"Arise fire and light the way. Guard this place and all who stay. Before your glow our foes will flee, to those belonging, Blessed Be."

Blain watched as Afton stood by the fire and chanted. He wasn't close enough to hear the words she spoke, but he could certainly hear the comments coming from some of the crowd.

Bonny leaned over his shoulder. "Poor Afton. She's about to make a fool o' herself. I feel sorry for her. She can't even light a match, much less a fire the size o' that one." She clucked her tongue. "'Tis a nice man she needs. But she's tryin' to impress you, Blain, and you're warrior class. Afton should be takin' up with someone like herself. Too bad she didn't inherit her family's powers, the poor wee thing."

From several tables away, a man slammed a tankard down upon a table and shouted for others to keep quiet. When Blain turned his head to see who was causing the commotion, it was Gawain. He was trying to quiet the crowd so Afton could concentrate. Apparently, many of the people around her brother shared Bonny's opinion of Afton's abilities and felt she shouldn't try something as ambitious as relighting the huge fire.

Blain shrugged Bonny's hand off his shoulder and stood. Intending to show Afton support, he tried to make his way toward the table where Gawain and his family sat. Suddenly, the entire sky lit up. The fire before Afton not only burned, its flames shot more than thirty feet into the air and glowed iridescent blue before falling back to a more controlled height and turning bright orange. The entire time, Afton stood before the fire, summoning it to do her bidding. Controlling it as if it were a living entity. When the flames were where she wanted them, she lowered her hands and turned to face the crowd. Every single man, woman and child present, including Afton's family, had gone completely silent. Blain looked around and saw people back away, staring at her. What had she done? If this was an example of not having powers, Blain didn't want to know what someone like Shayla or Hugh could do with the flames.

"I knew she had it in her," Shayla murmured, suddenly appearing beside him.

Blain turned to look at the Sorceress. "What's happening?"

She shrugged. "Afton is just coming into her powers a little late. But then, so did I."

Blain glanced around. People began to whisper. Many smiled and began to applaud. Afton stood demurely in front of the fire. Before anyone had a chance to speak with her, she lowered her head and walked into the woods.

"Music. We need music to dance by, and good wine to drink," Shayla commanded.

Slowly, the revelry began again. Blain glanced at Afton's family. Her mother was sitting at a nearby table with her head in her hands. It appeared she was smiling and crying all at once. Her husband was grinning like an Amazonian python. Her brothers laughed and toasted while men approached the entire family. Blain guessed that they might be suitors. In the very short time he'd been in their midst, power seemed to mean a great deal to these people, and Afton had just proved she had it.

Glancing around, he saw Morynn and Bonny pointing at the fire, apparently discussing what they'd witnessed.

"Now shut up, the lot of you! Don't ever say anything insulting about my sister again, or you'll answer to me," Gawain shouted. "And bring me some damned ale!"

"Shayla, where did Afton go?" Blain asked, when he found the Sorceress in the crowd.

"She might need to rest. It took a lot of energy to do what she did. There aren't ten in the entire Order who could have done it. She's finally a warrior." She beamed at the pronouncement.

"I'm going to find her," Blain declared. Without waiting for Shayla's response, he turned and walked toward the woods.

Afton walked as far as she could then sank into the grass. In her anger, she'd pulled out all the stops and had started a fire that would have the entire Order talking for months. She hadn't meant to show off, just put some wagging tongues to rest. In doing so, she'd surprised even herself. What more was she capable of? There would be hours more of practice ahead of her so she could gain control over the other elements. No one, especially her family, would ever have to worry about her after this. She could choose any man she wanted. That had her grinning like a fool as she attempted to close her mind to everything around her except the clean smell of the forest.

When Blain saw Afton his heart almost stopped. Her small figure was so still. He ran forward and knelt beside her, placing his hand on her cheek. "Afton, are you all right?"

Afton heard Blain calling to her, but her mind was so tired. It took everything she had to pull herself back to consciousness. "Blain...where did...you come from?" she managed to mumble.

"Honey, are you okay? Can you sit up?"

"I think so. Just give me a moment."

When she tried and failed, Blain took her in his arms and held her to him. "Lie still. Don't try to move if you're too tired. Just rest." He stroked her hair as he spoke. Where were her parents and her brothers? If they knew such an effort physically cost her so much, why weren't they with her? "Don't worry, Afton. I'll get help if you need it."

"No. That isn't necessary. I just need to sleep for a few minutes, that's all." She snuggled against his chest.

"I'll hold you, then. You shouldn't be alone after exerting yourself so much." He thought of what could have happened to her if she'd tried such a thing in New England. He began to understand why these people were so secretive and wary. "You're vulnerable right now."

"Not anymore," she whispered. "You're here. I'll be safe."

Blain's heart warmed at the trust she showed him. He held her for about an hour and gently stroked her hair. During that time, Afton didn't move. Her breathing seemed normal and her pulse was strong. He couldn't sense anyone in the vicinity, but his anger grew with each passing moment. Where the hell was her family? If she agreed to handfast with him, he'd never let her be alone after using so much of her strength. He'd guard her with his life until she recovered. For a family who was supposed to be so close, this didn't make any damned sense.

He let his wings enfold them both, shutting out the world and the distant sound of merrymaking. Finally, she stirred.

"How long did I sleep?"

"Quite a while. Are you feeling all right now?"

"Yes," she sat up but kept her arms wrapped around his neck.

He stood, lifting her into his arms. "Tell me how to get to your cottage. I'm taking you home since no one else seems to give a damn about checking on you."

"Why are you angry?" She tilted her head and gazed at him in confusion.

"Afton, you were lying in the middle of the woods in the dark. You used almost all of your energy to start that damned fire, and not a single soul has come looking for you. Not one of your family has shown any interest in finding you. They must have known this was going to happen. Shayla did."

"Blain, if they saw you come after me, they probably thought we wanted to be alone."

Blain stopped walking and gazed into her eyes. The starlight reflected in their blue depths, calling to him. He hadn't thought of that. All he'd been able to think about was making sure she wasn't hurt or ill.

"Do we?" he murmured.

"What?"

"Want to be alone? I seem to recall you saying something earlier today about seeing me later. That was right after I almost threw you to the ground."

She smiled at the memory. "I'd like to be alone with you. Very much." She leaned her head against his shoulder.

He slowly lowered her to the ground but held her close. "I've missed you all day. So many things have happened to me, but it looks as though you were putting your time to good use, too. Shayla says you've finally got your powers."

"I was never able to call upon so much power before I met you," she said. "I think you must inspire me."

He cupped her cheek in his palm. "Maybe I can give you other inspiration." He lowered his mouth to hers then brushed his lips across her soft cheek. His hands caressed her back through the thick fabric of her robe, and he heard her moan so softly he thought he might have imagined the sound. "Afton," he breathed, "I want you, but it might be a good idea if I took you home. You used too much of your energy starting that damned fire. I don't want to hurt you."

"You would never hurt me, Blain. Sleep and contact with the earth renewed my strength. Please—I want you, too. No one will interrupt us here. We've all the time in the world." When she saw his green eyes glowing for her and the indecision within them, she placed her hands behind his neck and pulled him down to her level. "Don't make me beg, Blain. I want you."

His mouth came down on hers with crushing force. He could taste her innocence as if it were sweet, spring wine. Going slowly would be hard, but he had to hold back. She was as new to making love as he was to this magical Order he'd entered. And in fairy form, he was more powerful than ever. He pulled away from her far enough to help her stand, lifted her robe over her head and let it fall to the ground. She was naked, and moonlight illuminated her beautiful body making his heart pound and blood rush to his groin.

He took her hands in his, placed them over his hardening member and saw her smile bewitchingly. When her slender fingers unlaced his pants and touched the solid flesh beneath, he thought he'd go insane. He dropped his head back and savored how her hands moved over him. Exploring, learning. She knelt before him pulling down his leather boots and then his pants. He stepped out of the clothing. His calves tingled at her touch. Her soft palms lingered there, massaging. She leaned her cheek against his lower thigh.

"Blain...Blain," Afton whispered over and over until he pulled her into his arms and molded their bodies together with his strong hands. The kiss he bestowed on her made her weak and replenished all at once. The world spun out of control. All she knew was her love for this man. There was no earth, no sky, and no boundaries for them.

Go slow, he reminded himself. She's a virgin. He wanted to make her first time very special. In a way, it was his first time, too. He felt he had the strength of several men and the endurance to go with it.

Her hands moved to one of the most sensitive places on a fairy's body—the base of his wings. She traced a small pattern with her fingertips, and he felt his control flee. He lowered her to the sweet-smelling grass and covered her body with his. He devoured her with his mouth, teasing at each nipple until she cried out and writhed beneath him, and he could no longer stand the sweet torture. Still, he had to make sure she was ready for him. He ran his palms down her thighs then between them, stroking the sensitive flesh there. Afton cried out again, and he knew she was finally ready. She cradled him between her soft, smooth legs and gently, ever so slowly, he pushed forward.

Afton knew a moment of tearing pain, which quickly diminished. Blain crooned sweet words of encouragement until she nodded. Then, he began to gently thrust. Just small strokes at first, then more deeply. Her breath left her. His green gaze seared into her heart, warming her body. Then an incredible pressure began to build, and she wanted more. She clawed at his shoulders to bring him closer.

Afton's soft cries and the instinctive rocking motion of her body told Blain she was quickly reaching climax. When her womb began to contract, he lost himself with her, and the world fell away. She lay in his arms, trembling from the beauty of it.

He held her against his chest and rocked her in a slow, easy motion. When he felt moisture against his skin, he lifted her chin and kissed away her tears.

"Did it hurt that much?"

"It didn't hurt but a moment. It was wonderful, Blain. It was…I have no words."

She hid her head against his chest and wept again, but Blain knew this was her way of dealing with the emotions besieging her. Nothing in the world—not man nor beast nor magic—would ever take her away from him. She was his sweetest desire and hope for the future. He was determined to make a life with her somewhere, somehow. No challenger would ever part them.

"Blain?" she called his name in a soft voice.

"Yes, sweetheart?"

"I eavesdropped and heard what you told Rhiannon the night you sent her away. You said I could never be more than a friend to you." She paused and waited for his response.

"Honey, how could you remotely think such a thing after what just happened?" He held her tightly. "Sweetheart, I was lying to myself and Rhi. Rhiannon and I never cared for each other the way I care for you. She's just one of those people who like having things their way, and I went along with it because I felt so alone." He realized that with crystal clarity now. "I'd already begun to fall in love with you, but I didn't want Rhi confronting you. She can be vindictive. I was also afraid that if the Order didn't accept me, I'd lose you. I didn't want to get close knowing I might never see you again. And while I do need your friendship, little Druid, you're far more than any friend to me. I love you, Afton."

"You love me? Really? And you've accepted the Order without any reservations?" She looked up into his eyes and smiled.

"Afton, I accept it all. And I love you so much it hurts to be separated for even a short time. I want to handfast with you.

That's why I wanted to make love with you tonight. I don't want anyone challenging me for you. But can you love a man not born into your world? Someone who'll spend the rest of his life learning what he is?"

"I do love you, Blain. I do. And I don't care where you're from, or what you have to learn along the way." She sighed and kissed his chest and neck.

"You're so damned sweet. I could lie here with you forever and let the world just rotate away." He pulled her into his arms and rolled them onto their sides. She cuddled close, and he felt pure joy and wonder in this, the most precious moment of his life. Like someone lighting a candle in the night, Afton's warmth reached out and led him to a safe place. He could sense the strands of it weaving a protective cocoon around his lonely soul, and he had been lonely for so long. But all that had been missing in his life fell into divine place. She would be in his arms forever, and he in hers. He was finding a place in this amazing world and wanted to know everything about it he could. Afton was the perfect person to help him. Her patience and tenderness brought as much peace as her lovely body brought passion. He ran his fingers down her side to her slender waist and pulled her even closer. Life with her would be an adventure.

Afton ran her hands over every inch of Blain. He was hers. He loved her. Because of him, her powers had finally emerged. And they would make a future. She sighed and kissed his broad chest again.

He placed a finger beneath her chin and lifted her face. "You're so beautiful. So soft."

Soon the kiss heated, and their passion renewed. This time Blain took her more powerfully. The sensual motions she made with her hips soon had him breathless and crying out in ecstasy. She wove such an exotic and exciting spell, that he'd never doubt a moment of his life with her.

Afterward, they lay facing each other, learning how to please and be pleased. Touching and telling each other those sensual places only lovers know.

"I shouldn't have taken you again, love. You're exhausted," he spoke softly as he held her to him. His hand lifted her long hair and let it sift through his fingers back to her shoulder.

"I'm not made out of china. Just because I'm new at this doesn't mean I can't keep up with you, my man. I want to stay with you all night. And I even wish we could find Shayla and handfast now," Afton murmured.

Blain smiled when he heard her throaty admonition. "I was told we have to wait until the next major celebration. That's a few weeks away, isn't it?"

"Yes. But it's so long to wait."

"Don't worry, sweetheart. I'll meet you every night if you want. Right here. As far as I'm concerned, we already belong to each other. The vows have already been spoken."

"Oh, Blain, I love you so much," she turned her head into his shoulder and wrapped her arms around him. Then she smiled. For tonight, she was one of those women who had so annoyed her in the past. She'd vowed never to cry over a man, yet here she was, lying in Blain's arms and about to sob all over him. She tried to stem the flow of tears and couldn't.

"Hush, sweetheart. It's all right," he comforted as his arms encircled her. "I think I'd better get you home. It's almost dawn, and you need to sleep."

"Do we have to?" She looked up at him and grinned through her tears.

He smiled back. "I'm afraid so. Your family will be missing you, and I don't want those brothers of yours beating me to a pulp because I kept their beautiful sister in the woods all night."

"They wouldn't dare. They'd answer to me."

"After that display you put on with the fire, they might have seconds thoughts about it at that. I'll have to get you to show me how to call the elements. I don't know if my powers extend into the Druid realm."

"We'll find out together," she promised.

"Together." He grinned and rubbed noses with her. "I like the sound of that."

Blain changed back into human form, but dressing took awhile as they kissed and caressed each other during the process. Finally, he placed his arm around her shoulders and they walked to Afton's cottage. Dawn hadn't yet arrived, but it was fast approaching.

When they reached her home, he pulled her into his embrace, intending to kiss her once more before leaving. They were nearly as close as two beings could be when the door to the cottage swung open and Gawain stalked out.

Before Blain could say a word or even move, Gawain strode forward, pulled Afton away and threw a roundhouse blow that hit Blain squarely on the jaw. It sent him flying a good ten feet back. Blain landed on the ground, shook his head to clear it and was up in an instant.

"Gawain!" Afton cried out. "What in bloody hell are you doing?"

"Stand back, honey. I think this was bound to happen sooner or later," Blain told her as he swiped a line of blood from his lip.

"Stay away from my sister," Gawain growled. "I won't warn you again."

"No, you won't," Blain countered. He walked forward and punched the man back.

The fight was on, and all Afton could do was watch. It was like seeing two bulls charging each other. The sound of the fighting soon had the entire household awake. Afton watched her remaining brothers and parents file into the front yard.

"Father, do something," Afton pleaded as she raced to him. "They'll kill each other."

"It's best to let them have this out, lass," he shouted over the melee. "Gawain's been spoiling for a fight ever since he saw this man near you."

Afton turned to her other brothers. "Taurus, stop them. Drew? Sean?" When there was no response other than mischievous grins, Afton turned to her youngest two siblings. "Ian, Bolt—do something!"

Bolt looked at the two fighting men and back at Afton. He shrugged and would have moved forward, but Drew and Taurus stopped him. Afton was about to put her powers to the test again and stop the fighting herself. But her mother appeared and latched on to her arm.

"Come inside, darling. Let the troglodytes fight it out. We can talk."

Afton tried to resist her mother's strong grasp, but was caught off guard and hauled inside the house. Continuing the fight, Gawain shook his head after a particularly clean blow from Blain's huge right fist. "Try that again, bloody Yank!"

"Kiss my ass, limey!" Blain charged at him.

For the next five minutes, Blain heard the hoots and howls coming from the others. They were hoping Gawain would get in his licks. He was tiring, but so was the megalith who was hitting him. "Had enough?" Blain panted as he circled his opponent.

"Not nearly," Gawain cried out as he charged yet again.

"Stop this instant!" a loud voice called from the perimeter of the woods. Everyone, including the two battling men, stopped what they were doing. Shayla walked into the light from the cottage. Pluck and Hugh stood on either side of her.

"Gawain, what is the meaning of this?" She crossed her arms and glared at the man.

"He's been in the woods all night with Afton. The celebration has been over for some time. If I hadn't had too much to drink, I'd have found 'im and bloody well pulled his head off!" Gawain swung his arm in Blain's direction. "I want to know what his intentions are."

"Can you answer him?" Shayla turned to Blain.

"Why on earth is that his business or anyone else's?" Blain angrily responded.

"Though I disagree with their method, Gawain and his family have a right to know what you want of Afton," she calmly responded. "We don't exactly do things here the way they're done in the outside world."

"We're both adults, Shayla. Afton and I don't have to answer to anyone but ourselves."

"In this place you do," Gawain insisted.

"Tell him and his family about your feelings for Afton, lad," Hugh said. "If she were your sister or daughter, wouldn't you be concerned that she'd been in the woods all night with someone?"

Put that way, Blain could hardly blame them. "I love her. She agreed to handfast with me. Are you satisfied?" He looked everyone straight in the eyes after he spoke. Even Pluck.

"Aye, lad. I am." Afton's father grinned. "That's all we wanted to hear. Now, come into the house, and we'll let Afton and her mother tend those wounds. You too, Gawain."

Afton's family filed back into the house taking Hugh and Pluck with them. Blain was left standing on the lawn staring at them in bewilderment. Shayla smiled at him and patted his arm. "Come inside, Blain. Afton's family will accept you wholeheartedly now. All they wanted was your promise to love Afton. And, I suspect, they were trying to see if you'd put up a good fight for her."

"Why in hell didn't someone just ask? Gawain almost tore my ass off, pardon the language."

"No pardon is necessary. And you know as well as I that you wouldn't have answered their questions if they had asked." She paused. "As you can see, some of our ways are rather different from anything you're used to. Now, come along. Your face is bleeding rather badly."

Blain began to wonder if anything about his life would ever be normal again. When he would have walked into the cottage, a breeze blew through the trees. He hesitated and turned to watch the branches move.

"What's wrong?" Shayla asked and turned to follow his gaze.

"There are other men out there who want Afton, aren't there?"

"Quite probably. Especially after last night's display."

Blain curled his fingers into fists, prepared to do battle until the last drop of blood fell from his veins. Afton and he were meant to be together. In his gut, he knew it. And something urged him to be with her as much as he possibly could. If he had to fight armies, then that was the way it would be.

The dark, ominous feeling came back, just as it had when Lore mentioned that he needed to guard those he loved. It was almost as though he was operating on borrowed time. As if something else was about to happen and the event waiting for him would take Afton as well. It was an urgency that wouldn't go away. The future was still out there. Closing in. Blain wondered how soon he would finally be confronted with the nameless, faceless horror.

Chapter Eleven

ഔ

After Blain entered the cottage, he was surprised how easily everyone seemed to cast aside the fight. Everyone but Gawain. Afton's mother and Shayla took them to the kitchen, but wisely seated him and Gawain at opposite ends of a long table. He stared at Gawain as the man stared back. But there was no longer any hostility in Gawain's gaze. Just a kind of curious intensity.

When Afton entered the room, carrying bandages, herbs and water for their wounds, Blain kept his full attention on her. He needed to make sure Gawain knew he was staking a claim for good. And it was hard to take his gaze off Afton. After making love, she had a kind of lovely golden aura around her. Maybe it was just his imagination, but she was so beautiful. Like some kind of nature angel who hovered over him, seeing to his wounds. Eventually, everyone drifted away leaving him, Gawain and the object of their battle alone.

Afton stood before Blain and shook her head. She continued to clean the wounds on his face and hands. "You look as if you've been battling an army. You'll have bruises for days." Then she turned to her brother. "Gawain, what in the world is wrong with you? Have you lost your bloody mind?"

"I just wanted to make sure he wasn't using you, Afton," Gawain growled. "You're not like some nymph who passes her favors out like pastries."

"And I suppose you've never sampled your share?" she accused.

"Well...I...that's different," he defended.

"Why? Because I'm your sister? Aren't the women you play around with someone's sister or daughter?" She glared at him.

Blain grinned. This wasn't an argument Gawain was going to win. He got great satisfaction out of seeing the other man lower his eyes in guilt.

Gawain yielded. "You're right. All I wanted was to hear Blain tell us his intentions where you were concerned."

"Well, now you know them. If you ever put a hand on him again, I'll never speak to you for as long as I live. Is that clear?" Afton put her hands on her hips, glaring while waiting for his answer.

"All right. I get the point." Gawain grinned. "No more fighting."

"And you, Blain?"

When she turned to him, Blain saw her blue eyes flash with anger. "Me? What did I do? I'm the one who got attacked, remember?" As he tried to defend himself, Afton stared at him, her gaze icy and adamant.

"No more fighting with Gawain or any of my brothers. Not for any reason. And certainly not over me. Is that clear?" She spoke between clenched teeth.

Blain grinned then immediately winced. The cut he'd received to his lower lip was deep and stung, but still he had to smile. Afton was adorable when she was angry. But he had to remember she had powers that could go a long way toward convincing him of the error of his ways. Especially if he didn't sound repentant. Still, all that anger made him want her more than ever. It would be fun making up after they argued. "All right, honey. No fighting."

"Good. Now, apologize—both of you." The stern look she gave them made it clear she expected them to follow her order.

Gawain rose from his chair and walked toward Blain with his right hand extended. "Sorry, Blain. Didn't know I'd be pummeling a future brother."

Blain took his hand and shook it. "It's okay. I agree with Hugh. If Afton was my sister, I'd have torn a strip off anyone taking her into the woods for the night."

"That's better." Afton smiled. "By the way, Blain, is the axe handling well for you, the balance good?"

Blain stared at her, totally confused. "Uh, yeah, it's fine. Incredible piece of workmanship."

"Thanks," Gawain blurted, then winced as Afton grabbed his right hand and continued to clean his shredded knuckles.

Blain looked at the man, then back at Afton. "What's he got to do with the axe?"

"He made it," Afton explained. "Along with fighting," She pushed Gawain's wounded shoulder hard enough to make him yelp, "my brother's more civilized talents include being a master at metalwork. He's renowned for his artistry, and you'll hear him referred to as the Craftsman."

"That just about figures," Blain said with a sigh. Now he'd have to thank the man who'd just cleaned his clock.

"Pardon?" Gawain asked, his eyebrows rising in sarcasm. "Didn't catch that comment."

"I should thank you for the axe. It's an awesome weapon," Blain admitted grudgingly.

Gawain smiled. "I didn't know it would end up in the hands of someone with such a good right hook."

"Idiot!" Afton smacked Gawain on the back of the head. "Try to act like you have some manners and say thank you."

Blain started to chuckle. "I've seen hints of it before, but I didn't know she had this sharp a temper."

Gawain winced while rubbing the back of his skull. "She gets her way. A lot."

Afton glared at the both of them, then continued to tend their wounds, finally calming down. Blain's heated gaze had her pulse racing, and Gawain gave her the apologetic expression he always wore after pummeling a suitor. Only this time his expression was sincere. By the time she was through, the sun was just coming up. Hugh, Shayla, Pluck and the rest of the O'Malley family came into the kitchen after being assured everything was under control. Afton and her mother fixed them all a large breakfast and they talked well into the morning. Her mother offered Blain a spare bed for the day, but Afton knew he preferred the woods. He rose to leave and she walked him to the front door.

"I'll see you tonight, my love. The same place?" she added in a whisper.

"I'll be there, Afton. Nothing could keep me away! Sleep well, sweetheart. I love you." Blain bent to kiss her softly on the lips and left.

Afton walked back into the kitchen, poured herself some tea and sat with the rest of her family. She'd never felt so tired and wonderful in her entire life.

"Afton, darling, you and Blain will have to keep your plans very secret. Since you exhibited so much power last night, you'll have young men calling on you in droves from now on, especially near Lughnasadh. You don't want Blain having to fight them all on your handfasting night," Deirdre warned.

"Yes, Mother, I know. I just wish I didn't have to wait so long." She sighed and smiled dreamily.

"Go to bed, Afton," Shayla said. "You're tired, and you need your rest so you and your mother can start making plans for your handfasting. We'll speak later."

"I'll run you a hot bath," Deirdre said.

Afton turned to go, but hesitated and let her mother walk out of the kitchen alone. She turned to face her mentor and watched as Shayla drained her teacup. "You're very pleased with how things have worked out, aren't you, Sorceress?"

"Whatever are you talking about?" Shayla asked with a smile.

Shayla's innocent tone further fueled Afton's courage. "You wanted Blain and me together. That's why you had me go to the States with you. This is another one of those situations I've heard about where you easily manipulate people into doing what you want. You're very famous for this kind of thing." Outside the kitchen window, Afton heard a subdued chuckle and realized Hugh had been standing there, listening.

"Hush!" Shayla ordered him in a loud, commanding voice. Then she turned her attention to Afton. "I've been doing things my own way for a great many years, my girl. How I do them isn't your concern. Just be happy." She rose and kissed Afton's cheek, then hugged her.

Afton watched her mentor walk out of the kitchen. She walked to the open window and saw her strolling away with a smiling Hugh. Shayla didn't need to tell her to be happy. She already was. Deliriously so. But as she turned, something made her look out the window again. Shayla and Hugh were entering a very thick part of the forest and were quickly out of sight.

But something made her feel as though she was being watched. And it wasn't a pleasant sensation. It wasn't like the feeling she got when one of the guards was on duty in that part of the forest. Maybe it was a strange side effect to the previous night's use of power. Maybe she'd overdone it. But whatever it was, it dampened her newfound feelings of happiness. Try as she would, Afton couldn't sleep for the rest of the day.

* * * * *

Blain found a nearby oak tree, stretched out on the grass at its base and slept. It was the most peaceful and refreshing sleep of his life. Afton loved him. Her family had accepted him. Even

Gawain had made peace with the fact that his little sister was going to handfast with him. He didn't know what the future held, but Afton would be in it. He dreamed of her loving him and couldn't wait to see her again.

Later that day, he retrieved his battle axe from its forest resting place. He went to the clearing where he was sure he'd be seen. There, he practiced with it and every other weapon he could get his hands on. He wanted to make sure that if anyone was thinking of challenging him for Afton, they'd think twice about doing so. Lore had told him these fights were no longer to the death, but he wanted to establish his abilities publicly.

It was three in the afternoon when he had the sudden urge to either fight or run. It was like some switch inside him had been flipped to survival mode. Lore and others of the fairy faction stormed from the woods, but he knew they were coming before they ever got to his location. The doomsday feeling came back and crashed down on him like a wall. It was so overpowering he almost sank to the ground with the weight of it. This was what he'd been waiting for. The horrendous event had finally arrived. That certain evil he had sensed so many times before crawled through the forest like a disease. But as the instinct to protect flooded him, he pulled himself together and prepared to fight. He knew he could kill if he had to. He saw the fairies were all carrying the same kinds of weapons he'd been practicing with, but this was no practice. It was real.

"Blain, come quickly," Lore called and motioned to him. "Something's happened on the far side of the forest. Pluck's been injured. We need everyone there."

Without pausing, Blain picked up his axe and followed the other fairies. Their faces were filled with trepidation. They were rapidly joined by other factions of creatures, and it took all of them several hours to get to Pluck's location. The growth was thick in some places and the paths were very narrow. Some of the fairies were able to use their wings and glide short distances over the most difficult parts where thickets and thorns grew. He even mimicked them and was able to do so as well. But centuries of never using such powers had genetically weakened them all. Flying even a short distance seemed to sap the fairies' strength more than walking did, so they stuck to the earth most of the time.

As they moved on, he finally got up the courage to ask someone about Pluck. But no one seemed to know what had happened. Lore didn't look as if he was in any mood to talk about anything. The man's face was a mask of fury and rage. Apparently, whatever had taken place wasn't an accident. Blain could have told them that. It had to do with the blackness that was now invading their forest home. He only hoped friendly little Pluck was all right.

When they finally reached the other side of the woods, Blain saw the O'Malley family standing in a circle. Afton was on her knees beside a small figure in the grass. Concern for her caused him to push his way forward. What he saw sickened him. Kind little Pluck lay in the grass, a large, bloody gash in his chest. But the bleeding seemed to have stopped.

"Pluck. Oh, Pluck," Afton cried.

"Did anyone see what happened?" Lore searched the faces in the growing crowd.

"Pluck was guarding the northern entrance to the forest. I went to the west. I heard him cry out and found him like this," Gawain explained. "I would have moved him, but he was in too much pain. I thought it best to leave him where he could rest rather than risk making him worse."

"The Sorceress is here, let her pass," someone in the crowd announced.

The crowd parted, and Shayla and Hugh walked forward. Shayla knelt beside Afton and placed a hand on Pluck's chest.

"He's alive. You did the right thing in letting him rest against the earth, Gawain. Remaining in contact with it renewed some of his strength and stopped the bleeding. Had you moved him when he was first injured, he would have died," Shayla explained as she gently stroked the unconscious elf's cheek.

"He's been resting for some time. Will it be safe to move him now?" Gawain asked.

"We'll have to. Something tells me he won't be secure in this place much longer. Take him to the nearest cottage." Shayla looked around the woods and pulled her cloak tightly around her body.

Gawain moved forward and lifted the small man. Blain watched him walk away, wondering what could possibly have happened to have hurt Pluck so seriously. But he knew it had something to do with the dark presence he sensed. Who could hurt a man, then move away so that a Druid couldn't have seen or heard anything? Pluck's elf powers, whatever those were, hadn't helped him avoid this injury.

Shayla pulled Afton to her. "I want you to concentrate. You're the person Pluck most cares for. Together, you and I might be able to sense what happened."

"You know this was no ordinary mishap, Sorceress. Someone attacked him," Lore said as his gaze scanned the area, searching for any clue.

"Yes. But we must be certain before any blame is assigned," Shayla warned.

Suddenly, Blain felt sick. Weakness engulfed him. It was the same feeling he'd had when he'd been hexed back in New England. He shook his head to fight off the feeling, but it became more intense as the seconds passed. He would have said something about the sickness, but it was an impairment he didn't want to display in front of these people, particularly under the present circumstances. Pluck was hurt and that needed to be addressed before his own physical problems. He could, however, relate what he knew to be most important.

"Someone was here, Shayla. Someone with powers like those used on me back in the States," Blain said.

Everyone turned to look at him. Shayla walked to where he stood. "Tell me," she commanded.

"Whoever it was, they're still nearby. I can feel it." He knew he was connected with whoever this presence was. The others weren't. Despite his illness, they needed him to stay strong.

Without waiting another second, Shayla began to take action. "Fairies, take the northern path and search every clearing and glen. Those of the Druid factions go to the west and take Gawain with you after he has seen to Pluck. Everyone else spread out to the east and south. We meet back here when the search is complete. If anyone finds anything, relay a signal through the woods immediately. Take no chances. Hugh, you and Afton stay with me and Blain," Shayla ordered.

At her bidding, the entire assemblage moved in their assigned directions. Blain could see raw anger in their faces. That anyone would attack and hurt Pluck so grievously was inhuman. He felt angry himself. The man had only been guarding. Who would want to hurt him?

"I know now that Hannah Biddles wasn't the only enemy you had," Shayla told him.

"Even if that's true, how could anyone have found me here?" If the elf had been hurt because of him, then no one around him would be safe. And that included Afton.

Shayla took Blain's arm. "Someone with the kind of black powers we're speaking of could find you anywhere if they wanted you badly enough. And, for a time, they could hide their presence from us. How do you feel? And don't try to hide anything from me."

Blain shook his head. "Like someone or something's sapping my strength again."

Afton moved beside him and took one of his hands in hers. He looked into her eyes and saw tears of pain for Pluck and concern for him. "Don't worry, baby. Whoever hurt Pluck will pay. I promise!"

"Come with us, Blain. We need to get to the center of the forest again. We're too close to the edge here. Outsiders might see us," Shayla explained.

They trudged back the length of the forest, to the large clearing. Even though hours had gone by, the feeling of weakness was increasing. He tried to shake it, but it was getting worse. The evil power attacking him was stronger and more crushing than anything he'd felt back in Maine. He tried to keep Afton from knowing how bad off he was, but she wouldn't be fooled.

"Please stop, Shayla. Blain can't take much more." Afton wrapped one arm around Blain's waist as he leaned against a tree.

"I...can...go on," Blain gasped.

"Don't be daft, lad, you're shivering. We'll stop here. Lass, start a fire, will you?" Hugh quickly took Afton's place to support Blain. Then he took Blain's battle axe and leaned it against a nearby tree.

As Hugh helped Blain to the ground, Shayla placed a hand on his forehead and shook her head. "I've never seen any conjuring so powerful. Someone wants Blain very badly. Whoever it is injured Pluck to get past him. Unless we find them, this will continue until Blain grows so ill he won't be able to move."

"Perhaps that's what someone wants. Maybe they want us to stay put," Afton suggested.

Shayla turned to Afton. "Explain."

"Maybe we should try to wait here. See what happens."

"We'll have to. Blain is almost unconscious," Hugh said, his voice thick with concern for his nephew.

Afton turned and began to gather small stones to circle a fire and wood to fuel it. When she finished, she raised her hands and quickly had a bright blaze burning.

"She's something, isn't she?" Blain rasped as he watched Afton's efforts.

"Shhhh, darling. Don't talk. Just rest." Afton knelt beside him and pulled his head against her shoulder. She stroked his long hair away from his face and kissed him tenderly. Nothing must happen to him. Nothing.

"Good, Afton. Stay with him. Hugh and I will search the immediate area, but we won't be more than a short distance away. If you see anything, call us."

"Be careful," she called out as they left.

"Afton, I love you. You know that, don't you?" Blain opened his eyes to look up at her. His voice was no more than a whisper.

"Yes, my heart. I know. I love you, too. Now rest." Afton caressed his cheek and tried not to cry. He needed her to be strong.

"You're so gorgeous."

"Hush, Blain. You have to sleep." He was weakening so much Afton wasn't sure if he knew what was happening or what he was saying anymore. She could hear Hugh and Shayla as they moved farther away and pushed undergrowth aside. They were searching for anything that might give them a clue as to what was happening or who was doing this. Whoever it was, they'd have to kill her before getting to Blain. And she'd destroy whoever tried.

Without warning, Blain opened his eyes and sat up. It was as though he'd been jerked into position. She saw him reach for the battle axe, and it appeared he was using his fairy powers to order up the very last dregs of his strength.

"Get behind me, Afton!" He quickly got to his feet.

"Blain, what's happening?"

"Do it now!" Blain brought his axe up, ready to swing. His enhanced eyesight scanned the nearby tree line. Afton did as she was told, but only so far as to stand back and to the side of him. If something was about to happen, she'd add her strength to his. Blain wouldn't have to fight without her help.

From behind a nearby tree, a strange mist appeared. It floated toward them ominously. Blain held his axe tightly. Afton watched as a fierce expression covered his face.

"Shayla, Hugh," she called.

"Don't waste your breath, Afton. I don't think they can hear us," Blain growled. "Besides, I know who it is now." He could sense her malevolent presence. Oh, he'd been an idiot.

"Recognize me, do you, lover?" a voice whispered from the mist.

"Show yourself, Rhiannon. Stop playing games," Blain demanded.

"Rhiannon? What are you talking about?" Afton stared at him, convinced he'd lost his mind.

"It seems your anemic little sweetheart doesn't remember me, Blain. But then we only met for a few moments."

"Show yourself," Blain repeated.

"All right. Here I am," the voice from the mist murmured.

Blain backed away, pulling Afton with him. From the center of the mist a shape emerged. The clear outline of a woman formed, and Rhiannon stepped forward. She was wearing a long black gown. There was a bloodied knife tucked in her belt. The smile she gave Blain was menacing. He saw her lips curl cruelly, and he wondered how he could have ever thought her beautiful.

She was an evil, grotesque aberration. He could feel her depravity like a disease surrounding him. His weakness was quickly dissipating. Whether it was because she had halted her torture on his senses, or because his anger was too great, he couldn't be sure. In one hand, she held a staff which had a crystal ball mounted on the top. Her palm gripped it until her knuckles turned white, indicating her fury. Blain watched her movements closely as he gripped the handle of his axe with equal force.

"You almost killed a friend of mine." Blain glared at her and thought of Pluck's horrible wound.

"What? That insignificant little toad?" She tapped the knife in her belt. "He was nothing. None of these rejects from a fairy tale mean anything to me." She tilted her head and considered Blain in his fairy form. "Speaking of fairy tales, I see you've joined Shayla's little band of merry men and women. Those wings are quite lovely. I think I'll mount them over a fireplace in the castle."

"Don't even think about it," Afton growled. "And you're going to be sorry for hurting Pluck. He didn't deserve what you did to him, you savage." She would have lunged for the woman, but Blain held her back.

"Ah, yes. I remember that night at your party, and how the little white Druid showed her claws." Rhiannon paused. "Well, let's see how well she does fighting a woman with real power." Rhiannon raised her staff and pointed it toward Afton. A beam of dark energy shot from it and struck Afton in the chest. The force knocked Afton to her knees.

"Afton!" Blain knelt to help her.

"I'm all right. It'll take more than that to do me in," she croaked bravely.

"That was nothing compared to what I'll do to you when I'm through dealing with Blain. He's the real reason I'm here." Rhiannon circled them slowly.

"You're behind everything that happened at the farm aren't you, Rhiannon?" Afton glared at her. "Hannah Biddles was working for you, wasn't she?"

"It was actually the other way around. I worked for Hannah and actually called her Mistress. I tried to tell her that what she was doing wouldn't work, but she was a fool. Just like him." Rhiannon motioned toward the woods, and Reverend Myers stepped forward.

From the look on the man's face, Blain could tell he was under Rhiannon's power. His eyes stared into the distance, and he moved mechanically. Myers either couldn't or wouldn't make a sound. It was as though he was in some kind of zombie-like state from which he couldn't awaken.

Rhiannon waved a hand in a contemptuous gesture. "Hannah's powers were really quite mediocre. All those stupid little hexes. She was careless, fell for Shayla's trap and got caught. And I used her just like I'm using the Reverend. I can make him do anything I want and never have to take the blame for his actions. He's not calling me names anymore."

"I don't understand, Rhiannon. What's this all about? What do you want from me?" Blain tried to keep his attention on both Myers and Rhiannon. He didn't know what to expect from either of them.

Rhiannon gave him a sarcastic smirk. "I could say I just wanted you for the wonderful sex. But I'm afraid all good things come to an end sooner or later." She affected a sigh. "Such is life. But all that lovemaking was just a ploy to get you away from the house and your uncle so Hannah and I could weaken you. Hannah just wanted Shayla to come to your aid. You see, a long time ago, Hannah's older sister died trying to keep her place as Sorceress of the Ancients."

"Freyja was Hannah's older sister?" Afton whispered.

"That's right, little girl," Rhiannon replied derisively. "But when Freyja died, Hannah believed she should have succeeded her for control of the Order. She believed it was her birthright, but the Order chose to let a usurper be their Sorceress. Freyja had the right idea all along, though. The only way to rule is to make sure the laws are strictly obeyed. And the only way to make sure the laws are obeyed is through fear. That's how to truly maintain control over so many magical beings. Any of the Order who breaks the law should die, and allowing factions to intermingle their blood is breaking the law. Freyja knew it, and Hannah knew it as well."

"If Hannah thought she could do a better job as Sorceress, she could have challenged Shayla," Afton said. "That's one of the laws, too. Or maybe the only laws Hannah would have enforced are those she deemed worthy. She and Freyja wanted to keep the power in their bloodline. Is that it?"

"That's the way it should be. Shayla has no right to rule. She won that battle by cheating," Rhiannon responded angrily. "That's the only possible way she could ever have defeated Freyja. Hannah knew that, and she knew she'd be cheated in any fight as well. So she didn't challenge for the leadership." Rhiannon paused a moment, then continued. "The day that fight took place, Hannah saw Freyja would lose. She and a few others left the Order. Some of Hannah's cohorts altered the records of who died that day in all the fighting, so no one even thought she was alive. But all that was years ago. Now the Order has a weak, useless Sorceress. Shayla isn't feared as Freyja was, and members of the Order should fear the position of Sorceress of the Ancients. Whoever holds that title is a Goddess. She can make laws and enforce them as she pleases, and one of the laws that should have been enforced had to do with *his* parents." Rhiannon pointed at Blain. "Blood shouldn't be mixed the way his is. It defiles the Order."

"You're not even arguing rationally. All you want is to have your way whatever the cost. You want to kill Blain the way Freyja and Hannah would have," Afton declared.

Rhiannon shrugged. "Actually, it was Hannah's idea to go after Blain. Though it took her years, she used the black arts to find out where he and his family were hiding. But she didn't want Blain to die quickly. She wanted revenge. His parents' resistance to the law is what eventually cost Freyja her position as Sorceress and her life. When Syndra and Arthur defied Freyja and successfully hid themselves from her in the outside world, others began to resist Freyja's commands as well. That was the beginning of the end for her."

"That explains Freyja's and Hannah's actions, but what about you, Rhiannon? What has all this got to do with you?" Blain asked.

"Hannah wasn't just my Mistress, though that's what she forced me to call her. She was my mother. Jed was my father." She shrugged again. "I, as Freyja's direct and only living descendent, should now be Sorceress. Hannah became too impatient, moved in at the wrong time and got herself killed. Unfortunately, I have to finish the job here. With Shayla's warriors all over the place, it will be much harder, but I *will* succeed."

Afton gasped. "Listen to yourself, Rhiannon. You're not even making sense. Even if you had been born within the Order, there's no guarantee you'd have ever been Sorceress. If Shayla hadn't deposed your Aunt Freyja, someone else surely would have. It's obvious that your whole family is crazy, including you."

Rhiannon tilted her head and simply stared at her. "That's not true. It's not true…not true…"

Blain shook his head in disbelief. Confronted with reality, Rhiannon just stood there in front of them with her head at an odd angle, mumbling. As Afton had said, there was no logic in her argument. She was insane by anyone's standards. Rhiannon seemed to be interpreting things the way she wanted them to be. Whatever was the most comfortable reality for her to deal with.

"You'd have eventually killed your own mother to be Sorceress, wouldn't you?" he asked, watching her slowly come back to reality. He saw her shake her head and the glazed look left her eyes.

"I've wasted enough time explaining myself to fools who won't ever understand. Come with me." She beckoned to Blain and Afton with her staff.

Against his will, Blain dropped the battle axe and felt himself being pulled forward. His mind didn't seem to control his body any longer. Glancing at Afton, he saw that she seemed equally impaired. The two of them were forced to walk behind Rhiannon and Myers.

"Where are you taking us?" Afton asked, struggling against the force propelling her forward.

"Mother told me—yes, that's it. An entrance to the crystal caves is just ahead. Her description of this woods was very accurate. Shayla will have to follow me into the mines to get you. That means there won't be room for her to bring all her warriors. I'll send Myers to her with an ultimatum. She comes alone, or you both die."

"The Order won't accept someone who takes control this way, Rhiannon. They'll hunt you down for sure," Blain warned.

"And you're suddenly an expert on what they'd do?" She paused as they approached the cave entrance. "Just keep your mouths closed, and I promise you both a quick death. Keep talking and you'll linger in the most horrible way I can imagine."

Blain and Afton were forced through the cave's entrance while still fighting against the power which controlled them. The ground began to slope gradually downward, and the passageway became more narrow. They walked for what seemed like ages. Torches lit the walls where the workers had left them. Afton knew the miners had probably dropped what they were doing as soon as they'd found out about the attack on poor little Pluck. When someone entered the forest and got past the perimeter guard, every man, woman and child old enough to know how was assigned to a position of defense— even if that position was to hide those too young or old to fight. That meant she and Blain would be on their own against a woman using black magic.

But Afton knew that kind of magic would eventually eat the user alive. Though it was horribly powerful, its practitioners always suffered the most excruciating diseases or deformities toward the end of their lives. It was why no sane soul in the Order ever wielded that type of magic. Even now, its influence was taking away every vestige of human emotion Rhiannon may have ever felt, along with her sanity. All that was left of her was a cold, evil monster with a rock where her heart should be.

If Rhiannon's plan succeeded, the Sorceress of the Ancients would die. The Order would be left in the hands of an evil witch who would destroy thousands of years of culture. Afton couldn't let that happen. She glanced at Blain and could see in his eyes that he was thinking much the same thing. If they got a chance to destroy Rhiannon, they'd have to take it.

After walking for some time, Rhiannon stopped in the middle of one of the main chambers. Clear quartz crystals coated the walls and ceiling. They shimmered brilliantly in the torchlight and reflected rainbows of color everywhere.

"A beautiful place to die, isn't it?" She smiled coldly. "Both of you, against the far wall." At her beckoning, Afton and Blain stumbled backward into the wall and sank to the ground, unable to move. "It's pure hell being in such an impotent position, isn't it? Doesn't it just make you want to scream?" Rhiannon laughed sarcastically. Then she walked a few yards away to recite an incantation to the catatonic Myers.

"Afton," Blain whispered, "how can she control us so easily?"

"Black magic is very powerful, but it exacts a high toll. It may be that Rhiannon is using a great deal of energy to bind us to her this way."

"What can we do?"

"I don't know unless…" Afton stopped to think and began to chew on her lower lip.

"What?" Blain urged her to continue.

Afton looked straight into his eyes. "Shayla will try to get to us if she can."

"I was hoping she wouldn't." Blain nodded toward the roof of the cave. "There are a lot of people up there who depend on her. If I were her, I'd consider us expendable."

Afton smiled. "But you're not her. Ours lives aren't expendable to the Sorceress."

"If that's the case, she'll die right along with us," he reasoned.

"If that happens, the Order might not survive. I'm glad I'm with you, Blain."

"I'm sure as hell not. I want you a few thousand miles from here. Right back on the farm leading animals all over the place."

Afton shook her head. "I belong with you."

"I love you, Afton."

"Shut up!" Rhiannon called out. She turned back to Myers and lifted her hand. The motion caused him to stumble back the way they'd come. Rhiannon walked behind him for a short distance, making sure he followed her commands. The crystal ball in her staff began to glow as she conjured. Blain watched Rhiannon and remembered what Afton said about needing a lot of power to hold them so helpless. It gave him an idea.

"Afton, honey, whatever I do or say, stay out of it." Before she could question his intent, Blain called to Rhiannon. "Hey, Rhi!"

Rhiannon made one last gesture toward Myers' retreating figure, then angrily turned around and stalked to where Blain sat. "I thought I told you to keep your mouth shut!" She leaned over and slapped him hard.

Blain shook his hair back and grinned up at her. "I just had to ask one question."

She straightened, put one hand on her hip and arched a brow. "Not that it matters, but go ahead."

"What was all the sex really for? I mean, you came to Harvest to kill me. You didn't have to screw my brains out just

231

to weaken me. All those hexes were doing a pretty good job. Or was Myers' opinion right on the money?"

Rhiannon's lips twisted. "What are you talking about?"

"I'm talking about the real reason you had sex with me. Couldn't a worn woman like you find a man in New York, or did you have to come all the way out to the sticks to jerk off some country boy?"

He saw Rhiannon's expression shift from insipid boredom to pure fury. She raised her staff and pushed it toward the wall. Blain's body was instantly jerked from his seated position and slammed into the side of the cave.

"Oh, come on, Rhi," Blain gasped as soon as his breath returned. "You have to know the real reason I dumped you." He watched her eyes turn black with rage. "Word all over town was, you'd been sleeping with every man you could find. Hell, sweetheart, even a country boy like me has to have his standards. I think men refer to women like you as sloppy seconds."

Rhiannon's scream of anger echoed off the chamber walls. She dropped her staff and threw herself at Blain, her nails extended like talons. She sank them deep into his chest. Blain was able to move again. Getting her angry enough to drop the staff and physically attack him had worked. He pulled her hands away from his body and tried to pin them behind her, but she twisted away and quickly backed up.

Before he could rush her again, Rhiannon grabbed her staff. "I told you I'd have your wings mounted over a fireplace. Well, I can't think of a better time to pull them off! You're going to die very, very slowly."

Blain charged, but Rhiannon aimed the staff at him. The same kind of white light that had incapacitated Afton hit him in the left shoulder. He cried out but kept trying to move forward.

Afton gasped as her body was finally released from Rhiannon's hold. She raced to help Blain. He was doing this for her.

"No, Afton! Get out!"

He threw himself at Rhiannon once more. She was more physically powerful than he could imagine. It had to be the magic she used. As he struggled with her, its dark source physically sickened him.

Afton watched in horror as blinding light shot off the crystal walls. Rhiannon's staff directed bolt after bolt of power at Blain. But he was moving too fast, grappling with her to take away the staff, which was acting like an amplifier. Shadows appeared against the walls as they struggled. Afton tried to get closer without being struck by the staff's powerful light. One of the shadows didn't move with the fighting couple. It seemed to leap toward them. Then another did the same. Afton backed away as the dark figures seemed to come to life and move toward Rhiannon. This was an unholy magic Afton had never known existed.

"See the powers I have at my beck and call, Blain? See them do as I bid?" Rhiannon gasped.

Blain might have won the battle, even though her strength had been augmented by the powers of the staff and its crystal, but he couldn't fight off the shadow figures that pulled him against the wall and held him fast. They were very much like the same red demons Hannah had summoned. Realizing Afton was finally free gave Blain some hope.

"Run!" he yelled.

Afton shook her head in refusal, and Rhiannon slowly turned in her direction.

"Afton, if you love me, go!"

"I won't leave you."

"You couldn't hide from me anyway," Rhiannon snarled. "No matter where you went, I'd hunt you down like an animal." Rhiannon summoned more power and sent a beam of it straight toward Afton's chest.

Blain watched in terror as her slender figure folded to the ground.

Rhiannon stood over Afton, laughing. "There goes your little English bitch. Too bad. Now I'll just have you to use as a lure."

Blain roared in anger. Afton's still form enervated him in a way he'd never known possible. From the depths of the earth he drew powers. Something in his intuition told him these were the powers of his father. Powers of a Druid. He focused on strengthening himself and felt the very forces of nature entering his muscle and sinew. He pulled free of the shadowy demons, charged Rhiannon and struck her to the ground. The woman was so stunned she didn't have time to react. Blain put his hands around her neck. He only had a second to squeeze before people were pulling him off her choking form.

"Lay off, lad!" Lore ordered. "This woman's punishment is left to the Sorceress."

Blain struggled as Lore and several other large men held him fast. "If Afton's dead, so is Rhiannon," he gasped and tried to pull free.

"Calm down, Blain!" Shayla commanded as she hurried into the chamber, knelt beside Afton's body and checked her pulse. "Afton isn't dead. She's just badly injured. It's lucky for the both of you that Rhiannon didn't know there are other entrances into this chamber. Quickly, bind Rhiannon and take her to the castle," Shayla ordered some of the men. "Lock her away from Myers. Someone help me with Afton."

"Let me have her!" Blain tried to reach out for Afton's body, which was lying before Shayla's kneeling form. But Lore and the other men held him back.

"Only if you calm down," Lore told him. "Getting Afton to safety is our main concern right now. You need to release your anger over that evil woman. Don't pass it on to Afton."

Blain nodded and extended his arms.

Lore ordered his men to let Blain loose, and one of them picked Afton up off the cave floor and handed her to Blain.

"I'm here, baby. It's all right," he whispered as he took her body in his arms and quickly followed the others out of the cave.

Chapter Twelve

ॐ

Blain watched as Shayla, Hugh and Afton's parents fussed over her. She was so pale it frightened him. "She'll be okay, won't she?"

"She's absorbed quite a dose of evil energy. We'll have to wait and see what happens," Shayla responded. "If she makes it through the night, then I believe everything will be well."

Blain watched Afton's mother cry. Her father tried to console his wife and not give way to his own emotions. In the hallway, six large men waited to hear what would happen to their little sister, and Blain felt the entire situation was his responsibility. He had brought this horror to these good people. To the woman he loved. And he was in agony over it. He should have known when he saw Rhiannon's twisted reflection in the gazing globe and said something, but it was too late to look back now. His only consoling thought was that none of the more powerful creatures around him had been able to home in on Rhiannon as the source of their problems, but that really didn't make him feel less responsible.

After the struggle with the crazed woman, Blain discovered that the amethyst fairy stone Afton had given him was one of the reasons he'd survived. It glowed after having absorbed some of the powers Rhiannon had tried to use against him. As an element from the earth, it gave him strength. The same as it would have done his father or any other Druid. By giving it to him, Afton had probably saved his life, and he vowed to never again take it off.

He'd been told that little Pluck was fighting for his life. One other perimeter guard had been found injured, and two more were dead. That was why it had taken Shayla so long to get to him and Afton. They'd been tending the other wounded guards, trying to save their lives. Rhiannon had used her magic to conceal Myers' and her presence until they got close enough to attack. Blain cursed himself for ever having anything to do with her.

He sat down beside Afton, took her hand and waited. No one would ever persuade him to leave her side. All through the night he whispered to her and held her hand. Cleansing incense was burned near her bed, while herbs were scattered beside her body. Her brothers were allowed in toward the early morning hours when it looked as though she wouldn't rally. Gawain placed a hand on Blain's shoulder, and Blain finally took his gaze off Afton long enough to see the big man's eyes filled with tears.

His heart was breaking, and Blain truly understood how loved Afton was. He leaned closer to her. "Don't you leave me, dammit! If you do, I'll come after you. Do you understand, little Flower?"

Afton's eyelids fluttered open, and she moved her lips. Everyone stood absolutely still and held their breath. Blain leaned closer to her and gently pushed her hair back. "What did you say, honey?"

"Wh-what did you call me?" she croaked out in a very soft voice.

In his excitement, Blain couldn't talk. He just gazed into her eyes and placed a soft kiss on her lips.

"He called you Flower." Gawain looked down at her with a tearful smile.

Afton's tired gaze focused on her eldest brother. "Gawain, you didn't tell him that silly nickname?"

Everyone laughed as she wearily smiled and squeezed Blain's hand. It was her way of letting him know she was going to be all right.

* * * * *

"Here, drink this," Blain said as he placed a cup of herbal tea into her hands. "It'll make you feel better."

Afton shook her head in frustration. "I'm fine. It's been three days and I want to get up."

He adamantly shook his head. "No."

"Couldn't I just—"

"No, you can't."

"If I could just sit by the window and see outside…" Afton's voice trailed away as she looked beseechingly at him.

Blain sighed, considered the window seat then carefully picked her up and carried her to it. "There. Now you can see outside."

He tucked a warm blanket around her, walked across the room and placed some cookies—or biscuits, as the English seemed to call them—on a small plate. "Eat these. You need to get your strength back."

Afton watched him place the small offering on a table and move it close enough so she could reach the food. "How long are you going to keep coddling me?"

He smiled, knelt in front of her and kissed the backs of her hands. "Forever."

She lost herself in his green gaze and finally smiled. "Blain, haven't you slept? You need a shave. Please don't make yourself sick over me."

"I got a little sleep when you did." He passed a hand across his face and felt the stubble. But going to his room meant leaving her even for a few minutes, and he just couldn't bring himself to do so. Still, the way she was wrinkling her nose made him think he might need a shower as well as a shave.

"Okay, sweetness, I'll go clean up. But I won't leave until I can find one of those brothers of yours to stay with you while I'm gone."

"For goodness' sake, Blain, I'm perfectly capable of—"

"You're perfect." He kissed her and made his way toward the door.

As he suspected, Gawain and the rest of his brothers were in the hallway. They'd long since given up trying to stay more than a few minutes with their sister. Blain had chased them all out as soon as Afton's father had taken her very tired and distressed mother back to their cottage. Since the castle had been closer to the caves and immediate medical attention was available there, that was where Afton, Pluck and the injured guard had been taken. Afton's family had haunted the place until they were absolutely sure she was out of danger. Still, those brothers of hers weren't going far from their baby sister. Blain understood it wasn't a question of his being in her room that fostered their constant vigil. They just loved her.

"I've got to get cleaned up or I'm afraid Afton won't let me near her. Who wants to go in and—" Blain grinned. Before he could finish the sentence, all six hulking men had pushed past him and into the room, smiling like idiots. Gawain was last and nodded at him in appreciation. In the past few days, a bond had formed between him and the brothers. It was a bit like having brothers of his own.

As he walked toward his room, he found he was grinning, too. Since Afton's family had taken him in, he now felt as though he belonged with them. In the long hours as she'd slept, they'd talked and come to know each other better. That was how he'd found out about her silly nickname. He suspected that when Afton was able to put up a good fight, Gawain was going to catch hell over that indiscretion.

Blain whistled as he showered, changed, and hurriedly left his room. He was in the hallway and on his way back to Afton when Shayla, Hugh and Lore approached him from the far end of the corridor. His good spirits sank when he saw their leaden expressions. They stopped as soon as they drew close.

"What is it?" Blain asked, his gaze moving to each of their faces. "Is it the other injured people?"

"No. Pluck and the other injured guard are going to be all right," Shayla told him, "but there's something you had better know."

"Is something wrong with Afton you haven't told me about?" he asked, anxiously.

Shayla placed her hands on his forearms. "No. This has to do with Rhiannon and her mother, Hannah."

"I don't give a damn about them." Blain tried to step around the Sorceress only to have Hugh and Lore block the way.

"You'd best know, lad," Hugh said.

There was a kind of barely controlled anger in his uncle's tone that immediately alerted Blain. Shayla beckoned him and the others to follow. He anxiously glanced back down the hallway toward Afton's room, but it was clear he wasn't going to be able to go back there until whatever business Shayla had planned was over.

They walked, continuing a steady course down corridors, stairs and winding passages. A floor below ground level, Shayla stopped before a large oak door where two Herculean guards stood watch.

"Go in," she ordered.

Blain looked into the Sorceress' eyes, hesitating when he saw the anger there, then entered the room. Inside, Rhiannon was secured to a heavy chair, her hands tied behind her. The rest of the room was empty of any furnishings. Its stone gray walls and floor confirmed the place had once been a dungeon. Herb bundles lay on the floor, circled around Rhiannon. Blain guessed they were warding off whatever magic the woman might use. The Sorceress wasn't taking any more chances with her.

Rhiannon smirked when she saw him. "Well, well. I was wondering when you'd come."

He'd have turned and left, but the heavy door slammed closed. Apparently, he was supposed to stay and hear her out. "I take it you have something to say to me? 'Cause I sure as hell don't have a damned thing to say to you."

"I imagine your Sorceress wants me to tell you what I told her."

"And why would I care?"

"You should. You see, Shayla intends to pronounce judgment on me for coming here and attacking and killing her people." She paused, then continued when Blain didn't respond. "You know what that means?"

"I've got a pretty good idea, but you made that bed yourself."

"Yes, well, before she has me killed, I wanted you to know the entire story."

The smile she gave him could only be described as sickening. Something in the pit of Blain's stomach turned. "Get it over with," he bit out.

"Do you know why your father and mother stopped moving on after reaching Harvest?"

Again, Blain didn't respond. He didn't like the expression in her eyes, or the maliciously evil tone in her voice.

"They knew they'd finally been found by those of the dark side. They intended to stop running and make a stand," she announced.

Blain turned to leave. His heart throbbed out a warning, and he wanted to get away from her and back to Afton and her pure brightness. But Rhiannon's next words stopped him.

"You were on a trip to purchase seeds when your father suddenly died. Don't you wonder why your parents insisted that you go on so many trips alone?"

Though his heart was turning to ice, Blain turned back around to face her. "Go on," he responded in a low voice.

"Arthur had never been ill, had he? Syndra told you he just dropped dead while working." She stopped long enough to toss her long hair over her shoulder, smile wickedly at him and let her words sink in. "That story Hannah told you and everyone about being angry over the sale of her land was the truth. But not all of it. You see, Jed, my bastard of a father, sold the land to Arthur without my mother's knowledge. Since Father put the deed in his own name, it was easy enough to do. Jed was a Druid just like your father, but like my mother, he was a practitioner of the dark powers. He left the Order the same day my mother did."

"Get to the point."

Rhiannon continued as if Blain had never spoken a word. "I think Father once actually thought he loved Mother, but that quickly passed. He was afraid to go back to the Order, even though he wanted to, and one day he started drowning his sorrows in booze. Later, he found out he was dying. I think he correctly suspected that Hannah was slowly killing him with magic and potions. He couldn't do a thing to stop her or find a way to safely leave. He was a weak man, and there was no room in Hannah's life—or mine—for weakness."

Blain's throat went dry. The clean forest called. He wanted to be anywhere but standing in this gray cell.

Rhiannon tilted her head back against the chair. "Hannah had a plan. After she finally found Arthur and Syndra, she was going to kill them, lure Shayla to Harvest to protect you, then kill Shayla, you and your uncle. We knew there would be those of the Order who would never accept us, so we decided to buy up all the land in the area and start our own version of the Order. A place where only those of the dark arts could reside. With all our powers put together and Shayla dead, we could eventually attack the Order, finish off anyone who tried to stop us and regain control. But that stupid father of mine came to believe that if he got the land out of the hands of those practicing the black arts and into those using white magic, he could redeem himself for whatever afterlife awaited, and, of course, take revenge on my mother for poisoning him. So he made a deal with your parents behind our backs."

"What happened?" Blain angrily asked as he stepped closer to Rhiannon.

"When Jed thwarted her plans, Hannah passed around that trumped up story about Arthur buying the land from her drunken husband who'd wasted all his money. It was the only way to explain why the best farmland in the area was suddenly sold. It also garnered my mother sympathy from the townspeople. Some believed the poor widow-woman had been taken advantage of by Arthur. Hannah planned to later use that sympathy when the rest of her cronies were supposed to arrive and take up residence. A lot of strangers in a small town encourage gossip. She wanted people to think they were old family friends come to help her in her time of need."

"And where were you while all this was happening?" Blain questioned. The tone in his voice should have warned Rhiannon, but she kept going.

"Here and there. New York, Massachusetts and sometimes to Harvest to visit dear old Mom. But the rest of the community never knew I was Hannah and Jed's child because we were never seen together." She paused and tilted her head. "But that's not important. What is of interest is the way your father and mother really died."

Blain's hands clenched into fists. His heart was beating so hard it hurt.

Rhiannon smiled when she saw him go pale. "Jed ruined everything my mother planned. He simply admitted that he was a black magic Druid and told your parents that masters of the dark arts were preparing to gather nearby. Somehow, he was able to convince them of his sincere motives for their safety. Frightened for your future, Arthur and Syndra decided to stop my mother's plans. They were tired of running. Of course, they sensed the presence of evil long before they knew its source. Up until Jed decided to spill the beans, Hannah did a good job at keeping them from knowing who she was and what was going on. Just like we did a good job of hiding everything from you, Shayla and everyone else."

Blain took a threatening step toward her, but she shook her head. Warnings echoed from deep inside him. He didn't want to accept what his mind was already telling him.

"You need to hear the rest of this, darling," she drawled. "Before Arthur could learn more, we decided to take action. One day, we found him working alone. Arthur couldn't defend himself against both of us. His death looked like a heart attack, and the local authorities didn't question it. Your mother wouldn't have said anything to the contrary because no one would have believed her. Then she had to worry about you. You had absolutely no knowledge of the Order or any powers you might have. She couldn't tell you what was happening without you believing she was insane. Or worse, you might actually believe her and try to fight us. I suspect that was her worst fear. Taking us on would have meant certain death for you. So, without your father there, Syndra did the best she could to fight us with her puny fairy power, but it was only a matter of time before the amulets that weakened you killed her. Your parents were dead with no one being any wiser."

Blain was frozen with pure fury. He could do nothing but listen to the horrible sound of her voice.

Rhiannon persisted, only to torment him more. "But you know it wasn't your parents we really wanted, lover. We needed them out of the way, because it was you we were really after. We could have killed you sooner or later, though your powers are stronger than we expected. But keeping you alive and ill was the easiest way to carry out our plans. There would be no resistance from you because you had no idea what you were up against, which made you so much easier to deal with than fighting your parents. And you were what we needed to draw Shayla out. We knew Hugh would find you when the magic wasn't there to hide you any longer. Your loving uncle would try to help you when he knew you were being hexed, and the best way he could help you would be to summon the Sorceress. Shayla would soon show up, and if we could kill her, the Order would one day fall. There wouldn't be time to find someone powerful enough to replace her. We'd have our revenge against your parents and get Shayla out of the way all at the same time."

Blain began to shake, and something in his soul broke down and screamed in grief. He knew hatred the likes of which he'd never felt before. It was as real as the air he breathed.

"When Mother screwed up and got herself killed, Shayla wasted no time bringing you back to the Order. So, I had to come here to try to kill the Sorceress by myself."

"You're lying!" Blain spit out through clenched teeth. "My parents died of natural causes."

"You know that isn't true, and if you're honest with yourself, you've probably known for a long time. You're in what's called denial, but Shayla knows I'm telling the truth. Why do you think she sent you to see me? And she knows one more thing." She paused for the shock her words would cause, smiled slyly and then said, "You see, Blain, no matter what happens to me, Syndra and Arthur are still dead. But you want to know what the funny part is?"

Blain was so overcome with rage, he couldn't speak. He felt no remorse in knowing Shayla would kill her.

Rhiannon leaned as close to him as she could. "You see, lover, Syndra and Arthur kept themselves so well hidden that they never knew Shayla was the new Sorceress. For whatever reason, that drunk father of mine never told them that old Freyja was dead. I suspect Jed thought that if they knew the truth, Syndra and Arthur would leave for Britain and he'd have no one to help him get even with Mother—no way of getting back at her for slowly killing him. But several days after your clueless father was dead, I paid a friendly little visit to your mother. I told her that her dear friend Shayla Gallagher had been in charge of the Order for years. Then, I placed the most powerful binding spell on her I could. It was my once-in-a-lifetime best achievement with black magic. That spell left her physically incapable of contacting the Order and warning Shayla, and there was nothing Syndra could do to fight it. Again, she wouldn't tell you because you'd most certainly try to avenge your father's death. She probably believed you'd get yourself killed trying. So she fought until the last and tried to hide it all from you. Your mother died knowing she and Arthur had run for no reason. That if they'd only gone back, or contacted people they'd once called friends, the two of them would be alive today. And I told her that once we were done getting Shayla to come to your aid, you were next. It was my little way of sending her off, and a rather inventive way to punish her one last time for running from Freyja and bearing a half-breed like you. Brilliantly cruel, don't you think? You see, lover, I'll always find a way to win. You still lose!"

Blain finally understood why his mother had told him someone would come to defend him and be on his side. Why her last words had been so odd. They were both a warning and a message of hope. She hadn't the strength to say more. It ripped his heart into a million pieces knowing she'd died fearing for her son's safety.

When Rhiannon saw his stricken expression, she began to laugh. The chilling sound of it echoed off the stone walls and into Blain's heart. He slowly turned, walked to the door and opened it. The guards were gone and the hall was empty. His battle axe was leaning against the far side of the corridor. He reached for it and mechanically walked back into Rhiannon's cell. The laughter died on her lips when she saw the massive weapon.

Blain raised it and swung once. The double blades sang out as he slowly lowered it back to his side.

* * * * *

After Blain trudged out of the castle dungeon, word quickly spread that Rhiannon was dead and the Sorceress had sanctioned the circumstances surrounding her demise. Those members of the Order who were waiting for him silently parted as he made his way from the main castle entrance. Blain didn't look at their faces and didn't respond to their questions. He only stopped when he saw someone put Myers into the back of a large black sedan and drive him away.

"Myers is being taken to a hospital where he'll be left anonymously," Lore explained. "He was an unwilling dupe in this situation, but his mind is gone."

Blain didn't respond. He simply stared at Lore then turned his attention to the woods.

"Come back inside," Lore pleaded. "It's over, and there's nothing anyone can do now."

Blain simply walked away and didn't turn around when Lore called out to him.

* * * * *

For almost two days, Afton watched Blain from a castle window. He stood like an oak, facing the forest and refusing to communicate, eat, or rest. The battle axe was still in his hands. He gripped it as though he was ready to swing again, and she was afraid he might lose his mind. To kill someone in the heat of battle was one thing, but what had happened with Rhiannon was grisly.

After learning how Syndra and Arthur died, she couldn't blame him. Some of the Order even held him in awe because of his actions. But that wasn't helping Blain. She couldn't begin to imagine what he was feeling, or the kind of pain that was tearing him apart. What had happened to his parents made no logical sense, and that was the most tragic part of the story. They didn't have to die. They could have come back at almost any time. But even if they'd known about Shayla being in charge, Afton believed they might have wanted peace for themselves and their special child. Perhaps contacting the Order again would have been too difficult once Blain was born and became accustomed to the outside world. And maybe they needlessly blamed themselves for the fighting and death their running had instigated, although that battle would have had to be fought sooner or later. Or maybe they thought any old comrades or family they contacted, like Shayla or Hugh, might suffer for befriending them.

Despite Rhiannon's confession, Afton knew the real reason Syndra and Arthur never contacted the Order lay dead with them. But because of the man Blain was now, she also knew Syndra and Arthur had loved him fiercely. They had raised him to be strong and good, and she knew instinctively that they would have given up everything to keep their son safe. Perversely, fears for Blain's safety might have blinded his parents to the possibility that things might have changed within the Order. It was a tragedy no matter how one looked at it.

Afton understood she and everyone else could speculate forever about Arthur's and Syndra's motivations. Blain was still suffering and she couldn't stand it any longer. From her window in the castle, she watched as Lore approached him time and time again. Blain acted as though the man wasn't present.

Finally, word came to her that the Sorceress had ordered him to be left alone until he was ready to speak. Even Shayla's efforts to communicate with him had produced no response. And all Afton wanted to do was hold him. To let him know he wasn't alone.

"How are you feeling, Flower?" Gawain put a concerned hand on her shoulder.

She shook her head. "I'm worried sick about him. How long can he keep this up? Can't someone please try again?" she asked with tears on her cheeks.

"You chose a good man. His conscience is probably eating him up, though he knows his parents were murdered and he would have been used to kill the Sorceress. This is one of the saddest things I've ever seen happen to one man."

Afton turned to her older brother and saw the look of sympathy on his face. "Gawain, help me go to him. I'm still a bit weak, but I could make it if you helped me."

He considered her request for a moment. "All right. I'll take you. I don't think the Sorceress would object if you talked to him."

"Would you do me a favor and go to the cottage first? I need the package that's under my bed." When Gawain looked as if he'd question her, she raised her hand. "Just get it for me, please?"

"Sure. Anything you want."

Afton impatiently waited for him to complete the errand. When Gawain returned, he handed her the small package, which she cradled as though it were priceless. "I'm ready now."

Gawain carried her most of the way. When they got to the foyer, he gently put her down and watched her walk toward Blain. As soon as she was within a few feet of Blain, Gawain closed the castle doors. His little sister didn't need his protection anymore.

Afton stood before Blain waiting, searching his face for some sign of recognition. His expression seemed tired and distant, as though he didn't want to be where he was.

She put out her hand and touched his arm. "Blain, I love you. We all do. Talk to me." For a very long time he didn't respond. Afton was a second away from going back to the castle when he slowly turned toward her.

"She killed them, Afton. She killed them over something that happened years ago, before she was even born."

Afton moved closer to him. "Don't let her win, Blain. As long as you go on with your life, she can't win."

There wasn't another soul on earth who knew what Rhiannon's last words had been, but Afton's assertion flowed into him like water over the top of a dam. Deep inside, the horror, anger and pain came to the surface. Tired and confused, Blain sank to the ground. As he did so, the heavy battle axe fell beside him. He covered his face with his hands and wept.

Afton placed her package beside the axe and pulled his head against her chest. She stroked his hair with infinite tenderness. Then she untied the leather lacings on his jerkin and pushed it off his bare chest and arms. "Change into fairy form, Blain, and know from this moment forward that every time you do, it's a gift from your parents. Draw strength from the earth and elements the way your father would. See the beauty in nature that was your mother's legacy. Every time you do these things, they live in you, and no evil can win."

Blain did as she requested. When he stood in fairy form and pulled her to him, he could feel the future in his arms. A future that was strange and wonderful, full of secrets and magic. The past and the horror that went with it could never be changed. Things ahead might not always be easy, but as long as they were together, there would always be love.

The breeze began to gently blow. In it, he thought he could hear his parents' voices. Afton stooped and carefully unwrapped the package Gawain had brought her. Inside were the two urns containing Arthur's and Syndra's ashes. He gazed at Afton as she placed one in each of his hands and reverently removed the lids.

"Let them come home, Blain. Let it all end. They don't need to run anymore." Afton raised her hands, and the breeze she summoned blew warm upon their backs.

Blain upended the urns and let the wind take the ashes where it would. "They are home, aren't they?" he murmured.

Afton nodded. "Yes, and no one will ever separate them from here or each other again."

Blain smiled sadly and turned to Afton. "I love you more than anything on this earth."

She cupped his cheeks with her hands. "And I love you, too."

* * * * *

Shayla and Hugh watched the scene unfold from the castle's tallest tower room. "We have plans to make, Hugh. There are still those practicing black magic who would do everything within their power to destroy us. I let my guard down and many have suffered horribly for it." She thought of Blain, Afton, Pluck and the injured and dead guards. Their families would suffer forever. And she remembered Syndra and Arthur.

"It isn't your fault, my love." He took one of her hands in his. "What can anyone do when evil takes its course?"

Shayla looked out over the landscape. "What we can do is make sure we're not all in one place when that evil eventually comes again. I believe the Americans have an expression about not putting all your eggs in one basket. We must find other ground, sanctify it and place some of our people there. If the worst should happen here, the Order will go on." Her fist struck the top of the stone window casement in front of her. "I will protect our people."

"Aye, love. But who would leave our sacred places in this part of the world? Our kind have been here for thousands of years."

"Whoever is willing. I won't force anyone to move. After this incident, however, there may be those who will want to find another home."

Hugh nodded. "It will be difficult for you to make decisions with us scattered about."

"Not any more so than it is now. And this is a new century, Hugh. Remaining in contact is much easier if we use technology to our advantage instead of living in the dark ages.

England, Scotland and Ireland shouldn't be our main sources of sacred land. The world here is closing in. We'll need more room."

"Aye, Shayla. If your plans for the future are to be carried out, we'll need more land indeed."

Epilogue

ॐ

"Come quickly, lad. It's little Syndra," Hugh gasped as he ran into the barn.

Blain dropped his pitchfork and ran toward the house with Hugh puffing at his heels. For days now there had been signs that his daughter would be getting her first set of wings. It was comparable to a human baby's first steps, and he wasn't about to miss it. Once the little girl fell asleep tonight, those baby wings would disappear forever. She wouldn't get her permanent one until she was old enough to summon the change, and that wouldn't happen until the day she understood when it was and wasn't appropriate to reveal her true form. At least that was how it worked with other fairies. Of course, little Syndra wasn't like other fairies, Druids or anyone else in the Order. But whatever happened, he and Afton would support her.

He ran up the stairs and into the nursery. Afton was holding the baby and crooning to her. Blain remembered the first time he'd changed. The tearing sensation had been excruciating as it had knifed down his back and through him. All he wanted to do was hold his sweet little girl close. To let her know Daddy was there and that he loved her so much.

"Give her to me, Afton." Blain held out his hands. Afton handed the girl over. "She's been fussy all morning. I should have known this would happen today."

"Aye." Hugh spoke from the doorway. "She's always had such a sweet disposition."

There was the sound of footsteps in the hallway. Pluck burst through the door, panting. "I've told Afton's family. They were all by the small waterfall in the upper pasture. Gawain wasn't with them, but I found him in the barn. Everyone's coming!"

"Thank you, Pluck." Afton smiled at her friend. When the baby had shown signs of producing her first set of wings almost a week ago, her family and friends had all come to the States to celebrate the event.

"Where's Shayla?" Blain asked Hugh.

"I'm right here," the older woman said as she rushed in from the hallway and pushed her way around Hugh and Pluck.

The baby cried and rubbed her small fists against her eyes. Then she leaned into Blain, unable to tell her father what was wrong.

His heart went out to her. She was barely a year old. His baby was in horrible pain, and there wasn't anything he could do to take it from her. He cuddled her close to his chest and murmured soft words. She looked up at him with huge tears in her eyes as though she was begging him to make it go away.

"Soon, little girl. It'll go away soon. Daddy loves you," he crooned.

"Oh, Blain, she's hurting so." Afton stroked the baby's bare back. "Isn't there something we can do?"

"Wait! Maybe I know something that'll help." Hugh quickly left the room and was back again in a moment. He thrust Blain's flute toward him. "Take her to the garden and play for her, Blain. She loves to hear you play."

Blain smiled and took his flute from Hugh's outstretched hand. "You're a genius, Hugh. I know this will help."

Hugh was right. The perfect place for his baby to be right now was in the garden that Afton, Shayla and Hugh had planted for him over eighteen months ago. The same garden where he had first seen the gazing globe. He carried the baby down the stairs and out into that special place. Afton, Shayla,

Hugh, and Pluck followed. Everyone else who wanted to witness the event would know to follow the flute's music.

Blain handed the baby to Afton, and she sat on a stone bench close to the gazing globe. The baby turned to look at it as she always did when taken into the garden. She was fascinated with its reflective qualities. She soon stopped crying, rubbed her eyes with her fists again and smiled.

"Blain, look. She's feeling a little better now." Afton confirmed this by holding up the baby so he could see her.

He touched Afton's cheek and gazed into her beautiful eyes. When he turned his attention to Syndra, the baby looked up at him and reached out when he showed her the wooden flute. Their beautiful baby had her mother's blue eyes and light brown hair. It curled around her little head like a small halo. There were already tiny freckles on her upturned nose, and she promised to be every bit as lovely as Afton. He loved them both with all his heart. There was peace in this place. No evil entered, nor would it as long as he lived.

He stayed very close to Afton and Syndra as he lowered himself to the ground. The baby watched every move he made as though she was transfixed. Blain began to softly play his flute. Syndra tilted her small head and listened.

"It's working," Afton whispered as she rocked Syndra in her lap.

Blain was aware of everyone crowding into the garden, but he ignored them and played for his daughter. He put his heart into each note, and the sounds of the flute filtered through the garden. Even the birds ceased their song and listened as he played. The breeze blew the tops of the flowers. They swayed as though they were doing so in time to the music. Pink fairy roses and brightly colored foxglove dipped in the wind. There was a hint of thyme, sage and rosemary in the air. A large purple dragonfly landed on the baby's head as though it were offering itself up for a decoration. Sulphur butterflies vied for the child's attention with their more colorful cousins, the Monarchs. Somewhere in the surrounding woods, tiny pixies drew near. Blain could sense them watching. He played on.

Suddenly the baby leaned into Afton and cried out. Afton held her close and looked at Blain. "I think it's time," she whispered.

Blain stopped playing and touched the baby's head. Two tiny ridges appeared on her back. The ridges immediately grew outward and two, aqua-colored wings burst forth. They were gilded with silver like her father's. Blain quickly removed his shirt and changed to fairy form. With a tender expression, Afton handed the baby to him. Grinning proudly, he carefully cradled Syndra so as not to damage her tiny wings.

"Isn't she beautiful?" he boasted. "Have you ever seen wings like these?"

"Never in my lifetime," came a voice from the woods.

Blain turned when everyone else did and saw Lore and some of the fairy faction emerging from the woods. He extended his hand to Lore.

"I'm glad you made it. I wasn't sure we could get a message to you in time."

Lore clasped Blain's arm. "I wouldn't have missed it. She's the first fairy child to have ever received her wings on new ground."

Without the pain that had plagued her for the last week, the baby began to smile and laugh at all the attention. She looked up at Blain, all the love in the world in her innocent gaze. And Blain was thoroughly enchanted.

"Come, everyone. See Syndra's new wings and celebrate her life," he invited in the ancient fairy way. He placed an arm around Afton and drew her near. "I love you, Afton. My sweet Flower."

"I love you, Blain," she responded and stood on tiptoe to kiss him and then the baby.

"Syndra is a beautiful baby, just like her namesake." Shayla smiled as she spoke. She and Hugh stood in the background waiting for the baby to be properly presented.

"Aye, and everything has worked out exactly as you planned it. As usual," Hugh added. "Now that the babe has her wings, I was thinking of giving those two young ones time to be alone. They've had little enough privacy since coming back to the States. So many of the Order have decided to move here, and I'm glad of it. As you said, we're safer not living in such great numbers and on such limited space."

Shayla looped her arm through Hugh's and laughed as Pluck hopped around for the baby's amusement.

A smiling fairy approached Shayla and handed her a note. "I'm sorry I didn't pass this on to you earlier, Sorceress, but with the little one's wings coming, I got excited and almost forgot about it."

"It's all right, Paris. Join the others." She took the note and began to read.

"Bad news, Shayla?" Hugh asked, concerned.

"No, not bad. Just...strange." Shayla placed the note in the pocket of her robe. "It seems someone has hacked into our new database at the castle."

"Shayla," Hugh gasped, "this could be disastrous. Why we could be in serious —"

She raised her hand and smiled. "Hush, Hugh. No secure information was accessed. Just some legendary bit of tripe from our archives. Our people have taken the computers offline until the matter is cleared up."

He let out a sigh of relief. "For a moment, I thought my old heart would stop."

"It's a matter that can wait until we get home. For now, let's enjoy the moment, the love and the happiness. Look at Pluck's dancing." She laughed. "Isn't he a rascal?"

Hugh turned his attention to Blain, Afton, and tiny Syndra. As the warm breeze blew, a wonderful scent wafted through the air. "Sorceress, whatever you're wearing is quite…quite…"

"Alluring isn't it? It's a special blend of aphrodisiac herbs that Afton once used on Blain. Do they do anything for you?" Shayla asked with a sense of expectation in her heart.

"Tonight, after everyone disperses, meet me in the woods where the little stream turns into a grotto. You know the place?" Hugh murmured into her ear.

"I know the place," she repeated. "Don't be late. Pleasuring isn't just for the young, you know, and it's been some time since we made love."

Laughing, Afton rushed up to them, grabbed their arms and pulled them forward, saying, "Come on, you two. Come see the baby."

Shayla and Hugh held out their hands as Syndra was passed to them. The baby chortled happily.

"She's the best in us all," Shayla pronounced as she fawned over the lovely little girl. "Take care of her always. I charge everyone to take care of all our children. They're our future. Without them, there's no hope and our kind will perish. Teach them to be fair, honest and wise, to be tolerant of one another and their differences. They should learn to harm none except in defense of the Order, and to hold their heads proudly. Most importantly, they should know the meaning of love, harmony, and the blessings of family and nature. What they're taught, they'll one day teach. *So Mote It Be*."

Afton stepped forward and took the baby back. As she did so, fairies, pixies and elves began to play a variety of instruments. Somehow, probably by chartering a private plane or by some other covert means, Shayla had made it possible for some of the Order to find their way to this new land. Though only those who could shift into human form or otherwise hide while traveling were currently present, maybe others could eventually find their way to America. Forever after, the land would be blessed because of their existence. The magic was in this new place everlastingly, and they would reach out for outsiders to learn of it one day. And perhaps some of those outsiders wouldn't fear the creatures who had hidden from them for centuries. Whatever happened, Afton and her family would know love. It was all around them. It always would be.

Blain leaned toward Afton as she cradled the baby. "I want ten more just like her," he declared.

"We can start whenever you're ready," she replied.

With that, he smiled broadly and lifted her and the baby into his arms. He laughingly sat them upon a nearby bench, picked up his flute and joined in the celebration. He knew who he was and his place within this strange, magical world. And, with Afton by his side, anything—everything—was possible.

He stopped playing for a moment and waved a hand. Midnight blue fairy dust drifted toward his adorable little girl and her lovely mother. They laughed and held their hands up to catch the shimmering, star-like flakes. He'd even discovered his own special powers to share with them, but nothing was more magical than the love they shared. Each day, the love they knew vanquished all the sadness of the past. Blain felt he was the luckiest man alive, and as he caught his dazzling reflection and theirs in the gazing globe, he wondered what more could any creature want.

Why an electronic book?

We live in the Information Age — an exciting time in the history of human civilization, in which technology rules supreme and continues to progress in leaps and bounds every minute of every day. For a multitude of reasons, more and more avid literary fans are opting to purchase e-books instead of paper books. The question from those not yet initiated into the world of electronic reading is simply: *Why?*

1. ***Price.*** An electronic title at Ellora's Cave Publishing and Cerridwen Press runs anywhere from 40% to 75% less than the cover price of the exact same title in paperback format. Why? Basic mathematics and cost. It is less expensive to publish an e-book (no paper and printing, no warehousing and shipping) than it is to publish a paperback, so the savings are passed along to the consumer.

2. ***Space.*** Running out of room in your house for your books? That is one worry you will never have with electronic books. For a low one-time cost, you can purchase a handheld device specifically designed for e-reading. Many e-readers have large, convenient screens for viewing. Better yet, hundreds of titles can be stored within your new library — on a single microchip. There are a variety of e-readers from different manufacturers. You can also read e-books on your PC or laptop computer. (Please note that

Ellora's Cave does not endorse any specific brands. You can check our websites at www.ellorascave.com or www.cerridwenpress.com for information we make available to new consumers.)

3. *Mobility.* Because your new e-library consists of only a microchip within a small, easily transportable e-reader, your entire cache of books can be taken with you wherever you go.

4. ***Personal Viewing Preferences.*** Are the words you are currently reading too small? Too large? Too... ANNOYING? Paperback books cannot be modified according to personal preferences, but e-books can.

5. ***Instant Gratification.*** Is it the middle of the night and all the bookstores near you are closed? Are you tired of waiting days, sometimes weeks, for bookstores to ship the novels you bought? Ellora's Cave Publishing sells instantaneous downloads twenty-four hours a day, seven days a week, every day of the year. Our webstore is never closed. Our e-book delivery system is 100% automated, meaning your order is filled as soon as you pay for it.

Those are a few of the top reasons why electronic books are replacing paperbacks for many avid readers.

As always, Ellora's Cave and Cerridwen Press welcome your questions and comments. We invite you to email us at Comments@ellorascave.com or write to us directly at Ellora's Cave Publishing Inc., 1056 Home Avenue, Akron, OH 44310-3502.

Cerridwen Press

Cerridwen, the Celtic goddess of wisdom, was the muse who brought inspiration to storytellers and those in the creative arts.

Cerridwen Press encompasses the best and most innovative stories in all genres of today's fiction.

Visit our website and discover the newest titles by talented authors who still get inspired—much like the ancient storytellers did...

once upon a time.

www.cerridwenpress.com

Made in the USA
Lexington, KY
14 September 2010